worth every RISK

USA Today Bestselling Authors

TERRI E. LAINE &
A.M. HARGROVE

First Edition

Cover design by Letitia @ *RBA Designs* | *Romantic Book Affairs*

"Anger may in time change to gladness; vexation may be succeeded by content."
    —Sun Tzu, The Art of War

ONE

Andi—Where It All Began

My brother Mark waltzes into the kitchen to grab a milk carton, drinking straight from it. Normally, I would have called him out on it. Today, I try my best to ignore him and continue to stare at the paper in front of me like holes would appear.

"What's got you pissed off?" he asks. When I don't answer, his tone changes. "What's his name so I can kill him?"

I briefly meet his eyes, noticing he's dead serious, which shouldn't surprise me. Any guy who glances my way gets one warning that keeps him at a distance … as if I'm interested in any relationship with anyone. It might have been funny if he'd given me that look any other day but today. At my continued silence, he walks around to look over my shoulder. I'm not fast enough to close my book and cover the blank black and white paper-sized map of the continents in front of me.

"Oh, that." He chuckles. "They still make you guys do that?"

I roll my eyes. He thinks he's so mature since he's in college and I'm only in high school.

"It's no big deal. Mom's family is from Great Britain and

Dad's ..." He trails off, beginning to get why this stupid project has me staring into space.

I push back, the chair screeching over the floor. Then I'm out of it, because I don't want him to see me cry about being adopted as a baby. I know it's selfish of me wanting to know who my biological parents are.

He calls my name, but I'm running out the back door, needing air. I can't seem to catch my breath or see due to the tears blurring my vision. I run on instinct until my legs give out. My destination might not have been predetermined, but after I wipe my face, I'm not surprised to see where I've ended up. A swing dangles from a tree branch, mocking me, and I force myself to make the few extra steps to slump into it.

The sky is dark with clouds and it will be a long, wet walk home if I can't build up the energy to run back the way I came.

I close my eyes, wishing I'd gone to my room instead and had hidden under the covers. Then I could sleep away the ache in my chest.

"Hey."

I recognize the voice of the only other person outside of my family I'm connected with and snap my eyes open. Why does he have to be the most beautiful boy in school? All the girls think so. Even though I pretend not to notice, I see him, and not in a brotherly way. But it doesn't matter. He's also the only boy completely off-limits to me.

"Hey," I say, feeling stupid for coming to his house.

He moves on silent feet to stand before me and remove strands of hair stuck to my tear-streaked face.

"What's wrong?"

There's something so fundamentally different in the way he asks versus my brother. Even though we've only ever just been friends, I've never had a lot of those.

It's so hard to open up to anyone when you feel like leftover garbage so easily tossed away. Without answers as to why my real parents abandoned me, that's how I feel.

2

I shake my head. "It's nothing."

His fingers lightly trace my face from my cheek to reach my chin before gently lifting it so that I can't ignore his gorgeous eyes.

"You know I can keep a secret," he whispers, as if anyone were close. Though no one is.

I do know. Our brothers had sworn us to secrecy more than a few times over the years, like when they'd left us in kiddie movies to go hook up with their girlfriends in another one.

"Tell me," he says.

I'm not sure if it's something about him or the sheer need to get it off my chest, but I blurt out an answer.

"It's that stupid project."

I've held in my feelings for so long about that hole deep inside me, any longer and I might have imploded.

He looks puzzled for a second until he pieces it together, nodding his head as he speaks.

"The world history project, where we have to try to show as far back as we can how our ancestry down to our parents ended up here in Waynesville?"

I roll my eyes. "It's stupid."

My parents haven't advertised that I'm adopted, though they never kept it a secret from me. I could easily use Mom and Dad's family tree to do it. But as much as I hate to feel this way, I want to know who my birth parents are and why they gave me up. I haven't told Mom and Dad this because I don't want to hurt them. It's not like I don't love them. I do. But ...

"I can help you; maybe——"

I shake my head and snap out the next words. "Why should I even care who they are when they obviously didn't care enough about me?"

My rant surprises us both because we stare at each other for long seconds.

"I care," he says so softly I'm not sure I heard him correctly.

Then he bends down, and I let out a little gasp when his lips connect with mine. Because my mouth is still parted, his tongue easily sweeps inside. For the second time today, I'm at a loss for oxygen. I've never been kissed. Either guys don't think I'm pretty enough or my brother has left a lasting impression in our town that I'm off-limits.

I'm like a statue, still in shock, when he pulls back.

"I'm sorry," he rushes to say.

It shouldn't hurt, but it does. Why is he apologizing? Does he regret kissing me?

"Wait, no, I'm not sorry unless you are. Are you?" he quickly asks.

Chase can have any girl he wants, so I let out a giggle at him fumbling over his words. I cover my mouth when he looks confused.

"What's funny?" he asks.

He removes my hand, and of course I blurt out the first thing that pops in my head, which isn't remotely funny. But then maybe he's short-circuited my brain.

"My brother is going to kill you."

He scrubs a hand over his head. "True, then my brother will resurrect me and kill me again."

I watch him pace as I puzzle the consequences of our actions. He abruptly stops and faces me.

"I don't care. You're worth it."

He says the words casually without any clue how much they mean to me. And he's never lied to me before, so I believe him.

"You're my best friend," I say.

And my only true one. How could I risk that?

"I want to be more and everyone to know it."

I shake my head adamantly. "If we do this, we can't tell anyone."

I'm not ashamed of him. In fact, I'd be the proudest girl in school for everyone to know he's mine.

He stops his forward progress as if he'd planned to kiss me again to seal the deal and realized something.

"Why not?" he asks.

I have two good answers for him.

"One, I don't want you to die." He shrugs that off. "Two, if our parents get wind that we have feelings for each other outside of friendship, we will never get another moment alone."

The truth of my statement dawns on him. Our families spend a lot of time together.

"Fine, a secret. But no other guys. It's just you and me from now on."

Suddenly, the project is forgotten and I grin. "And no other girls," I say saucily.

"That's a given."

Then he's leading me behind the old barn. Every cell of my body is on heightened alert. I can hardly believe Chase is kissing me like I've imagined a hundred times over. I want to pinch myself to check that it's real this time.

But his lips are there, softer than I've imagined, and I gasp because I can't breathe. His tongue slips into my mouth and I want to melt. This is so much better than any fantasy I've ever had. He tastes vaguely of mint. I can't think beyond trying to mark this memory forever.

Chase Wilde is mine. What will the girls think? But no one can know if I want to keep him. So this—us—will just be another secret I hold close, which I'm good at.

Though I trust him with all of my heart, I hope he doesn't flake out on me. I'm putting our friendship on the line, which means more to me than anything else. He's my best friend. I don't want to lose that. But this feels like so much more. It feels right. And he's worth the risk.

TWO

Chase
___

HER VOICE WHISPERS the time over the phone. My excitement mounts. It's been days since we've been able to sneak away and be together. The mere thought of touching her silky skin makes my mouth water. But kissing her is another story altogether. Seeing her in school and pretending we're just friends has turned into the most impossible mental torture a guy can take. How am I supposed to fake this much longer? We've been hanging out since we were twelve and tagging along with our brothers. She was the main reason I wanted to be with them. I'd take all the crap both our big brothers dished out just to be near her. I used to love nothing more than to watch her long brownish-blond hair fly behind her as she ran while I chased her, letting her believe she was faster than me. She never was, but it was the view I was after. And the sound of her laughter when she'd thought she'd beaten me.

Each time I check the clock, only another minute or two has passed, and I have another hour to wait. Her parents are going out to dinner, and I plan to go over to her house where we will be alone. Then, all too soon, I'll have to leave and things will be as they are now—back to the two of us pretending we're just friends.

I nearly leap into the car when it is time. When I get to her house, I'm careful to make sure no one is there. If my brother or hers ever get wind of us being together, they will both kick my ass. It won't matter what she'll say to defend me. She's Mark's baby sister and off-limits to me. Those were the rules drilled into me when I accidentally made an offhanded comment about how pretty she was.

When I drive by to make sure the coast is clear, I park on the next block and then jog through the woods behind her house to her back door. The secret knock I use lets her know it's me.

She opens it and heaven stands in front of me—Andrea James, or Andi, the most beautiful girl in the world.

"Hey," she says. She always manages to look shy as though we've only first met.

"Hey back. I've missed you."

"Me too." She links our fingers and draws me into her house.

"How much time?" I only ask so I can be gone in time for when her parents get home.

"Around two hours if my parents don't bow out early."

Then my arms wrap around her and I breathe in sunshine and flowers. When I let go, she leads me to the back stairs.

"Where are we going?" I ask.

She glances at the floor and then finally back up at me. "To my room."

"Wait? What?"

"It's just you've never been to my room. I thought—"

She stops and starts to head to the den with her face in flames.

"No, I want to go."

I have no idea what this means. We've never gone very far beyond kissing. She's let me touch her, but not skin to skin. Now I want to see her room since she's dangled the carrot in my face.

When she makes no move either way, I cup her cheeks with my hands. "I'm good wherever you want us to go."

Her eyes are fathomless. But behind her armor is someone with a heart of gold. I love her, though I haven't told her yet. She hasn't said the words to me either. Then again, she keeps most things close to her chest. She never lets anyone see her vulnerability, except occasionally me.

A second later of saying nothing, I reassure her the best way I can using my thumb to brush over her hand that's clasped in mine.

Then she's steering me toward the stairs. My heart is thudding so loudly, I'm sure she can hear.

When she opens the door to her room, I stop, not sure what I expected. It's neat and orderly with very little that screams this is her space. What catches my eye is a stuffed bear I'd won for her out of the claw machine a few years ago when we hadn't been old enough to think about hooking up. It's the only thing on her bed besides her pillows. I walk over and pick it up.

"You kept it," I say, turning to face her.

She's stock-still in the doorway, nerves cracking her expression. She nods stiffly, no doubt expecting some sort of judgment. So I grin to hopefully put her at ease. I place the bear back down and make my way to the second thing that snagged my attention. It's a corkboard filled with pictures from the instant camera she got for Christmas a year or two ago. Most are pictures of her parents and Mark. But in the center is me, captured when I'd been flushed from a serious round of kissing. It was the first day I'd snuck over, and we made out for what felt like hours. Good thing it was dark and the only thing shown is my face.

"No one has asked about that?"

She shakes her head, still rigid at the door.

I walk over but leave some distance between us, sensing her fear of rejection—or maybe she's afraid of what might happen alone in her room.

"We can go back downstairs," I say.

There is nothing I wouldn't do for this girl.

Hesitantly, her head moves slightly side to side, and slowly she looks at me with her big blue eyes. Ever so softly, she says, "Please take the weirdness out of this by kissing me."

I step in and cup one hand around her neck and the other around her waist, drawing her close. When we kiss, everything disappears. I hardly notice I'm walking us backward to her bed. The backs of my knees hit the mattress and I sit, leaving her standing in front of me. I widen my legs and pull her in between them, not breaking our connection.

I'm not sure how it happens, but somehow in our urgency to get as close as possible, I end up flat on my back with her on top.

At the moment, my fingers skim the bare skin of her waist. She stops and sits up, straddling me. I want to squirm, sure she's about to notice how hard I am and rush to get off me.

Instead, she looks like she wants to say something. I lift one of her hands from my chest and brush my lips over the tips of her fingers. "What is it?" I ask, trying to coax the shyness out of her.

"It's just … Do you want …?"

We haven't talked about it, but these are words I've only dreamed of. I never thought she'd be the first to bring it up. "Are you sure?" I ask.

My question is two-pronged. I don't want to assume we're thinking the same thing, and if we are, I want her to know she has an out.

"Yes." When her face blooms with color, I know it's real. Her sure smile spreads warmth deep into my chest, behind my ribs, heating every part of me.

"I, uh … don't have anything." Because yeah, I hadn't expected the night to turn in this direction.

"Oh."

I deflate because I'm such a fucktard. Dad told me to keep a condom on me, but I hadn't wanted Andi to ever find it and feel pressured.

"Maybe Mark has one?" she says.

Then she's getting off of me and leaving the room. When she returns, she holds one up in between her fingers.

So this is it. I take it from her hand with more surety than I feel and toss it onto the bed. Despite the rep that surrounds me, I haven't ever gone all the way.

"I'm not very … that's to say, I may not be very … I mean—"

"You haven't done it before?" she asks, looking shocked. "I mean, I haven't, but I didn't think …"

At seventeen, I am probably the oldest guy in my high school still a virgin. All the other guys brag about how they are getting pussy. I've gone along, pretending I am. "I haven't. It never felt right."

"But with me?" she asks.

"I've never wanted anything more in my life." I can't believe I just said that. "But we can wait. I don't want you to feel like you have to or anything."

Her throat muscles work before she says, "I want it to be you, no one else."

Her confession spurs me into action. I grab hold of her face and kiss her like tomorrow might not come. When our connection breaks, she steps away from me. It's surreal-like when her fingertips catch the bottom of her shirt and she slowly lifts it, sliding it over her head. I've seen this much of her before, but it still feels like the first time. Now she stands before me in her white cotton bra and oh, is it ever sexy. I have to swallow the bale of cotton in my throat. I ache to touch her, but she holds out a hand, stopping me. Her arms reach behind her to unclasp her bra. Now I really want to touch her. My poor dick might not make it.

So she's not the only one on her way to being completely naked, I hook my thumbs under the elastic of my soccer shorts, sliding them past my hips. Her eyes enlarge when she sees my boner. I cover it with my hands because I don't want it to scare her.

Her hand hesitantly lifts. "Can I touch it?"

I'm pretty sure I'll come the very instant, but I let my fists drop to my sides.

She steps forward, and as she gets a grip on my dick, I palm her tits. Bending down to suck on one, I swallow my groan as she starts to stroke me.

I have to stop. I need to see her naked too. I want to kiss her all over. I'm sure I'll shoot off like a bottle rocket, but I don't care. I've been waiting for this moment forever, and I'm not going to waste a single second of it. She seems to understand without me asking and takes off her jean shorts.

I draw her back to the bed and guide her to lie down. Then with a confidence I didn't think I would have, I situate her and spread her legs. I've only heard about this and am probably going to royally fuck this up, but whatever. My fingers spread her to reveal slick pink flesh, and I press my lips to her warm skin. She's sweet and salty as I gently lick her seam. I locate the tiny nub I hear the guys talk about and concentrate on that. She digs her fingers into my hair and moans. Her hips thrust upward so that my mouth is over her entire pussy.

"Yessss," she hisses.

I don't stop. I'm actually afraid if I do, I'll disappoint her. Her clit swells and it's not long before she starts to quiver. Her breathing changes and she must be climaxing. I lift my eyes to peer above the landscape of her body. Her head is thrown back onto the pillows, extending the column of her neck, and her mouth has formed an O—for orgasm, I hope.

When her spasms subside, so do I.

"Chase." She's still panting.

I crawl up her body to face her. "Is it okay if I kiss you now?"

She answers by pulling my mouth to hers.

"You can still change your mind," I say, though I would have to leave so I could rub one out. I'm ready to detonate.

"No, I want this, you."

She glances at the condom that landed on the bed near her head. I grab it and put it on, following the directions drilled in my head. No mess-ups here.

"I'm sorry if I hurt you doing this."

She only nods.

I nudge against her entrance and find resistance. Opening her legs a little wider, I go again, not one hundred percent what I'm doing is right, though this time I'm able to slip in a little. I put my fingers down there to see how wet she is. That's what I heard you should do.

"You're soaked," I say.

"Is that bad?"

I push her hair back and smile. My heart is near bursting. "No. It's good. Very good. Tell me if I hurt you too much."

She gives a slight shake of her head and I push again. I watch her face for any kind of signal to indicate she's in pain. There are two little lines between her eyes and it almost looks like she's analyzing this whole thing.

"Tell me what you're thinking," I say.

Her eyes focus directly on mine with so much trust, I'm speechless. "Maybe you should just go for it."

"But I'm afraid I'll hurt you," I admit.

"Probably, but I trust you."

Why did she have to say that? She's giving me everything, and I feel a supreme responsibility to do it right. I decide to distract her with a kiss, and when she's all into it, I make the move. Thrusting forward with my hips, I push deep inside. I suffer for it because she sinks her teeth into my tongue.

We both say, "Shit," at the same time. I taste blood and she has an apologetic expression on her face.

Then we both say, "Sorry," at the same time.

"Are you okay?" I ask.

"It burns. And feels super weird."

It's probably not the best time for a discussion, but I ask anyway.

"Like how?"

She deadpans, "Like I have a huge dick in my vagina."

Then I laugh. And she does too. That doesn't stem the incredible pressure crawling up my balls. I can't hold back any longer because I'm about to bust one. Her tight as hell pussy squeezing my dick is by far the most fantastic thing I've ever felt. No one could've prepared me for this. My balls have to be the color of an eggplant by now. I inch out, then back in. I gauge her pain by her facial expression. So far, so good. I don't know how much longer I can hold back. I use my fingers between her legs to stroke her nub—a tip I'd heard from somewhere—because it won't be long. Whoever said it was right. That does the trick. Her eyes close and she moans. Not long after, her pussy tightens so hard around me, I groan out her name along with my orgasm and hope the neighbors don't hear.

When I can think again, I ask, "Are you okay?"

Her head bobs. I'm not sure I want to know the truth, but I say it anyway, "If you didn't—"

She silences me with a kiss. When we part, I roll on my back and pull her to lie on my chest.

"Next time, I'll make sure it feels as good as my mouth, I swear." If I have to read and watch every sex book and porn video I can to learn the right techniques, I will.

The smile she offers me is the best reward a guy could ask for. "It was good. Better than I expected."

She's never lied to me before, so I have to trust her. "You're everything to me, Andi James."

"You're everything to me too."

"I wish we didn't have to keep us a secret," I say.

"Some secrets are worth the risks."

❄

14

Two Years Later

She stands with her back toward me and I stare at her for a moment. If only I didn't have to tell her this. I know what she's going to say. I know in my heart what her answer will be. Andi has always been the logical one out of the two of us. As I gaze at her silken strands, my fingers flex to touch them. I can almost smell the sunshine in them. A quick flashback has me seeing us running up the hill in her parents' backyard, me following her just to watch those locks of hers fly through the air. The breath leaves my lungs like I've been punched in the sternum. How can I do this? All of a sudden she turns.

"Chase. I didn't hear you come in."

"Uh, yeah. I just arrived."

She is running toward me, her arms out. And then she's kissing me. "I missed you. I hate being apart. Why didn't we choose the same schools?"

"Because you're smarter than hell and got an awesome scholarship to Northwestern, and I got a scholarship to USC."

"Oh, yeah. I forgot." Her hand cups my cheek. "And they're a million miles apart."

My brow furrows, and she's not one to miss anything. "What is it?" she asks.

"It's ... well, I have news."

"News?"

"Yeah. I've been contracted with the pros."

Her eyes turn into the brightest of stars. She throws her arms around me and jumps up and down. "Oh my God, Chase, that's fantastic! I'm so excited for you."

When my reaction doesn't match hers, she takes a step back. "What's wrong? You should be ecstatic."

"It's just that the contract is in Italy."

"Did you say Italy?"

"Yeah. You know soccer in Europe is the rage. We've talked about it, right?"

"Yeah. It's just that I was expecting you to play here first."

"I was too, but when they talked to me last year and said they wanted to see how I did after a year in college, I guess they were pleased with my results."

She smiles. It's not her genuine smile, but she's trying hard to make it look that way. Only I know my Andi.

"Chase, you're going to be one of the best players that Italy's ever seen."

"Yeah?"

"You know it."

"So that means you'll go with me?"

Her eyes drop to the floor. "I can't. I have school. But maybe we can try after I finish?"

"But, Andi, that's three years. I want you by my side now. We've been apart this past year and I don't want that."

"Chase, Italy is half a world away. I can't just pick up and leave. But ... this is *your* chance to make a name for yourself. You *have* to go. You *have* to give it your all. I would never hold you back. Promise me you're going to show them just how talented Chase Wilde is."

"Promise you'll try to come after you graduate? Living without you has been ..."

"Chase, you know I love you, but let's be realistic. I don't want to hold you back and I don't want either of us to get hurt. So much can happen in three years. Let's not fool ourselves."

Leaving her is never something I wanted but sometimes you have to let go. They say if love is meant to be, it will be. I hug her even though it's not answer I'm looking for. It feels more like a goodbye than a possibility that we'll have a future together.

"I believe you and I are meant to be ... and even though Italy is halfway around the world, you and I are worth it ... we're worth that risk."

Two And A Half Years Later

"Chase!" I look up to see Fletcher, my brother, calling out my name.

"Hey," I say as I man-hug him.

"What a nice surprise having you here for Christmas," he says.

"Yeah, I had a break so I figured what the hell."

My mother claps her hands and adds, "You're just in time. Everyone's about to arrive. Ryder and Riley should be here, along with Mark. His family's coming too."

Ryder and Riley are twins and my cousins. Ryder plays baseball, and his sister, Riley, is a golfer. In true Wilde fashion, everyone is heavily into sports.

"His whole family?" I ask.

"Yeah."

That means Andi will be here—the one who got away. The girl I can't stop thinking about, the one I've crushed on for and have loved for as long as I can remember. Before I can think anymore, the door swings open and the room fills with people I haven't seen in ages. Family, friends, and there's not much time to ponder over how I've rubbed one off—okay, not one, but a hundred—to images of Andi.

And then she's standing in a halo of sunlight right in front of me, looking like an angel ... and someone fucking taped my tongue to the roof of my mouth.

"Chase, when did you get in?" she asks.

A grin tickles the corners of my mouth as I ogle the woman. Her brown hair is dusted with gold and the smile she gives me could light up a room at midnight.

"Chase?"

"Oh, yeah, about an hour ago." Then she hugs me and I want to throw her down on my parents' kitchen floor and bang the hell out of her. "My bang landed at two."

"Excuse me?"

"Plane. My plane landed at two." *Pull it together and calm the fuck down.* "So how've you been? How's school? Nursing, huh? I could use a nurse around me." *Shut it now, Chase.*

She tilts her head and gives me an odd look. No fucking wonder. I'm yapping at the mouth like a Yorkshire terrier.

"Yes, nursing. I love it. I'll graduate next spring."

Everyone calls us in to eat, so Andi and I sit next to each other. My appetite takes a hike—well, the one for food anyway. I only want to soak up Andi. Everything she does has me on a high. And unfortunately, it seems to have attached a string to my dick. And the fucker won't stay still. Wouldn't you know I get the squeaky chair too? Every time I squirm, which is every ten to fifteen seconds or so, everybody's head turns my way. I should give them a Queen Elizabeth wave.

The meal seems to last forever, but the moms get up to clear our plates. I offer to help, but they won't allow it. Once the table is cleaned, they cart in all the desserts. Andi carries my favorite, lemon meringue pie. She holds it up for me to see because she knows I love it.

"Did you bake that?" I ask.

She laughs. "You're kidding, right? Mom did. I'm the worst at baking." Then I watch as she cuts me a huge slice. She hands it to me and our fingers touch. I almost drop the plate.

We both catch each other's gazes and there isn't a hint of humor between us.

As I eat, my eyes drill holes into hers. God, I love her blue eyes. Large, with lashes that are endless, I want to lose myself for days in them. And for some reason, when I go to take another bite of pie, my plate is polished clean. I have zero recollection of tasting a single bite of it.

I jump up and carry my empty plate into the kitchen, then

load plates into the dishwasher. Why hasn't another woman ever made me feel this way? Ever since we were together in high school, no other woman can expunge her from my mind. Wiping off my hands, I turn around to find Andi leaning on the counter.

"Would you like to take a walk?" she asks with a glint in her eye.

"Yes. I'd love that."

We practically sprint out of the kitchen, not bothering to tell anyone we're leaving. No one has a clue that anything has ever happened between us. The only thing I know is I want to kiss this woman … this woman who I've never forgotten over the years.

We get to the barn and run inside. We barely close the door before my mouth crashes onto hers, rediscovering everything I can about it.

Andi tastes sweet and spicy, and I intend to find out if she's the same girl I used to know. Has she changed and lost the innocence she used to have? She tangles her tongue with mine, and soon we're both panting hard, struggling for air. The kiss turns slow, sensuous, sexy, and deliberate. I slide my hand beneath her shirt, waiting for her to give me the word to stop, but it never comes.

"We don't have much time until they notice we're gone, but damn, Andi, I've missed you. And hell if I don't want you like I've wanted you ever since those long ago summer nights."

"I want you too. Don't stop."

Pushing her bra up, I find a nipple hardened to a peak. When she moans, my dick responds. It's already hard as stone. The last thing I need is to bust a nut in my pants. Better move south. I walk her against a wooden post.

Opening up her jeans, I tug until they slip down. I drop to my knees, burying my face in her sweet pussy. Spreading her lips with my thumbs, I tongue her slit, concentrating on her nub. When I know she's ready, I find a place we can sit.

There's a stack of wooden crates against a wall so I take her there, get rid of my jeans, and put her on my lap, her back facing my front. Her ankles are still bound by her pants and shoes, so she kicks them off. Then she guides me inside of her, and oh, fuck, I have to put my hands on her shoulders.

"Stop a sec, or I'll come."

She sits still for a second but pulls away and spins to face me. "I'd rather see your face when we do this since it's been so long."

"So would I."

She spears herself with my cock and rides me like a rodeo queen. Thank God she is close, because it doesn't take me long at all. After I shoot off, I grab her face and kiss her, long and slow.

"I'm not sure I can tell you how much I've wanted you. You've been the center of my fantasies for years," I confess.

She runs her hand through my hair. "I hope I lived up to them."

"You surpassed every last one. Do you have any idea how sexy you are? You were always beautiful, but now, you're even more so."

She traces the outline of my lips. "I'm pretty sure you're the one who has sexy covered."

If only my sexy had been enough to keep her … had been enough to get her to come to Italy with me, I wouldn't have been so lonely being half a world away. "Thanks, but I hope my sexy in action satisfied you." I wink at her.

She playfully pats my shoulder. "You really have to ask, tiger?"

"Well, a guy can never be too sure. So, this may be a terrible time to tell you, but I have a game in three days. I'll be heading back to Italy tomorrow."

Her smile fades and the light disappears from her eyes. "Oh. Right."

"I'd love for you to come with me. Back to Italy, I mean."

"I … I can't. School. I'm almost done. Only one more semester. And I love Chicago. I've already been offered a job after I graduate. I want to settle there. For a while, anyway. And we haven't talked. Lately, anyway."

Who can blame her? She hasn't done any exploring yet—really lived.

"I see. Any chance I can change your mind? I mean, after you graduate, of course. This wasn't a simple for old times' sake thing for me, Andi."

She pinches that little place at the top of her nose. "I … it wasn't for me either, Chase, but I can't just run off to Italy either."

"Will you think about it at least? Maybe when you're finished with school?"

"Yeah, sure."

"We better get back before someone finds us half-naked."

She lets out an uncomfortable sounding laugh. The moment —the amazing moment we shared—is gone. Evaporated, like morning fog.

We get dressed and walk toward the house together, but I can't let these be our last words.

"Andi, I just want you to know that this meant something to me. You've always meant something … everything to me. You … if you change your mind, please call me. I'll be there for you. We can make a great life together. I know we can. I feel it in here." I pound a fist to my heart.

She squeezes my hand.

As the two of us walk hand in hand back to the house, a big part of me wishes I had stayed here and not gone to Italy. Andi means more to me than anything. If only there was a way to persuade her to join me when she graduates. I won't give up until I'm in the car heading to the airport.

THREE

Andi—Present Day

WHEN THE ALARMS BLARE, I move into swift action. Carefully, I use the armholes to reach my patient. With delicate hands, I stroke the baby's chest, and just like that, he remembers to breathe again. I sigh as the alarms go silent without any more help from me.

The charge nurse pops her head in. "You need any help?"

After glancing over my shoulder, I shake my head. "We've got this." Looking down at my patient, I say, "Don't we?"

Of course, he can't answer. Not yet, anyway. About the size of my palm, he's too small to be outside of the womb. I will do everything in my power to see he survives.

Peggy walks in. "You're putting your heart on the line with this one."

I glance again at the tiny person struggling to stay alive.

"He's going to make it."

The demand falls on deaf ears. He's here because of his mother's choices.

"She hasn't come in, has she?" Peggy asks.

I shake my head. "She's fifteen and scared." I close my eyes as I exhale.

"I hear she's given up custody."

I purse my lips. "She lives on the street. No way to raise a child."

"True," my boss says. "But who's raising her?" She waves off any reply from me. "Anyway, expect a social worker to come sometime today."

She leaves me alone and I can't help but think of my own mother. Not the wonderful woman who raised me, but the one who gave me up. I have to be a shit for craving to learn her identity when my mother gave me everything I could ever need —love, family, and the tools to be successful in life. Yet, it's like a hole exists somewhere in my heart.

To carve away at the ache, I do more than my duty as I take care of the tiny infant. I give him the physical contact that's shown to help babies thrive through touch, words, and even a song I hum.

By lunchtime, I'm starving. With only thirty minutes, I scarf down food as my friend, Beth, fills me in on the latest gossip.

"Five o'clock." She subtly points. "Dr. McDreamy."

I glance up in time to see said hot doctor all the nurses swoon over.

"First of all, he looks nothing like that actor. His hair is blond and he's a lot taller," I point out.

"And he's perfect."

"And married."

She lets out a long-suffering sigh. "I would so have his babies."

"Doesn't he have like eight of them already?" I tease.

Though eight is an overstatement, it's not by much.

"Is eight really enough?" She speaks like her head is in the clouds. "He's so nice. I swear, they broke the mold when they made him."

"You realize you have no chance. Have you seen his wife? She's gorgeous."

"With a body that couldn't have had one child, let alone all those kids." Although her words seem filled with jealousy, there isn't any malice in them. She smiles to herself. "Then again, I'd let him mount and ride me every night of the week. I'd stay pregnant."

"That's why they have so many kids," I concur.

"And when I wasn't, I'd maintain my figure knowing there were several women waiting in the wings to take my place."

"Exactly. But I've never seen him look at anyone like he looks at her."

Beth exhales. "So unfair. I swear."

"Set your eyes on someone else."

As if his ears were burning, a different doctor hottie walks over. "Ladies."

Beth moons at him with big eyes. "Joshua."

His focus connects with me. "Andi, how are things in the NICU?"

"Busy."

"Too busy to say——"

I stop him before he can ask. I can't be completely sure he's about to ask me out, but shut it down anyway.

"You know, I have to get back or Peggy's going to be all over my shit." I take my tray and head to the door with a wave.

Joshua doesn't totally give up and calls after me. "The NICU is boring. You should join us in the ER."

Half-turning, I continue my retreat. "I'll leave all that fun to you and Beth."

I wink at her and she gives me the biggest grin before flashing Joshua with it.

When I make it back to the neonatal unit, a girl way too young to be here stands before my tiny charge. I take the opportunity to introduce myself.

"Hi, I'm Andi."

I hold out my hand. She turns slowly with eyes that haven't seen enough years, but feel ancient.

"They're kicking me out of this joint today. I thought I would say goodbye."

She hasn't introduced herself, but I know her to be the yet-to-be-named boy's mother. Curiosity had me walking through the maternity ward on my way out yesterday in search of her.

"It's better this way," she says, though it's obvious she's trying to convince herself and not me.

"How do you know?"

Part of me wishes I'd said nothing. I shouldn't be trying to convince her not to give her son a better home. Then again, I ask because I can't ask my biological mom, whom I haven't found yet.

Her eyes morph into steel. "I live on the streets, lady. That's no life for him."

I know this, but the abandoned child in me needs absolution.

"Where are your parents?"

Her face turns cynical. "You mean the woman who would have sold me for her next hit had I not run? I mean, if someone was going to get paid for my virginity, shouldn't it have been me?"

A pain so deep has my eyes burning, but I know that if I cry, she'll make like a scared rabbit and flee.

"There are places you can go that will help you."

She laughs bitterly. "Yeah, where some foster dad can get touchy-feely. No thanks."

Her feet shift and I hold up my hands. "Wait. At least write him a letter."

"For what?" In her expression, there is a desperate hope that I have answers.

"So he knows why you gave him up."

Her chuff is more cynicism that I can't fix in the few minutes I'll have with her. "He'll get that I couldn't take care of him. Why else would I give my kid up? I wish my mother had given me up."

She wipes tears from her face with the back of her hand as I swallow the bitter pill of her words.

"It's better if he hears it from you."

"Who's to say his new parents will give him the letter?"

I shrug. "They may not. But when he comes looking for you—"

"I'll be dead." There's such a fierceness in her eyes, it's easy to see she believes it.

"When he finds you," I begin again, "you can say with a clear conscience that you wrote him explaining why you did what you did out of love."

For a second, hope flashes in her eyes as they search mine. Her lip trembles and her voice is a mere whisper. "I don't have any paper."

As much as I don't want to leave her for fear she'll run, I nod and go out to the desk. When I come back, she's facing the incubator with one hand on it as she peers down at her son.

"You can touch him." She shakes her head and I ask a different question. "What's his name?"

She doesn't look back at me when she speaks. "I didn't want to give him one. You know, so his parents could name him. But they said I had to fill out the birth certificate." I wait and say nothing. Time is like a gift. I wish I could give them both. "I named him Liam, like his dad."

"Where is he?" It's a risk to ask, but I feel some sort of responsibility for both children before me, the mother and the son who equally have no one but me at the moment.

Guilt meets me eye to eye. "He got locked up trying to get me something to eat."

And my heart cries for the child's mother and the pain that fills her eyes.

I don't push anymore, saying nothing, and watch her write for a long time filling the page with her truths. It's like I can physically see the burden lifting from her with each stroke of the pen. When she hands the paper back to me, I trade her. I give her cash, all that I have in my pocket, and a number for a teen shelter. Her tears are painful until we are both crying. By the time she leaves, she promises to use them both wisely, but we both know better. I keep hope when I watch her walk away and wonder if I've done enough.

When the social worker arrives, I explain my visit and hand her the letter. I can only pray it doesn't get lost. Maybe one orphaned child won't wonder why his mother left him.

My heart is heavy when I make it home later. I lie sleepless with the glow of the lamp next to my bed and run an envelope around and around in my hand. Inside it contains words I wrote so long ago. I remember each and every one as though I'd only penned them today. All it needs is a stamp and I can confess all my secrets, like how I really feel about the only man I've ever loved and what I've been doing all this time without him.

I'd been strong enough to do it two nights ago after sharing a bottle of wine with my neighbor. But then scrolling through the channels, a flash of Chase's picture had me stopping and turning up the volume. He hadn't been alone in the shot. A woman, beautiful like a supermodel, stood next to him. The headline—*Chase Wilde Engaged to Be Married*—was beneath the picture.

Tears fall from my eyes as I shove the letter back into the drawer. The strength I need doesn't return. Though I wonder for the millionth time if I did the right thing by walking away so long ago and not contacting him. I can't selfishly change the course of his life. I love him enough to want him to be happy. I loved him that much when I let him go. Deep down I know I could have gone to Italy with him when he asked. I'd chosen not to. At the time, I thought what I wanted was independence from my family and a degree that could lead me to a career of my own. Who am I to selfishly want him back when I had blown my chance? How could I spring my carefully written words on him almost three years too late?

FOUR

Chase

———————

It's New Year's Eve when I leave my cousin Riley's place to find Andi. I don't tell anyone where I'm headed. It may be a little awkward. None of my family knows Andi and I ever had a thing, and since Riley dates Mark, Andi's brother, it could get a bit sticky. It's better to keep it under wraps unless something develops between us. For all I know, Andi will tell me to go to hell. At this point, I just have to know, one way or another.

How many letters have I written her—a dozen or more?—only to be tossed in the trash because she could have moved on. And the burning question I've asked myself over and over still haunts me—why did I ever walk away in the first place?

All the flights are booked so I end up having to charter a plane. It doesn't matter. I am ready for this unbearable wait to finally end. At this point, I would fucking walk to Chicago if I had to, but it would take too long and I don't have the time right now.

Luckily enough, a friend of mine was able to book me an Airbnb. It's in the vicinity of Andi's apartment so it will be more convenient and comfortable than staying in a hotel room. When my flight lands, the car service I hired is waiting. It's almost ten at night so I have the driver take me somewhere to grab a carryout for dinner on the way to the rental. By the time I make it inside, I collapse on the couch because it's now eleven p.m.

I'm polishing off my sandwich and channel surfing when my phone rings. When I check to see who it is, I do a double take. What the hell is Lucia doing calling me at this hour? It's eleven here, which means it's five a.m. in Italy.

"Hello?"

"Ciao, Chase."

The last person I want to talk to. "Lucia, why are you calling me?"

"Sei l'amore della mia vita."

"English, please. I'm too exhausted to think in Italian."

"I love you, Chase. I missed you and wanted to hear your voice."

"Lucia. We've been through this. You and I have never been a *we*."

"Ah, but I know you could not mean that. Voglio stare con te per sempre."

"There is no forever for us. You knew that from the start." My frustration rockets to an all-time high and I'm barely controlling my temper. When is she going to understand?

"Promise you won't be angry with me. I hate when you are angry with me."

"What's going on?" My tone carries a warning note. "I'm already angry and will be more so if you don't tell me."

"The lady with the camera. She saw me and I told her ..." As she speaks, her accent grows heavier and heavier until the only thing I can gather is something about a fiancé.

"Let me get this right. You told someone that we are engaged?"

"Si. She asked me about my ring and I explained, 'È il mio fidanzato.'"

"I never gave you a ring, Lucia."

"But, Chase, I was wearing one and she asked me. What could I say?"

"You could've told her the truth, dammit."

This is just great. She told the damn paparazzi I was her fiancé. Wonderful. Now the world thinks we are going to be married because of a ring I never bought for her. I'll be the asshole tomorrow when the world finds out she was jilted only one day later. I did nothing wrong except mess around with a lunatic.

It takes to the count of ten until I can speak. She keeps calling out my name, but I don't respond. Then finally I say, "This is what's going to happen. I'm going to call my agent, Max. I will explain exactly what you did. He'll be in touch. And then you will retract what you said. We are done, Lucia. Finished. Don't call anymore. If you do, don't expect me to answer."

I tap end and stare blankly at the TV screen. I made it plain from the beginning that there would never be anything permanent between us. How did I end up with that mess of a woman? She's beautiful—a fashion model who can have any man she chooses. But for whatever reason, she only wants me, and I don't want her. I don't know how else to explain that to her. She refuses to let go.

Poor Max. He's going to have to deal with the fallout of this. I shoot him a text and quickly explain. I end it with a, "don't call me until at least nine a.m. *my time*."

I flop into bed and try to get some sleep. Try. I lie awake and think of what Lucia did. That shit will be all over the tabloids by now. Football in Europe is huge, and so is Lucia. Christ. I throw off the covers and hunt down my phone. Scanning the internet, I find it's already on the major Italian news networks. Her little video saying how thrilled and excited she is, flashing her stupid ring, and then a picture of me on the football field pops up. It's the one where I scored a goal in the World Cup. Fuck my life. I text Max back, amending what I said earlier, telling him he can call me anytime. I won't be sleeping much tonight. Then I throw my phone. Why the hell did I ever get involved with her in the first place?

In the morning, Max calls and he has a plan established. He's going to have her retract what she said. If she doesn't do it, he'll make her sound like a stalker, which could damage her career. At that point, I will make a statement saying that our relationship ended over a month ago, when we parted ways, and it's unfortunate Ms. Mazzanti remains under the delusion we are still together, even though I have urged her to seek professional counseling.

"You're sure this will work?"

"Chase, if I read this to you, wouldn't you retract your statement?"

"Yes! But, Max, she *is* delusional!"

"Don't worry. I will pay her a visit, with a witness of course, and persuade her to do what we ask."

When we end the call, I'm still uncertain she'll do it. I won't be satisfied until I see her statement. Damn, a thought just plows into me. I grab my phone and pull up TMZ, just to make sure that shit hasn't hit over here too. And fuck if it hasn't. What if Andi has seen it? What will she think? Probably that I'm a fucking asshole. If Lucia does the retraction tomorrow, maybe she'll change her mind. But I can't worry about that. Hopefully, Andi will give me a chance to explain things and I can make it right. That's a huge *if* right now.

Andi ... being this close to her makes me want to charge over to her apartment, tear down her door, and ... and do what? What exactly would I say? I've come all this way and I need a strategy, a game plan. I can't just show up out of the blue and not know what words will pop out of my mouth. It's been too many years and so much has happened to both of us for that. I have to come up with the right things ... show her what's in my heart. And it can't sound whiny, but dammit, I *will* beg if I have to. This is something I've thought about for *years*. And it all goes back to that afternoon in the barn … the last time we were together. I should've stayed or figured out a way to make it work between us. Long-distance relationships are difficult, but not always impossible. We could've done it. I would've done it. I'm still in love with her after all these years and if that doesn't say something, I don't know what does.

Checking the time, I notice it's around nine. My plan is to shower, grab some breakfast, and then go find my girl. I have no idea if she'll be home. It's New Year's Day, and who knows what she's up to. Maybe she had a date. Or worse, what if she's involved? My gut is razored as I conjure up a million unpleasant possibilities. At this point, food isn't even appetizing. Liquid courage is more of what I need.

As I shower, I clear my head of everything. It's a tactic I use before a game. If I don't do this, I'll be on the first plane out of Chicago and lose my chance with Andi forever. Then I head out of this place and find the first breakfast joint I can. I force a strong cup of coffee and a bagel down the hatch and then I take off in the direction of her apartment. It's game time and the winner takes all. If she takes me back, we'll both end up winners of this match.

FIVE

Andi

─────────

USING MY KNUCKLES, I knock lightly on my neighbor, Owen Kazynski's, door who lives down the hall. When he opens it, his smile warms the hallway.

He studies my face before asking, "Hey, you. Did you get enough sleep?"

He's an attractive man with a kind soul. We quickly bonded as friends after our first meeting.

Sheepishly, I smile back. "Thanks for helping me out."

He swings the door wide and I enter his apartment, which is a mirror of mine. We stop at the kitchen space to the left of the hall.

"Are you hungry?"

My stomach gives out a shout. I tilt my head to the side in a half-shrug. "Sure."

He moves to the microwave and pulls out a covered plate. "I saved some breakfast for you."

He's a blessing and a godsend. Sometimes I wonder if he's not an angel in disguise. "You're too good to me."

He's always doing little things like this. We look out for each other and have since he moved in a few years back. His wife died of cervical cancer, leaving him a single dad. With mounting bills for her failed treatments, he'd been forced to sell their house and move here.

"I was cooking anyway. Not too hard to add a portion for another person."

I take the plate and sit at his small table to dig in.

"What are your big plans for your day off?"

Holidays are pooled each year. I'd worked Christmas, and for that, I got New Year's Day off.

"I don't know. What about you?" I ask between bites.

"My in-laws have offered to babysit."

My eyes widen. Since his wife's death, they haven't exactly been close. "You should totally take advantage."

I think about my parents and how much I miss them. It's been over two years since I've been home. Owen can read me well and is quick to ask about them.

"Have you told them yet?"

Guilt assaults me. I slump, putting my chin in my palm as I rest my elbow on the counter. "My brother, Mark, is furious with me. He says I'm making Mom cry. He's even offered to pay for my flight if that's what it takes to get me home."

"So go." He makes it sound easy with his cheerfulness.

"How can I have him pay for my flight when I'm using money to pay a private detective to find my birth mom?"

Though my search isn't the primary reason why I'm staying away from home. I cover my face with my hands, willing myself not to cry. I'm torn between my parents and searching for a part of me I need to know.

"Andi."

Owen's patience is like a smoothing balm, but my soul has been in chaos these past few years.

"No, I'm such a bad daughter. How can I keep secrets from them?" My voice comes out soft and muffled as I speak more into my hand than to him.

"So tell them the truth." He pulls my hands from my face

and I stare into his earnest one. "From all you've said, they'll forgive you."

I nod. "They will after I endure their disappointment in me. Besides, Mark forced my hand by giving me an open-ended ticket to come home as a Christmas present. And with Ryder and Gina's wedding soon, I'll have to go back and face the music anyway."

"Who will you take as your plus one?"

"No one, I guess."

There has only ever been one guy.

"What about that guy, Chase?"

Hearing his name makes my heart grow tight in my chest.

"No, he's getting married." I gaze into space a second before blinking. "And I should be happy about that."

As I stare a hole in the wall, wondering if I could go to Chase's wedding, Owen cuts into my thoughts.

"You know what? You and I should go out and have drinks."

I'm about to answer when Holly comes tearing around the corner to her dad.

"Daddy, *Vilet* doesn't know where Clay Park is."

Holly has yet to master saying Violet's name. Owen's amusement reminds me what's important, and it's not despairing over a guy I gave up. He gives his daughter a concerned look to mirror her own. "Let's go and help her find it."

He stands and takes Holly's hand. I follow, hearing *Dora the Explorer* playing in the background. Just around the corner, another doll-faced girl stares at the TV. Dark brown ringlets crown her head. She turns when Owen sits on the sectional. Holly joins him on his lap. Violet beams at me and runs over with her thumb in her mouth while pointing at the screen.

"Clay Park?" It sounds reasonable, like the words if you've mastered two-year-old speak.

Owen launches into questions about the story and the girls answer him eagerly. For a second, I allow myself to wonder what it would be like if Owen and I became a couple. It's so easy to be with him, talk to him, and bonus—he cooks. What more can a girl ask for?

Only we are just friends. He hasn't exactly gotten over his wife yet. And I haven't exactly gotten over Chase.

I let those thoughts drift away as we search with Dora to find Clay Park. The girls giggle when we learn we must cross Troll Bridge first. Eventually, the Dora episode ends. *Go, Diego, Go!* comes on next before *Barney*. Before you know it, our morning has dissolved in animated conversation with toddlers and I wouldn't have it any other way.

Later, after I make lunch for us all, my phone rings.

"Mom," I say into the receiver after holding up a finger to Owen and excusing myself to step in the hallway.

"Andi, honey, how are you? You never call."

I sigh. I have to give her credit. She hadn't given me the third degree when I didn't come for Christmas.

"I'm sorry, Mom. I've been busy."

"I get that you're an adult and you have your own life but, sweetheart, we miss you. Have we done something to upset you?"

There's no condemnation in her voice, only a deep-seated sadness.

"No." I want to blurt out the truth and beg for her forgiveness. "Look, I'm coming for Ryder's wedding. I need to tell you both something."

"Can't you tell me over the phone?"

This is the kind of news better said face to face.

"It's better if I explain in person. I hope you'll keep an open mind and maybe eventually forgive me."

Dammit, Andi, if that doesn't sound ominous.

But Mom being Mom only says, "Andi, there is nothing you can do to make us not love you. We miss you and want to share a part of your life at least occasionally."

Tears well up in my eyes as my voice cracks into a million pieces. "I miss you too. And I'm sorry."

"There's nothing to be sorry about, sweetheart. I'm glad you're coming home. You're going to stay with us, right?"

"Yes, please."

"Let me get your dad. He'll be thrilled to hear you're coming home."

Just like that, I resolve to confess everything to my parents. Though they will still love me, what I have to say won't go over easily. That much I know. I'm just not sure how Chase will feel when he learns the truth.

After I talk to my dad, I walk back to Owen's. Violet comes running over to me.

"Mama, outside and play."

Her steel gray eyes are so much like her father's.

"It's cold outside. Maybe we should stay in."

Her head moves side to side, curls bouncing along.

"Holly, me are 'plorers," she says, pointing to her chest and then in the direction of her friend.

The last word she said might have been a little hard to understand for anyone else, but a year or so of baby talk and I'm fluent.

"Okay, but we can't stay long."

The girls squeal in delight and Owen says, "Let me get our coats."

I nod and say, "I'll grab Violet's and meet you in the hall."

He agrees, and for the second time, I wonder how easy it would be for Owen and me to become a family. We are halfway there, considering we have keys to each other's apartments. He trusts me with his most precious possession—his daughter. I trust him with mine.

Once the kids are all bundled up, we head outside to the park conveniently located across the street. It's one of the million reasons I picked this place. Owen guides me with a hand at the small of my back. Even though he's never given me the vibe that he's into me, I search for my reaction from his touch. There aren't any electric currents, no butterflies in my belly, and

I wonder how disappointed this makes me. Only one man has ever made me feel like a live wire.

Chase.

Until I can let him go from my heart, no other man stands a chance.

SIX

Chase

BREAKFAST HAS LONG PASSED and I've tried to eat lunch. I manage a few bites, but I'm edgy as hell. I'm sitting when Mom calls.

"Honey, what's this I hear about an engagement?"

Just when I think my gut's settling down, bile flares up again.

"It's not what you think. There is no engagement."

"But, Chase, your father and I saw Lucia on the news and she said—"

"I know what she said, Mom, but it's not true. We stopped seeing each other a while ago. She's not listening to anything I tell her and insists we're still together. But we were never really close like that to begin with."

It was even less than that, but I can't tell my mom she was only an occasional fuck.

She snaps into momma bear mode.

"Good Lord. What are you going to do?"

"Max is handling it."

"Handling it? How?"

I explain Max's plan, leaving out the most sordid of details. "Honestly, I think she needs help."

"Oh, honey, that's awful. It sounds like she does. You didn't do anything to warrant that behavior, did you?"

"No, Mom. I swear I didn't. I told her from the start that there was never a chance of anything permanent with us. When I told her I didn't want to see her anymore, she sort of went crazy. She just won't leave me alone."

"Your brother had trouble like that until he settled down with Cassidy. When are you going to settle down?"

I want to blurt out that I'm in Chicago to do that very thing. "Mom."

"Okay, I'll let it be. Maybe Max can persuade Lucia to seek counseling."

"I hope so. She needs it." Personally, I think she needs more than counseling, but I hold my tongue.

"So where are you now, honey?"

Shit. I was hoping she wouldn't ask me that. "I'm in Chicago."

"Oh? What are you doing there? Are you planning to visit your aunt and uncle? Or your cousins, Kaycee and Landon, while you're there?"

"No, I'm just getting away from it all. I needed a breather. I'm not planning on staying long."

"At least call them. They'll be so disappointed you didn't stop by. And, honey, if you need a break, you can always come back home to the mountains. Dad and I would love to have you."

"I know. And I'll get there soon. I promise."

"Okay. I love you, Chase. Keep us posted on how things go. And call your brother and Cassie. They're worried about you. They heard this news too and were wondering about it."

"I will, Mom. Tell Dad I said hi and I love you both."

My parents are the greatest. They've always been supportive of both my brother and me. If I ever needed them for anything, they would drop whatever it was they were doing and catch the next flight out to be by my side. I sit and think about what she said. Getting Lucia into counseling is a joke. She doesn't think anything's wrong with her.

It's a relief that after another round of messages to my agent after Mom's urging, Max finally calls and tells me he has Lucia under control. I can finally breathe easier. I won't be fully satisfied until she makes her statement and I witness it myself.

Though I've made it to town, I find myself sitting in a local bar, not too far from Andi's, imagining what she's doing today. Is she alone, or with someone? God, the thought of that makes me fucking insane. If she's with someone, I have no damn idea how I'll handle that. Probably get on the first plane out of here. Where the hell would I go? Back to Italy? And face the paparazzi and Lucia? No, back to the mountains in North Carolina is where I'd head. Mom and Dad would be the perfect antidote for me. Grabbing the bartender's attention, I order a beer. Maybe this will calm me the fuck down.

Then I think back to all the time … all the wasted time I've spent doing nothing but this. Thinking. And look where it's gotten me. Sitting alone, in a bar, practically stalking the girl I've loved for as long as I can remember. What the hell is wrong with me? Why didn't I just pick up the goddamn phone, call her, and spill my guts? Even if she had told me to kiss her ass, what difference would it have made? At least I could've moved on and not been this miserable fuck all this time.

When I go to toss back my beer, I notice the bottle is empty. Motioning to the bartender, I have him bring me another. This is my last one, and then I'll steel my balls to make my move. I didn't come all this way to sit in a bar and get plastered. If I'm honest, this isn't making me feel better either. It's only bringing me down. After I settle my tab, I head out the door into the cold January air.

The sky is dark gray and I briefly wonder if it's going to snow. There are a couple of inches on the ground already, and the sidewalks are slick with patches of ice. I'm not much of a fan of this kind of weather, which is why I love living in Rome.

Right as I think this, my feet go flying and I nearly land on my ass. Luckily, my quick action saves me and I skip over the ice to safety, almost as if I'm dribbling the ball downfield.

As I round the corner on the block where her apartment is, I check my phone to look up the address. There's a park across the street where several people are playing with their kids. That's when I notice her. She's just as I remember her from the last time I saw her, or maybe more beautiful. I also observe she's not alone. She's there with a man and two children. My feet momentarily freeze to the sidewalk as I watch them make a snowman, or try to, with the little amount of the white stuff that remains on the ground. I'm close enough to overhear.

"We need some sticks for his arms," one of the kids says.

"He doesn't have much of a body to put the sticks on," the dad says. In truth, the thing is lopsided and really only one giant blob of snow.

"Yes, he does, Daddy," the same kid says. "We can make him a head now."

Andi laughs as she plasters more snow on the thing. The smaller child doesn't speak a word, except runs around and around in circles. I almost get dizzy watching her, but can't help it when the corners of my mouth turn up. They can't be Andi's kids. Mark would've mentioned them to me. She must be dating that guy and those are his. Realizing I'm still rooted to the concrete, I propel myself into action.

First small, then larger steps land me almost right next to them. There's something surreal about this, almost as though it should be me in the middle of it and not that dude. How would it feel? Would I want to be him? A father? This is uncharted territory for me. I've never put a lot of thought into it. Hell, my brother's kid seems like an alien. Besides, my schedule is so booked up with practice, games, and appearances, not to mention endorsements, how would I ever work being a father in? But seeing Andi with these kids opens a door I never imagined existed.

Even though it can't be more than twenty degrees, I'm not cold. In fact, I'm the opposite. My bones are filled with heat and it dives all the way down to my soul. Just seeing her infuses my heart with joy and makes me want to do things … crazy things, like tell her I love her. Only I know that's not possible yet. Considering the scene in front of me, she may never be mine to have.

Focusing my gaze on her, it's hard not to see how much enjoyment she's getting out of this snowman thing. Perhaps I should turn around and leave. Go away and leave her to the life she's built. However, fate has different plans—plans that need to be settled. Right then, she looks up and our eyes connect. The hand that was smashing more snow on the blobby snowman stills and she drops the little pile.

"Andi? Are you okay?" the lucky bastard with her says.

She doesn't answer him. She stands and walks toward me. Slowly at first, but then faster until there's less than a foot of space that separates us.

"Chase? What are you doing here?"

I blink a few times because my fantasy of seeing her again has come true.

"I … I came to see you."

"Me? You came to see me? Why?"

It takes everything I have, every ounce of control in all my muscle fibers, not to pull her into my arms and kiss her perfect lips.

"Why wouldn't I have?"

"It's been so long. Why now?" she asks.

And when I go to answer her, the little girl, the one who was running around in circles, comes teetering up to us, yelling, "Mama, Mama, poopie, poopie. Nowwwww."

Andi gives me a look that's somewhere between desperation and apologetic. My thoughts are the scrambled eggs I couldn't stomach this morning.

"I'm sorry, Chase."

I watch as she grabs the child, picks her up, and carries her across the street at a run. Next thing I know, the dude comes over to me and says, "Kids, you never know when they gotta go." He follows with the other child, leaving me to stare after them.

The scene nails me in the heart. Andi's a mother, and clearly that guy is the dad. The two add up to a family and that seals my decision. With hands stuffed in my pockets, I head back to the little rental. I need to get the fuck out of Chicago. All the plans I hoped for are lost. She's got her own life and there's not a chance in hell I'm going to screw anything up for her.

SEVEN

Andi

OWEN MAKES the girls hot chocolate with milk while I race back outside. Chase is nowhere to be found on the sidewalk or at the park across the street. I move quickly to the busy end of the street and check there. He's gone and my heart sinks. I pull my phone from my pocket, but then I realize I don't have his number. When he permanently moved overseas, he'd gotten a new one.

I feel physically sick as I walk back to my apartment. Having no other choice, I call my brother, Mark.

"Hey, stranger," he says by way of greeting.

"I deserve that."

Before he can answer, a female voice in the background says, "Hey, babe, come back to bed."

"Is that Riley? You guys weren't …" I can't even finish. Images of my brother and his girlfriend naked only make me want to gag.

"Having sex?" he asks, chuckling.

"I don't want to know."

"I can tell you I might not have answered the phone if it was anyone but you."

"Why?"

"Well, I don't hear from my sister that often. So when I do, I have to wonder if there's an emergency."

I sigh. "I'm not that bad."

"Really, I haven't seen you in two years, Andi. *Two years*. It's not like you live on the other side of the world."

I cover my eyes. "I know I owe you an explanation. But I need to explain to someone else first."

"Who? Mom and Dad?"

"Not exactly. Look, I don't want to keep you from Riley." I can hear her cajoling him back to bed in the background. "Do you have Chase's number?"

"Riley probably does. But she's not in a position to get her phone."

I get his meaning and push a hand through my hair.

"Yeah, no explanation," I say before he can add details. "Can you text it to me when you get a chance?"

"Are you going to tell me what this is all about?"

Over two years ago, I felt like a lone survivor on an island until Owen showed up. I've wanted to be strong to prove to myself I could handle my life—my choices—without help. But it's cost me. Seeing Chase reminded me how my decisions have separated me from the people I love.

"I will. I promise. Just get me the number."

He's silent for so long, I glance at the phone to see if we got disconnected. When he finally speaks, his voice is filled with too much emotion.

"I want you to know that I'm here for you, sis. I don't care that we don't share blood. I love you and you can trust me. I'll help you through whatever is going on."

My eyes burn and my throat seizes up. I croak out my next words. "I know. And I love you too. I promise we'll have a long talk soon."

After we hang up, I walk back to my apartment, replaying the look on Chase's face. Had he been surprised to see me, disappointed, shocked? So many things played over his beautiful face, I can't begin to figure out why he'd come. More than that, how had he found me? I shake my hands like they have goop on them. There is so much I need to explain to him.

I take a deep breath before I use my key to enter Owen's apartment.

"Everything okay?" he asks, appearing almost instantly as I open the door.

"Yeah, I'm good." But I'm so not.

"Who was that?"

When I meet his eyes, there is only concern in his. "Chase."

His expression turns almost cartoonish. "*The* Chase."

I nod slowly.

"Is he in your apartment? Did you two talk?"

My nod turns into a headshake. "No, he was gone by the time I made it back outside."

The pause is short before he asks another question, "Did you try to call him?"

I shrug. "I don't have his number. Not anymore."

He shocks me when he finally speaks again. "Are you still in love with him?"

I gape for a few seconds, surprised he went there.

"No." My face screws up in that *are you crazy* expression, because the lie is easier than the truth. "He's engaged. He's probably in town, maybe to see his cousins, and dropped by to say hi."

Owen must see something because he steps forward and envelops me in a bear hug. For a second, I let out a choked breath and a contained sob before I muffle it.

"It's okay," he murmurs, pressing a kiss to my temple.

Needing reassurance, I glance up. The moment changes too fast for me to comprehend. His mouth descends and his lips press firmly to mine. Like I've been electrocuted, I jump back because it's Owen and we've been friends for so long. Yes, I've considered the idea of us, but Chase is here, in Chicago. No matter what I say to Owen, I need to be sure there's no possibility of a reconciliation with Chase before I move on.

He holds up his hand like I'm a cornered cat. Maybe I am. Feeling that my face is tight, I relax it.

"No, it's fine," I say.

"It's not fine. I shouldn't have." He closes his eyes and blows out a breath. "I'm so out of practice. It's just, you ..."

He stops and I realize that I'm giving him the *please don't continue* look.

Before things can get any more awkward, I jump in. "It's getting late. I promised Violet some one-on-one mama and daughter time. There won't be a problem with you getting her from preschool tomorrow, right?"

I pray that we can just forget the kiss and go back to being single parent pals.

"Yeah, no problem. This never happened."

He waves a hand, dismissing it. But in his eyes, I see the disappointment. Still, I let out the breath I've been holding and go scoop up my daughter, who squeals in delight. When we get home, we play *one for you and one for me* with our dinner. It helps her to eat things she doesn't like.

"Yuckie," she says, scrunching her face at the green bean I offer her.

I pick one up. "One for Mama." I put it in my mouth and say, "Mmm, yummie. Now one for you." She shakes her head fiercely. "Then Mama will eat all the cookies."

Her lower lip trembles before poking out. I again offer her the green bean. Reluctantly, she eats it. And we play this game until she's eaten all her dinner.

"Cookie now," she asks with her grabby hands out.

It's times like this, her determination, she reminds me of her father. But when she flashes me a brilliant smile to add to her irresistible charm, I know she's the light of my life. I can't help the grin I give her because she knows she's won in some way. "Yes, cookie now."

I clean up while she devours her dessert. We play with blocks to build because girls don't always have to play with dolls. We also watch *Sesame Street* and *Barney* before I give her a bath and put her into bed.

When I pull out the princess book we've been reading, because I have no problems with crowns and princes, she pushes my hand and shakes her head.

"Picture book, please." Though it sounds more like *picture book peas*.

Because some wishes are automatically granted, I set down the book and go to the bookshelf. I pull out the scrapbook I began before she was born and have only added to it over time. We spend the rest of our nightly ritual going through it page by page. She asks lots of questions as she points to different pictures, like of me when I was pregnant and of my family she's never met. She falls asleep shortly after I finish. I set the book in its place on the shelf, emotionally spent.

Back in my living room, I sink into my sofa and replay the events of the day. The kiss with Owen, my conversation with my brother, and *Chase* … He's at the center of my emotional turmoil.

What am I going to say to him when we finally talk? I finally get a text from Mark, who has impeccable timing. It contains two numbers for Chase. One I recognize. It's his old number in the U.S. This one can't be good, because he'd contacted me shortly after he moved, letting me know he had a new number. Wallowing in hurt feelings, I hadn't written it down, assuming I wouldn't need it. It must have been the international number included in the text. I stare at it a long time before dialing it, intending to keep the call short. My budget is tight and international phone calls aren't included.

My heart doesn't beat as the phone rings and rings.

"Ciao," a female voice says.

I say nothing for a second, thinking I might hang up. Then I decide it doesn't matter if he's brought her stateside. I have to talk to him.

"Is Chase available?"

"Chase," the woman says with a thick Italian accent. Then she spouts off a string of words I can't understand before hanging up on me.

I try again, but no one answers. Before I give in, I take a chance and call his old number. It's answered by someone at a bar or club based on the background noise I hear. Another female voice greets me.

"Hello," she slurs.

"Is this Chase's number?"

"Ain't nobody chasing anything, honey," she says before disconnecting the call.

Clearly, Riley doesn't know the U.S. number is no good. I put my phone down, leaving it on the sofa cushion before heading to bed. *He didn't come for you*, I think. He came because he was in town, maybe to see family to introduce his fiancée. He dropped by to pay me a courtesy visit, nothing more. That doesn't mean I won't talk to him eventually ... and soon. But it does mean I need to move on ... finally.

EIGHT

Chase

WALKING HOME FROM ANDI'S, I decide to take a detour into a bar and drink myself into oblivion. There were several things I'd expected, but none of them included her being married with kids, and how did I not hear about it? Why the fuck did I wait so long to contact her? This is totally my fault. Yeah, I gave her my number, but I should've known she'd never call, as stubborn as she is. I should've followed up and pestered the hell out of her, insisting she come with me. But I did none of those things. Now I'm sitting in this bar alone, while she's in the arms of another man, enjoying her wonderful family life. Good for her. Or that's what I should be thinking, anyway, but the honest side of me is jealous of *him*. I envy what that dude has because Andi should've been mine.

Opening my phone, I pull up one of the many airline apps I have and try to book a flight out tonight. Only this particular airline is completely sold out. When I go to the next, I find the same thing. I move on to one of those travel apps, which searches all airlines, and it seems every flight is booked. What the hell is going on? Even trying to get a charter seems impossible.

"Can I get you another?" the bartender asks.

"I'd rather you get me a flight out of here."

He laughs. "Good luck with that. Haven't you been paying attention to the weather?" He motions to the TV where The Weather Channel is on, reporting about some big winter storm getting ready to nail Chicago. I've noticed it's been snowing, but this is Chicago, where the weather is usually like this in the winter.

"You've got to be kidding me."

"Where've you been? This is all everyone's been talking about. Planes are stuck all over the Eastern seaboard to the Midwest. Can't get here, and from the looks of things, won't be leaving any time soon, either."

"Damn you, Lucia." I spit out her name like a curse. If I hadn't been so focused on her, I would've paid attention to the weather and what was happening around me.

"What's that?"

"Nothing. And yeah, I'll take another."

None of the charter services are flying, which means I'm stuck in fucking Chicago. I'm so close to Andi, I can practically smell her. Goddammit.

The bartender slides another beer in front of me and I ask for a menu. Better get some food in me before I get too hammered. As I stare at the TV, watching the blue on the radar approaching the Chicago area, my phone rings.

"Hi, Fletcher. What's up, bro?"

"Mom says you're in Chicago. Are you stuck?"

"I am now."

"I just heard the news, so I thought I'd give you a call."

"Seems like I'm the last to know about the blizzard," I say.

"That's not what I was talking about. I was talking about your engagement."

"Did Mom tell you I'm not engaged?"

"Yeah. You've got a mess on your hands. Is your guy handling it?"

"He says he is. She's crazy, Fletch. There's nothing more for me to tell her. I'm done."

"Yeah, I get crazy. Make sure Max takes care of it. So how long before you can get out of there?"

"No idea. I was working on it, but no one can tell me anything. I can't even charter a flight. It seems everything is sold out, and my guess is this place will be shut down when the storm hits."

"I would send you my plane, but the pilot is on vacation. Besides, I doubt they can get into Midway or the Executive Airport, and O'Hare is out of the question. So hang tight and keep me posted."

I order a burger, drink more beer, and am pretty damn toasted before I know it. The place is jammed with customers and a girl wedges her way next to me to order a drink. It's more than that, though. She leans against me and starts hitting on me. There is no pretense or shyness about her demeanor. Even I can tell what she wants in my buzzed state.

"Hi, I'm Mickie, and you are?"

"Chase."

"And I certainly would. Chase you, that is. You alone?"

"Not anymore, it would seem." She laughs at my little joke. Bleached blond hair—which is not my type—hangs too close to my face. Her bright pink lips—which are also not my taste—pucker up as though she's going to kiss me. I jerk away, trying to avoid the contact.

"Calm down, Chasie boy. I'm not going to hurt you or anything. Although I wouldn't mind doing naughty things to you."

"I can imagine."

"No, I don't think you can." Her hands drop to my thigh, and that's when I notice her cleavage. It's as deep as the Grand Canyon. I wonder how much she paid for her boobs and I almost ask her when she hits me with, "You like what you see?"

"Uh, yeah." I really don't. Unharnessed, those jugs must hit the damn floor, but I don't want to insult the woman.

"If you want, I can show you the real things." She motions with her head toward the back of the room. "It'd only take a few, Chasie boy."

"Er, yeah, well, I think maybe another time."

"Aww, don't be scared. Mickie promises she won't bite. At least not too hard, anyway."

Why does this shit happen to me? I get all the crazies.

"I'm sure you won't, but I'll pass. Thanks just the same."

"You don't know what you're missing," she teases. For a second, I think she's going to tickle me because she has her fingers up in the air, wiggling them.

"Mickie, some other guy is going to be very lucky tonight."

"You're right, Chasie boy."

My phone, which is sitting on the bar, rings and Mickie grabs it before I can answer it. Then she says something about nobody chasing anything. It's so loud in here, though, I'm not sure if I hear her correctly. Before I can grab the phone from her, she hangs up.

"Why'd you do that?" I ask.

"Do what?"

"Answer my phone."

She shrugs and her gigantic boobs bounce. At first I think they're going to hit her in the chin, but they don't. "I dunno. Thought I'd save you the trouble."

"Don't do it again." Picking up the phone, I'm not really concerned because I figure I can return the call. Only when I check the recent call list, it was a private call. There's not a number listed.

"Hey, Mickie, was it a man or woman who called?"

She cocks her head and gives me a sly grin. "Why you wanna know?"

Grinding my teeth, I say, "Stop playing games and tell me."

"You don't need any other woman. Mickie can give you more than she can." Then she pushes her tits together again. My patience has just left the building.

"Mickie, you couldn't give me what I wanted if I were stranded on a deserted island and you were the only woman there with me. Answer the question."

"Ya don't have to get all huffy about it. It was a lady. And all she asked was if this was your number."

"Goddammit." Motioning to the bartender, I hand him my credit card and square up. There's only one person who might call like this. If it was her, I don't have a number to call her back because of some bimbo. I don't want to risk going back to her place and disturbing her home. There's no way I want to intrude on that.

"You're not going, are you?"

I don't bother answering, but head out into the cold. It's snowing now and the wind is howling. No wonder all the flights are booked. If this keeps up, I won't be getting out of here for a couple of days.

By the time I make it back to my little Airbnb apartment, I'm about frozen. I did not prepare for blizzard conditions. The first thing to do is try to reserve the next flight out. Every airline is booked for days. I spend hours on the phone, waiting and waiting. Finally, I'm able to get a seat, but it's not for five days from now. The agent explains that it may be wise to get to the airport six hours before my flight, because the airport will be a mess that day. Since Andi and I didn't work out, there isn't any sense in me hanging around here longer than necessary. And since I'm going to be delayed for so long, there's no sense in staying here and trying to see Mom and Dad. I've decided to head back to Rome.

It's after midnight when I crash, but my sleep isn't what one would call restful. I end up tossing and turning all night until I eventually get up around seven. It's so quiet, the building seems to be coated in a soundproof quilt. When I look out the window, I know why. There must be two feet of snow on the ground. It's pristine, gorgeous, and I'm fucked. I don't even have a pair of boots or gloves with me. What the hell am I going to do? Being stuck in Chicago is one thing. Being homebound is another. My blood is too fucking thin for this weather. Yes, I am a cold weather wimp.

Scrounging through the fridge, I come up with something to nibble on, but I'm starved. I need to go out and get some food. There's a small grocery store on the corner, so I decide to brave it. When I get there, they are out of almost everything, but they do have coffee, juice, and snacks left on the shelves. I buy everything I can carry back to my place. When I get home, my feet are numb. Running shoes are not a great choice for blizzard conditions. Thank God the unit has a washer and dryer. It doesn't take them long to dry, although it sounds like someone is getting the shit beaten out of them.

Mom calls to check on me. I assure her I am fine and there is nothing she can do since she is in North Carolina.

"Your uncle can come and get you."

"Mom, there is too much snow. I would never ask him to get out in this. They haven't cleared the roads yet. Honestly, I'm fine. I went to the store and stocked up. Don't worry so much."

"Don't ever tell a mother not to worry about her children. One day you'll understand, Chase."

That's not likely, but I don't mention it to her. We say our goodbyes and I turn the TV on. What great timing I have, because it's just in time to catch Lucia, or rather a recording of her, saying that we're not engaged after all. It was a misunderstanding. Only the way she says it, and then how she sobs afterward, makes her look like the spurned woman. Excellent. Fucking awesome. What else can go wrong? This has turned into an epic shit show.

My phone rings and Max is calling.

"Max, what the fuck was that?"

"Was what?"

"Lucia's retraction."

"It was the best I could get from her," Max says.

"Yeah, well, the media is going to crucify me."

"Maybe not. If we can capture her cavorting with someone else, who knows? So when are you coming back? We need to discuss your contract."

"I'm stuck here, Max."

"Stuck? What do you mean?"

I explain my situation.

"Shit." But when he says it, it sounds like *sheet*.

"Exactly. I have a reservation in five days, but the agent wasn't optimistic. With the way things are today, it doesn't look like anything will go out today. Not to mention, it's still snowing."

"Then the phone will have to do. You need to consider what Munich is offering. They're currently third in the world and in Europe. Rome is eighth in the world, I'm sorry to say. The contract is solid. Our attorneys have asked and received everything you wanted. You won't get a better deal." Then he chuckles and says, "Unless, of course, Madrid offers you something." Madrid is number one, so I doubt I'll be getting that call.

"That would be nice, huh?"

"My opinion is you're in a better position where you are. You have room for growth and your skill level is as good or better than the Madrid players. That's why we can negotiate such a great contract."

"How long before I have to tell them?"

"You'll have until the end of January, and then the opportunity will be gone. I don't want you to lose this, Chase. These kinds of contracts don't come along very often. Not with this kind of money attached."

"Okay. Thanks, Max. And out of curiosity, what kind of money could I get back here in the States?"

I hear a choking sound. "Did you say the States?"

"Yeah."

"You can't possibly want to play there. They aren't even ranked. They couldn't pay what you're worth."

"Aside from all that, what do you think I could get?"

"I'd have to check, but maybe a quarter of what you're making, if that much. If you want to play in the States, you should consider their football. You know, the fake one." He laughs.

"Hey, don't forget my brother is a quarterback for the pros."

"Then play for his team. Maybe he could get you on as a place kicker. You're such a great striker, I imagine you could be a great asset as one of those."

"Max, you're so fucking funny, do you hear me laughing?" I'm doing anything but.

"All the way in Rome. Call me, Chase, when you can give me an answer."

"I want you to check on those figures about playing back here first."

"You can't be serious?"

"Just check. You're my agent. That's what I pay you to do. And make sure Lucia doesn't make an ass out of me."

"I'm trying. Stay away from the ladies." Those are his last words before the phone disconnects.

My head pounds. Was I serious about moving back here and downgrading to a U.S. team? With Andi out of the picture, why would I even consider it?

I flip on the TV and channel surf, trying to come up with something to watch. As it turns out, the only thing worth watching is football, and not the kind I play. Before I know it, I wake up several hours later. When I peer out the window, it's still snowing. I feel like a caged animal. The skies are gray, telling me there's no break in sight. Staying in here for the rest of the day and night isn't going to work for me. I shower, dress in the warmest things I have, and head back out to the closest bar. It's only a couple of blocks from here.

To my surprise, the place is open, and packed. The TVs are on because the Bears are playing. After waiting in line, I get the bartender's attention and snag a beer. The guy standing next to me is an obnoxious fan and yells constantly. Maybe a few beers will dull his voice. Unfortunately, it doesn't work, so I move to another spot. Only it seems the place is filled with these people. Why shouldn't it be? *It's Chicago, Chase. These are local fans, you dumbass.*

Doing my best to ignore them, I keep drinking. I guess it's because I've always been on the field playing, or with my brother, and never noticed this kind of shit before, but damn, these people are loud. Really loud. It's dark out by now, and I'm getting pretty fucking drunk and pretty fucking sick of hearing them boast about their team, and blah, blah, blah. All I want to do is get the hell out of this town.

When I can't stand any more, when I've finally reached that point, the point where everything hits—the issue with Lucia, the fact that I came all this way to tell Andi I love her, only to find she has a family, and then the damn blizzard—I let it all out.

"I don't know why the hell you keep going on and on about this shit. This isn't even fucking football. The real football is played in Europe."

Everyone around me stops talking and stares at me.

"What the fuck did you say?" some burly guy stands up and asks. He's all geared up in a Bears baseball hat and football jersey, and he outweighs me by fifty pounds. Even though it's not muscle, I'm sure his fist is the size of a bear's paw.

"I'm pretty fucking sure you heard me."

The dude gets in my face. "You can't be talking about that pansy ass game where those pussies kick a ball around and can't touch each other, are you?"

My fists ball up. "I'm not sure I heard what you said."

"No, I think you did. That shit played in Europe, *soccer*, ain't football, dude. So if you don't like what you see, take your pussy ass out of here and go back to Europe and fangirl over there."

"Did you say fangirl?"

He grins. "You bet I did."

I don't blink or wait for him to think. My fist flies and I deck him in the kisser. He drops like a stone. Now I have a problem, because it's me against everyone in the bar and I'm not sober. Someone pops me straight in the nose and face a couple of times, and another person lands a few hits to my ribs because I'm being held from behind, but the fight is broken up before it gets started. Some big ass fucker grabs me and throws me out on the sidewalk.

"If you ever bring your face in here again, you're going to jail. Got it?"

Not bothering to answer, because there's no reason to, I stagger to my feet and stumble away. My nose is probably broken, and I'm not sure what else is messed up. I can't breathe, so my ribs might be cracked. Blood runs into my mouth and I hope my damn teeth aren't damaged. When I get to the corner, someone is there who asks if I need help. My shit show has turned into a shit storm and this part is my own making.

"Can you get me a taxi? I probably should go to the hospital." The words are so slurred, I'm not sure if he even understands me.

"Do you need me to call 911?" he asks.

"No! I'm not that bad off. A cab or Uber will do. Here, use my phone." I hope he doesn't steal the fucking thing. That would be my luck. Turns out, he's a good Samaritan and an Uber shows up. I'm a little surprised, given the weather.

When I get in the car, the driver says, "Hey, man, don't bleed in this car."

"I won't. Just take me to the closest ER."

"What happened?"

"Someone punched me."

"Wow, you should call the police."

"Nah, it was … never mind." The hospital isn't far at all, and I add a hefty tip to the Uber fee and thank him.

"Good luck with that."

As I'm weaving my way toward the door, all I can think of is what a disastrous trip this has been. It's then I hear my name.

"Chase?"

I look up and see a vision standing there.

NINE

Andi

BLOOD MARS his beautiful face and I can't stop myself from racing over to cup his cheek to make sure he's okay.

"Chase, what happened?"

His hands circle my wrists. "I'm okay, Andi. Just a little misunderstanding."

"Misunderstanding?" I repeat in disbelief. I lightly rub a fingertip over the bridge of his nose. "It's probably broken."

Glazed, but sad eyes hold mine with fierce determination. He removes my hand from his face and my heart cracks. Every other time I've seen him over the years, he's welcomed my touch. Not today. I drop my arms with no choice but to accept the boundaries he's drawn between us.

"That's why I'm here," he slurs.

The reek of alcohol permeates the air between us. I'm about to speak when he takes a wobbly step forward and winces. He presses his palm to his chest. Had his bloody nose been the result of him getting into a brawl? He nearly takes a tumble with his next step. I duck under his arm and help him inside. Thankfully, he doesn't push me away.

I use my employee card to get through the secured doors. I

recognize one of the nurses once we get inside. After seeing me, she waves me through to the back. I steer him toward the triage area when Beth sees me.

"Hey," she says with wide eyes and immediately moves to his other side to help me with the big man.

She guides us into the main emergency area and into one of the empty rooms. It's not protocol to skip triage, but working at the hospital and having my best friend be a nurse in the emergency department has its perks.

Relief sets in once he's seated on the bed. Beth gives me a *what the fuck* glance before turning her eyes on the patient.

"Can you tell me what happened, sir?"

I don't think when I cut in and introduce him.

"This is Chase."

Her jaw comes unhinged and her eyes bug out. "*The* Chase?"

I nod and glance over. However, my former flame isn't tracking our conversation. When he opens his mouth, it's clear he's been stuck at her first question.

"What happened? I'll tell you. The fucking asshole's friends didn't appreciate me taking down the guy a peg. Figures. They have to be stupid not to understand football by definition and logic is a sport you play primarily with your foot and not your hands." He chuckles and continues to speak as if each word was connected. "I showed them what you do with your hands. And well, I would have won if they didn't all come at me at the same time."

"Uh-huh," Beth says, used to multitasking.

She's checking over his face and notices his split lip.

She sighs. "Any other places you're injured?"

"His chest," I say before Chase can. He glares at me, so I add, "He might have a few broken ribs. He was grabbing it when I found him."

"Where?" she asks. I point to the spot he'd clutched earlier.

She directs her next question at him. "Anywhere else? Abdominal pain or lower back?"

He shakes his head and says, "No."

"Can you tell me your pain level from one to ten, ten being the worst pain you've experienced in your life?"

A lopsided grin forms on his face. "Does that include a broken heart?"

Damn him, the flirt. She gets his smile and not me. I don't want to be jealous, but envy grows like a weed in my chest.

"I bet you're the heartbreaker," she says.

"Okay," I say, annoyed and wanting them back on track. "One to ten, Chase?"

"I don't know." He ends with a little laugh, reminding us both he's drunk.

Beth shifts to the computer. "Let me get him in the system so we can get a doctor in here. Someone from up front will be in here as soon as I enter this for your insurance information. Your name?"

When Chase hesitates, I answer, "Chase Wilde."

"Address?"

"Rome," he says, thinking he's funny. Beth shoots him an exasperated look.

I rattle off his parents' address in Waynesville.

"Thanks. I need to get his blood pressure and temperature, and someone will probably be in to draw blood for labs."

Stepping back, I put more distance between us, giving Beth the opportunity to do her job. After she's done, she hands him a gown. "Get undressed and the doctor should be in shortly. Do you need assistance?"

"He's fine," I say, although with him being as drunk as he is, I'm not so sure.

She gestures with her head, asking me to follow her. Once we pass the boundary of the curtain, she closes it to afford him some privacy.

"What the hell?" she whispers.

"I have no idea. He came by yesterday and I haven't heard from him since. Not that he has to check in with me. I just happened to run into him in the parking lot as I was leaving after my shift when he stumbled out of a car."

"Are you okay? Did he come to see you?"

My shoulders slump. "I don't think so. Not that it matters. He's engaged."

She gives me a dirty look. "When were you going to tell me all of this?"

I shrug. Had he come here to tell me about his engagement? The thought makes my eyes burn. Beth, reading my thoughts, pats my shoulders.

"We'll talk later. I've got patients."

"Okay."

I take a moment before entering Chase's room. When I do, he's all tangled up in trying to get off his shirt. It's halfway up his torso, revealing a swath of lightly tanned skin with all its ridges and planes. Luckily, his face is covered. He doesn't notice my riveted stare or my hesitation. The idea that he might flinch from my touch is reason enough for my reluctance.

Finally, I help him. My palms burn against his skin as I push the shirt up until his head pops free, leaving his hair a static cling mess. For a second, we both freeze. We've never been this close without acting on our lust since that first time we were together. My heart beats a thousand times faster, skipping a few here and there. Finally, I move back, tugging at the cloth until his arms are out of the holes. What had tethered us together crumples in my hands as I fight my need to touch him.

"You need to remove your pants as well," I say.

For privacy's sake, I turn, giving him a view of my back as I fight to regain my composure. I have loved this man since the first day I laid eyes on him. He's been my biggest champion, my defender, and my first for so many things.

It all began so long ago and he's never treated me differently, always an equal. He taught me how to play all sports, including his beloved football, though then he called it soccer. Seems living overseas, he's adopted a new attitude about that, which brought him here today.

A loud thump jolts me from my thoughts. I spin around to find Chase bent over, clutching his chest with one hand. The other tries but fails at pushing his pants down while braced against the hospital bed.

In a rush, I'm at his side helping him back onto the bed.

"Lie back," I say, hating the pain etched on his face.

Then as clinically as possible, I remove his pants after I get his shoes off.

I want to sag after he's dressed in a gown with a blanket over him. I can't think of another time I helped him undress that we weren't on the verge of fucking each other's brains out. For a second, I close my eyes, trying to fight those memories. Hell, it's not just the sex I remember. It's the way he'd look at me after. The way he'd tenderly touch my face and how I wanted to believe I'd meant everything to him. I fight the urge not to cry at my stupidity. When I open them, I find his lids firmly shut.

Panic sets in. I may be a neonatal nurse, but I know all about concussions. Knowing his jaw might be sore as well, I place a gentle hand on his cheek and call his name. Those stormy gray eyes of his open. My name is a mere whisper on his lips before his hand snakes around the back of my neck, drawing me down. I plunge into the well of desire, drowning in lust and need for a man I can no longer have.

Before I'm lost and pulled by the undertow of lost love and heartbreak, I yank back, drawing in a lung full of air, needing it to breathe.

"I'm sorry," he slurs.

He blinks so rapidly, I'm sure he doesn't fully realize what he's done.

"It's nothing. You just need to stay awake until they determine if you have a concussion."

His head bobs. "I think I'm drunk."

His confession comes out of nowhere. I laugh from the absurdity of it. At least the tension dissipates.

"That's an understatement. Why were you out drinking in the first place?"

I need to keep him talking, but after I ask, I panic. Has he guessed my secrets?

"Because I'm stuck in a snowstorm and I can't fly."

He makes no sense. It hasn't been snowing. Clearly, he's had a few too many. Though there had been talk about an incoming storm.

His lids drift shut.

"Chase."

When he stares up at me, I'm sure he's seeing someone else. There's a reverence there that can't belong to me.

"I should have told you I love you," he says.

The most confusing thing about what he says is that it comes out coherently. Suddenly, my mouth is dry and I'm speechless. There's no way to respond because Justin breezes in. He glances between us before walking over to Chase.

He pulls a small penlight from his lab coat and says, "Mr. Wilde, I understand you had an altercation this evening."

Chase holds up an unsteady hand. "To be fair, I was outnumbered. But you should see the first guy."

Justin uses a light to make sure Chase's pupils are responding as they should. If they don't, it could mean that he might have severe brain injury. "I can imagine. Let's get some pictures to see what's going on with your nose and ribs."

When Justin doesn't linger on his eyes, I breathe a little easier. Before he finishes, a tech guy shows up to take Chase to X-ray. Because Chase is looking at me like he won't see me again, I mouth, *I'll be right here* before he disappears.

Knowing this won't take long, I use the opportunity to call Owen. "Hey, Owen."

"Andi, everything okay?" Owen asks during my pause.

"Yes and no. Something came up. I'm running late. Do you mind watching Violet for a little longer?"

"No problem. Are you working late?"

"Something like that. I'll explain when I get home."

"Yeah, sure. She's eaten dinner. I'll grab her pajamas from your place and she can bunk here overnight if you want."

"Thanks. I might take you up on that. You're a lifesaver."

I hang up and wonder why I didn't tell him about Chase. But I do know. Things are now weird between us. It's better if I fully explain when I see him. Potentially, Owen could be the next guy I date. The last thing I need is for him to come to the wrong conclusions wondering about Chase and me. The truth is, I don't want Owen to ask me questions I can't yet answer, like what my feelings are for Chase. The only answer I have at the moment is complicated …

Grateful for Beth and Justin expediting things, Chase's results come quickly. Justin's ruled out a concussion, and the radiologist arrives to report on the X-rays.

"Mr. Wilde, looks like only your nose is broken. Your ribs are bruised and will heal on their own, although they'll hurt like the devil. I suggest you not be alone for the next twenty-four hours just in case. We're waiting on the ear, nose, and throat specialist to get here so he can set your nose. It's an easy thing, really. We'll give you a local anesthetic along with something for the pain and he'll do his thing. It'll take him five minutes tops."

Chase asks, "You can't do it?"

"You don't want me to do it. You'll end up with a big hump on your nose. That's why we call in the experts. He'll send you home with a pretty bandage too. But you can't be alone tonight, understand?"

Justin glances at me. I shrug. Chase brought his fiancée. Though why isn't she here?

"I'm in town alone," Chase answers my unspoken question.

That surprises me.

"He can stay with me," I blurt. I hold up a hand when

Chase tries to protest. "It's not up for discussion. Your mother would kill me if I didn't watch over you."

That keeps him quiet.

"Good," Justin says. "I can have the pharmacy fill your pain prescription."

"Yes, please," I answer for Chase, not wanting to make another stop on the way home.

Justin leaves and the registration nurse comes in to get Chase's insurance information. He produces a black American Express and I'm not surprised.

While Chase is getting his nose taken care of, I head to the pharmacy to pick up his prescription. By the time I get back, he's chatting up a storm about nonsensical things that have to do with football and Germany. I can't make out a thing he says.

Later, when we stumble through my apartment door, I'm barely two steps inside before Chase makes a beeline for my couch. He's flat on his back and asleep before I can offer him my bed. I cover him with a blanket because there is no way I can carry him to my room. When I do, my heart hurts seeing him so vulnerable. I take a chance and brush my lips over his temple, whispering words he'll never hear. Then I dutifully set an alarm on my phone so I can check on him every few hours over the course of the night. With phone in hand, I almost call his parents. But there is no need to worry them. It's only a broken nose. So after one last lingering glance to ensure he's breathing, I exit my apartment to go to Owen's to get Violet and awkwardly explain why I'm late.

TEN

Chase

WHAT THE HELL! Pain shoots through my entire face, lighting it on fire. I blink open my eyes, and staring at me from an inch away is a pair of large gray irises. The cherubic face surrounding them makes me question where the fuck I am. I squeeze my lids tight in the hopes the image will disappear. Except my nose and face erupt into another spasm of pain, and now I've figured out the reason. A chubby finger, whose owner is the cute little face I was confused about, keeps poking it. Then it gets worse. I rub my nose in an attempt to figure out why the hell it hurts every time she jabs it. Because, come on, the little tyke is what? Three? Does she have SuperBaby fingers or something? Only as soon as my palm hits it, I nearly levitate off the couch I'm lying on and slam into the ceiling. The toddler, with her dark ringlets, breaks into a fit of giggles. I'm glad someone thinks it's funny.

What happened to my fucking nose? My fingers gently trace the outline of it, only to discover gauze, tape, and an impossibly swollen bulge. The source of my pain takes aim at me again, but this time I intercept it. That brings on another fit of laughter, and her grin is so wide I can count eight of her teeth. Even though my face hurts like a mother, I can't help chuckling right along with her. She's so damn cute, and when she jumps around in front of the couch, she's comical as hell.

I glance around the room, taking in the scene. I'm at Andi's place and vaguely remember coming back here after my trip to the hospital last night. It is with great difficulty I keep my eyes from slamming shut, but I recall making it to the couch, and then nothing. She must've covered me up and crashed herself. I guess her husband is still asleep too.

The little kid tears off to the kitchen, which is basically right across the room. She's jabbering away, though I have no clue what the girl is saying. She runs fast, and right when I think she's going to crash into something, she veers away and is saved. Finally, she heads straight for me and I put my hand over my nose for protection. I need a face guard around this one.

"Dada. Dada." She points at me.

"No, I'm not Dada. He must still be asleep, Little One."

"DaaaDaaa." The kid sure has a set of lungs on her.

I reckon it's time to get up. Since my nose throbs like hell, I grab the bottle of pain pills I notice sitting on the coffee table. Then I stagger into the kitchen. My ribs feel as though the old mule Dad used to have on the farm kicked me. No, make that ten of those old mules. It takes me several cabinets before I locate the one with the glasses. Then I guzzle down water, along with a pill. My head throbs, too, though I'm sure all the alcohol had something to do with that.

The baby girl is following me around everywhere. "Dada. Dada."

"No, Cutie Girl, I'm not Dada. I'm Chase. And Chase needs to pee."

"Potty. Potty. Poopie."

"No poopie," I say.

Suddenly, she squats down and says, "Poopie. Now."

Oh, shit. Does this mean she has to go?

"You have to poopie?"

Her head bobs up and down. Now what the hell do I do? I've never spent much time with babies or changed a diaper, and she has to fucking poop!

Then she pops up and runs down the hall. Following her, because I don't know what else to do, she goes into the bathroom and pulls down her pants.

"Do you really have to do this? Can't you wait until your mama gets up or something? I think I'm going to wait out there." I point to the hallway.

"Noooo. Poopie."

Clearly, I'm a moron here. She has the biggest grin on her face as she sits on this tiny baby toilet. Oh my fucking hell. She's going to poop in there, and then what? Where does it go? Is there a flush mechanism or something, or do I have to manually get rid of it? Fuck me now.

"Poopie gone." She points to a container on the counter. "Poopie gone." I check it out and it looks like a bunch of Skittles in there. Does she get Skittles in exchange for a poop? Is this what kids do these days? They poop and get Skittles? "Poopie gone," she reminds me again.

"Okay, I got it. I take the lid off the container, take one out, and hand her one. I'll be damned. I never got Skittles for pooping when I was little.

Then she just stares at me. Now what? She aims that finger —which I'm now coming to understand is a very useful tool for a toddler—at the roll of toilet paper.

Oh, for fuck's sake. Not that too.

"Poopie gone."

"Here we go." I try to close my eyes, but this is a job that requires full-on visual capacity. I make it quick and let her know she's ready to go. When she gets up, I shut the lid on that thing and get ready to use the facilities.

"Okay, let's wash our hands." She holds out her tiny hands and wiggles her fingers. I get the job done in record time.

But the kid looks at me like I'm not finished. Too fucking bad. I won't do the rest of the story, as they say.

"Go in the other room. Chase has to pee."

She stands there and giggles. By now, my bladder's about to burst, so I nudge her out of the room so I can let it loose. She's mumbling something from the other side of the door, but after a second, she loses interest and I hear her feet padding down the hall. Then I hear her yelling, "Dada pee-pee. Dada pee-pee." Oh, boy.

When I get back to the living room, she's running around, full of energy, and all I want to do is sleep. How do parents do it? I lie down and she pats me on the stomach with both hands about a dozen times.

"Dada. Hungy. Cherinos."

"What?"

"Cherinos." She slams her palms on my stomach. Then she picks up her shirt and says, "Hungy. Cherinos."

She's hungry and my guess is for Cheerios.

"All righty. Let Uncle Chase make you some breakfast." She follows me this time into the kitchen. I hunt through the cabinets until I find her favorite cereal. When I show her the box, she claps her little hands and jumps excitedly.

There's a high chair near the counter, so I pull it close and set her in it, making sure she's secure. Then I get a bowl, cereal, and milk, along with a spoon. And while I'm at it, I grab one for me too. We sit and eat together. Or maybe I should say I eat, because there isn't a word for what she does. Fucking hell, she makes a mess. That shit is everywhere. Cheerios fly all over the place. There is more food on the floor and her tray than in her stomach. Thank God I tied a towel around her neck or she would've been covered in the crap.

How do kids stay alive eating this way? I can't fathom her getting much out of this since most of it never made it to her mouth. Do parents just feed them every hour or so? Her spoon plunges into the bowl and scoops up a dose, but from the bowl to her mouth, she gets maybe one Cheerio. When her bowl is empty, she looks at me and says, "Hungy."

"No shit. None of it made it to your stomach."

"No shit," she repeats.

"Don't say that." Oh, God, Andi will have my balls if she hears her kid saying *shit*.

"More Cherinos."

I guess it's okay since she didn't eat much, so I load her bowl up again. Only this time I don't add as much milk. It doesn't help. The little rings of oats are all over the place. Andi must have the cleanest kitchen in the world, picking up after this one. But when she's halfway through this bowl, all of a sudden, she takes her hand and slams it on her bowl. And my question would be—who was the dumb motherfucker that invented cereal? He should be shot. Andi's kitchen looks like Little One and I just had a giant food fight. She's giggling at the mess she made, and I don't know if I should leave her there strapped to her chair and go home or laugh right along with her.

I go with the second, because she has the most adorable expression on her face, not to mention a Cheerio plastered to her chin.

"Has anyone ever told you you're a mess, Little One?"

"Messh. DaaaDaaa."

"Chase." I pat my chest and say, "Chase."

Her head swings back and forth and she counters with, "Dada."

For some reason, she thinks I'm Dada. Maybe she thinks I look like her dad, though as I recall, I don't resemble the guy Andi was in the park with.

"Chase needs to clean up Little One's mess."

"Messh."

I spy a roll of paper towels on the counter and go to work. Those pain pills have made me a bit loopy, and when I bend down, my head spins a bit. Cheerios have made their way clear across the floor. No doubt Andi will find these things for years after this kid stops eating them. When the cleanup on the floor is done, I tackle Little One. She grins like a goon the whole time. She sure is a good-natured little kid. After the catastrophe is taken care of, I let her out of her chair and suppose it's time to head out of here. But I don't want to go without leaving Andi a note, thanking her.

There's a notepad on her counter, along with a pen, so I jot down a quick note.

Andi,
Thanks so much for coming to my rescue last night and letting me stay here. Don't
know what I would've done without you. I owe you one.
Chase

There's another dilemma facing me: Little One. My friend used to crate his dog when he left, but I'm pretty damn sure you don't do that with a kid. What should I do with her? I don't want to barge into Andi's bedroom. What if she and the husband are, well, I can't think of that.

My ass falls back onto the couch as I try to figure out my next move. I'm sitting there thinking when I hear a key rattling the lock in the door. When it opens, I'm surprised to see Andi's husband walk in.

"Hi." He pauses before he says, "I'm Owen, and you must be Chase."

"Yeah." I stand and hold out my hand. We shake, then I add, "I was just about to leave."

We're interrupted by Little One yelling, "Mama. Mama."

I turn to see Andi walk into the room, sleepy-eyed, with bed hair, and fuck me, all I want to do is take her in my arms and kiss that sweet mouth of hers. And doesn't that make me the shittiest guy around when her damn husband stands not two feet away?

"Good morning, sweet Violet," she says, as Little One runs into her arms. Violet. That's the kid's name.

Andi casts a guilt-ridden look my way. "I hope she wasn't a problem. I never planned to sleep this late."

"No worries. She's a great kid." Maybe now's not the time to tell her about the little present waiting for her in the bathroom.

Then she asks, "You've met Owen?"

"Yes, just now."

Owen steps forward and says, "I was only stopping by to drop this off. You forgot this when you picked up Violet last night."

"Oh, thanks," Andi says.

This is weird. Why would she pick up Violet?

We all stand in a circle, when Violet breaks the silence. "Dada," she yells.

An awkward laugh comes out of me. Andi cocks her head and levels her eyes at me. She doesn't speak for a moment, but when she does, she says, "Owen, thanks for dropping by. Can I call you later?"

"Oh." Owen looks weird. "Yeah, sure."

Owen dips his head and leaves. Now I'm extremely confused. Why would her husband leave, unless he's not her husband at all?

When the door closes behind Owen, Violet runs around, as happy as can be.

"Chase, there's something we need to talk about ... something that's long overdue."

I couldn't agree with her more. But I need answers about this Owen guy.

"Why did you send your husband away?"

ELEVEN

Andi

"Husband?" I ask. His brow arches. I hold up a finger before catching Violet around the waist. I pick her up and carry her to the sofa where I retrieve the remote. "How about you watch *Doc McStuffins*?"

Violet claps. I set her down and turn to Chase. I crook a finger at him to follow me into the kitchen. I hope he doesn't go ape shit when I tell him the truth.

Once we are there, my hands shake. To hide it, I pour two cups of coffee and hand him one.

"You still like it black, right?"

He nods.

"What's going on, Andi? I know when you're hiding something. What's up?"

I let out a sigh. Over the years I've told myself I was doing the right thing. But seeing his questioning eyes, I know I've made a colossal mistake. I can't force out the words, so I start off easy.

"How are you feeling?"

His gaze narrows. "Fine." He speaks as if he's forcing himself to remain calm. My heart races and I feel slightly light-headed at the idea of diving into the past. "It's a little sore, but I'll live. Now what's this about? Why did you send Owen away?"

Despite the impending conversation, I reach up, touch his temple, glide my fingers down his cheek, and over to probe lightly at his nose. I have a feeling he won't let me near him when our conversation is over. He winces when I touch a sore spot.

"Sorry, occupational hazard. I need to make sure you're okay."

He snags my hand. When he doesn't let go, my hearts skips so many beats it's surprising I remain standing.

"As much as I enjoy you touching me, I need to know who Owen is before this goes any further."

I lick my lips, catching the lower one between my teeth for a second as I try to prepare myself for what's coming.

"He's my neighbor and a friend."

"That's it?" His face brightens and I hold onto that picture. He won't look that way for long.

As much as I don't want to, I pull free of his grasp and turn away. Tears prick the back of my eyes, though I have no right to cry. When I turn, I can see the wheels turning in his expression.

"When you walked away and went to Europe, I thought that was the end of us," I begin.

"Andi, I made so many mistakes. That's why I'm here."

I hold up a finger as he takes a step in my direction.

"When you left, you didn't leave me alone."

Confusion makes lines form on his beautiful face.

"What does that mean?"

I glance over at Violet to make sure she isn't paying any attention to us. I turn back to find that he's followed my line of sight. When our eyes meet, I see when the pieces begin to connect for him.

"I never meant to keep this from you. I thought I was doing the right thing. I even wrote a letter to you I meant to send a thousand times."

Every muscle in his body goes stock-still.

"What are you saying, Andi?"

He's put it together, but the frost in his tone means he wants me to say it. Without wasting another breath, I do.

"Violet's your daughter."

I'm not sure what he will do next. Chase can be the sweetest guy in the world, but he also can freeze people out with a single glare.

He points a finger at me and narrows his eyes.

"She's mine and you kept this from me?"

His disbelief only heightens the guilt I've felt over the years.

"Honestly, I thought I was doing the right thing."

"My daughter?" he repeats.

"Chase." I make the mistake of reaching for him, but he takes a huge step back.

So far, our talk, though fueled with emotions, remains in a conversational tone bordering on whispers at least with his last ragged words.

"Does Mark know? Your parents?"

I shake my head.

"You've kept this secret from everyone?"

Yes, and it's been eating away at me bit by bit.

"How could I tell anyone before I told you? That didn't seem right."

"That didn't seem right?" He laughs, though a humorless one. "But keeping my daughter from me is okay. She's what, three now?"

"No, she's two."

"Two years I've had a daughter. Here I thought I screwed up by walking away from you, only to find out you're nothing but a liar."

I step forward and plead with him. I hate the way he looks at me now, like I'm a stranger. "Please, I'm sorry."

"Sorry doesn't give me back two years, Andi. Sorry doesn't even come close."

"It's not like you ever made it a secret that you didn't want kids," I blurt. It isn't fair, but it had been part of my reason for keeping it to myself. "I didn't want you to give up your career or resent me later because I got pregnant."

His lips compress as he shakes his head in bewilderment. "It's your body. I get that. But I had a right to be in on your plans, assuming she's mine."

I move back, a gasp held in my lungs.

"Don't be an asshole, Chase. You know you were the only one."

He shakes a finger. "No, I don't know anything, least of all you. The Andi I knew wouldn't have kept this from me. I don't know who you are."

I rein in my anger. He has every right to be mad. I'll give him a pass for that bullshit comment because he's upset, rightfully so.

"I deserve that. I get you're pissed at me. But know this, Chase Wilde. Violet is your daughter. I would never lie about that."

He turns to find her. Violet's in her own world singing to herself while mesmerized by the show. I keep my mouth closed because what else can I say? When he faces me again, it's as if I'm staring into the face of an alien. All the tenderness is long gone.

"She called me Dada. Why?"

Nothing I say will help me in this moment, but he will get only the truth from me going forward.

"I have a scrapbook with pictures of everyone. She likes to look at it every night before bed. Your picture is in there."

He chuckles darkly. "So she knows who I am?"

I nod.

"Fan-fucking-tastic. She knows that I haven't been in her life, that I've been a ghost of a father, while I didn't even know she existed."

He pivots before I can answer, making short work of killing the distance between him and the door.

"Chase, wait!"

The door is open and the menace on his face stops me.

"I always knew you were good at keeping secrets. Hell, our family doesn't know about us. But this … I didn't think you could keep something like this from me."

"If I could do it over—"

Even when Chase thought Owen was my husband, in my heart I felt that he still cared for me. Looking at him now, it's as if I never meant a thing to him.

"What can I say to make this right?"

"Right?" Another laugh born of pain escapes him. "Honestly, I can't stand the sight of you right now. But know this, you've had two whole years with *our* daughter. It's my turn now."

Panic fuels my rapid steps in his direction. "What does that mean?"

The door is almost closed, but I hear him clearly.

"It means you'll be hearing from my lawyer."

I cover my mouth with my hand as a sob tears through me. Yes, I've royally fucked up. But the idea of losing my daughter scares the absolute shit out of me.

TWELVE

Chase

───────────

ANDI'S WORDS keep ringing through my head like a fucking bell. Two years. Two fucking years. Well, longer if you count the pregnancy, and that wasn't even mentioned. How could she do this? And then she had the nerve to throw in my face how I didn't want kids. Talk about hitting below the belt.

Not to mention her talk about doing this for my career. Keeping my child away from me because of my career? Like hell! All this time I thought I was the bad guy for walking away. I always wanted to bring our relationship out in the open, but she insisted on keeping us a secret, so I did it to please her. I would've done anything for her. Well, look where it got me. I'm the one who ultimately gets my face rubbed in shit.

I always thought I knew her, knew the type of person she was. Evidently, I was way off-base on that one. The Andi I knew and loved—yes, *loved*, because all the emotions I had for her were drained out of me when she revealed the truth about Violet—was nothing more than a sham.

Who am I kidding? I'm beyond pissed the hell off, but my heart aches for her.

The snow is almost knee-deep as I trudge my way through

it, but I don't give a fuck. My inadequate clothing isn't enough to ward off the chill, but that's fine with me. Bring it the fuck on. Even the cold numbing my cheeks is a blessing. I need numb. It's a necessity to get me through the next hours. How the fuck will I make it through until I can get the hell out of here? There has never been a time in my life when I felt this much anger toward one human being, and to think she's the mother of my child. Jesus C, I'm a father. A damn father.

That little sweet-faced girl is mine. MINE and I've missed everything in her life.

I stop and lean against a building, forcing myself to breathe. This is so fucked up. How the hell did I even get to this point? This was supposed to be a nice little trip, where I showed up on Andi's doorstep, told her I fucked up when I left, that I loved her, and then everything would be cool. She was my one. But now look at me. I'm gutted, shattered. My emotions are a goddamn train wreck.

Forcing myself to keep moving so my stupid feet don't get frostbite, I eventually see my street up ahead. When I get to my rental, I'm to the point when I practically have to drag my feet to walk.

Wouldn't my football fans be proud of me now? Shit. I rip off my clothes and take a hot shower, careful not to get my face wet. I'm not even sure if I'm supposed to get that shit checked again. I'll take a look at it when I get out of the shower. Once I'm warmed up, I turn off the hot water. The bathroom is so steamy, I have to wipe the mirror to see. My nose is definitely broken. Not the first time it's happened, and I'm sure it won't be the last. I do a little poking and prodding to find it's not too bad. Then I pull on some clothes and call the only person I know who can help.

"Fletcher, I need you."

My brother is the one person I trust even over my friends or any of my teammates.

"What's up, Chase? You don't sound so good."

"No, I'm not good at all. In fact, I can't remember a time when I've felt this … fucked up. How much time do you have, because this may take a while."

"I have all the time you need. I'm free. Shoot."

I begin with the real reason I came to Chicago and everything that transpired up to this morning. When I get to the part about Andi telling me about Violet, he interrupts me.

"So, wait. What you're saying is Andi has a kid?"

"Yeah, a daughter named Violet."

"Holy shit."

"You'd better sit down," I tell him.

"I am. Go on. But, man, I can't believe she has a kid. And two years old at that. No one knows either. How the hell did she pull that off?"

"No idea. But that's not why I'm calling. See, as I said earlier, Andi was my girl, right? Well, Violet is my daughter."

Fletcher doesn't say anything for a while.

"Fletch? You there?"

"Uh, yeah. Your daughter? Violet is your daughter?"

"Yeah. Imagine my shock. Andi never told me and I'm so furious right now. She totally fucked me over. I swear I could put both fists through a concrete wall right now. And the fucked up thing about it is I still love her, but I don't know what to do." Then I go into Andi's excuses of why she never told me. "I don't even give a shit about all her justifications. I want to be a father to my kid. Which means I'll probably have to go for custody because I've been cheated out of two years with her."

"Fuck. Fuck. Fuck, Chase."

"Exactly."

"You have a two-year-old daughter. Holy shit. What are you going to do?"

"It's why I'm calling. I need you, man. I need your advice. Like I said, she's my kid too, but I don't think Andi will let her go to Italy with me."

"You mean you'd go for total custody?" Fletcher asks. His voice tells me he isn't one hundred percent on board with that.

"I don't have a choice. I want my two years back. She fucked me out of them, Fletch."

"But, dude, she's her mother. You can't pull a kid away from her mother like that. Especially if she's a good mom, and I'm sure Andi is."

"Are you? Then why didn't she tell me? She even has a scrapbook of pictures and shows Violet, so my daughter called me *Dada*. She thinks I'm some kind of an absentee dad."

"Okay, let's think about this logically. You don't think you can work something out with her."

"I'm so fucking mad right now I can't see straight. She lied to me. The Andi I've loved all my life would never lie to me. How can I trust her?"

"Okay, I get you going for custody. But go for joint or shared. Not total. That's just wrong, brother."

"And her keeping this from me isn't wrong? I'm not sure if I should love her or hate her or somewhere in the middle.

"Chase, you going after total custody is you trying to get revenge against Andi, but who's it really going to hurt in the end?"

Though I know where he's going with this, I blurt, "Andi." I am emphatic about this.

I know it's a knee jerk reaction. But I want her to hurt as much as I am and that's wrong, but it's how I feel at the moment.

"No, you dumbass. It's going to hurt your daughter. And trust me. After you form a bond with her, you would never in a million years want to do anything to hurt that kid. Taking her away from her mother would damage her."

"Fuck. Goddammit. I know your right."

"And what will you do with Violet when you have her? You travel with soccer."

"Football."

"Whatever. Are you going to take her to Italy with you? Who will keep her? Will you hire a nanny? And is a nanny better than her own mother? There's so much to think about."

My brother poses a ton of things I haven't begun to process.

"Did I mention she has a guy who's more of a father to my daughter than me?"

He's silent for a second. "Chase."

"No, never mind. I get it. I just want to be there for Violet and you're making this whole fatherhood thing very complicated."

"Listen, I'm not saying not to go for some type of custody arrangement, but you need to do what's best for your little girl and not think about how Andi hurt you. It has to be difficult, I'm sure, but seriously, if you do this the right way and don't use her as a pawn, she'll grow to love you and not hate you. Whatever you do, do not pull her away from her mom."

"Shit. I didn't think of that. I'm glad I called. Hey, don't tell Mom and Dad about this. I don't mind you sharing this with Cassie, but please keep it between the two of you, at least for now."

"Sure, and if you need to talk to Cassie about motherhood advice, I'm sure she'd be glad to help."

"Thanks."

"And, Chase, for what it's worth, I'm really happy for you. Being a dad is awesome. There is nothing like it in the world."

After we hang up, I sit and ponder our conversation. The first thing I need to do is talk to Andi again. I also need to figure out my career. Having a kid changes things drastically. Going back to Europe will make it considerably more difficult to see Violet. If I play here, it would be easier, even though it's a ton less lucrative. I've saved and invested my money wisely. I could stop playing entirely and be fine, if it came to that. Maybe even coach if I had to. It's time to realign my priorities.

My first order of business is to call the airlines and change the reservation I have. Then I call Max to explain the situation.

"Chase, are you still under the snow?"

"Sort of. Something's come up. It's personal. I'm not sure when I'll be leaving."

"What? You can't do that."

"I have to."

"Germany has been knocking down my door."

"I need you to hold them off for me, Max."

He blows out a breath so long I can almost feel it in my ear. "You don't leave me with much choice, do you?"

"Not any. Just know it's a family issue. Tell my coach it can't be helped."

"If I didn't know you so well, I'd drop you."

"I know. Thanks, Max."

Now I'm left to my toxic thoughts, although they're not nearly as bad as when I left Andi. Fletcher's conversation helped immensely. There is still a hole in my heart that plunges to the depths of my soul. It's something awful to discover the person you always thought you knew, the one you loved for so long, could betray you the way Andi did. I simply cannot wrap my head around why she didn't tell me. Yeah, I love football. It's my career. But she always knew how I felt about her.

Or did she? Did I not make myself clear to her? I thought I did, but it was so long ago, maybe I didn't. God, I loved her, was so in love with her. How could she throw those feelings aside so callously and think a stupid career would take precedence over her and our child? Did she think I'd be so cold-hearted? If the answer is yes, then I have some serious work to do on myself as a human being.

I punch in Andi's number. Better to have this discussion now, rather than later. When she answers, I say, "Hey, we need to talk."

"Chase," she answers reluctantly.

"No angry talk."

"But you just left not too long ago."

"Right. That was angry talk. I've had time to think and speak to Fletcher."

"What? You told someone?"

"Andi, let's get one thing straight. This isn't going to stay a secret anymore. But I asked him not to tell my parents yet and he won't." When she doesn't say anything, I continue. "He made me realize a few things. One, my career. I have to make some decisions on that. Two, we need to be parents to *our* child. Not you or me, but the two of us. We need to do what's best for Violet. What you did was fucked up to the core. I'm not gonna lie. But, if I take her from you, is having her raised by a nanny the best thing for her? There are so many questions pinging around in my head. I know the answer to one, and that is I want to get to know my daughter. Missing out on two years was too much. I will not miss out on any more. So either we work together on this or we work against each other, but I will be a part of her life. Are we clear?"

THIRTEEN

Andi

───────

WHEN THE KNOCK COMES, I nearly jump out of my skin. I open the door, afraid of what I'll see in Chase's eyes. Violet runs over with her hands raised.

"Dada."

He glances at me only a second before giving her his complete attention.

"Violet."

She pats his nose and I cringe when I see him wince. I watch him for his reaction.

"Funny nose," she croons.

"Yes, Dada's nose is broken."

Looking adorably cute, she pokes her lips out. "Kiss … make better." She nods her head until he agrees with her. More patient than I expect of a man who's treated most kids like they are made of toxic waste, he leans forward and lets her press a kiss to his bandage. "Better?"

Her eyes are full of hope.

"Better," he agrees.

I have to turn away as emotions well up in me. Seeing the two of them together is better than I could have ever imagined.

Feeling the weight of guilt, I leave the two of them alone and clean up the remains of lunch when I wonder if he's eaten anything.

"Are you hungry?" I ask.

Chase looks over. "I'm okay. I can grab something after I leave."

I press my lips together, hating the coolness in his tone and that he won't be staying. He just got here. Would he leave so fast? I slice up some of the roasted chicken I have in the fridge and make him a double-decker sandwich with slices of tomato and fresh lettuce. The man could eat, or so I remembered.

"Violet, honey," I call.

She's been chatting away nonstop. Surely, he needs a break. I wave her over, only to see annoyance cross his handsome face. I bend down to her height and hold out the paper plate.

"Go give this to your daddy."

She beams a smile that has me blinking away tears from the brightness of it. I remain crouched and hidden behind the cabinets, listening to her present her father with lunch.

"Eat. Good."

I stand up in time to see him pressing a kiss to her forehead and then pulling back to stare at her in wonder.

"Thank you."

"Eat," she repeats.

His returning grin is genuine.

I have to turn away and busy myself with planning for the night. I prepare each portion of her dinner in the sectioned child plate, wrapping it up so it will be one less thing I have to worry about before I leave for work.

About to go to her room to pack an overnight bag, I glance up to have Chase standing in my path. Immediately, I seek out Violet, afraid he's about to give me another round of his fury. But she is engrossed in Dora on TV.

He starts to move to the sink and I take the empty plate from him.

"Thanks," he says.

I can tell even that is hard for him to say to me. I bite my lip, holding in the crazy emotions swirling in my head. Still, the love I have for this man hasn't disappeared. To have him hating me shatters every fantasy I had for our future.

"I'm sorry."

The words tumble from my lips like a prayer.

"Stop, Andi. Your apologies mean nothing. I'm here for my daughter, nothing else."

I nod, holding back the waterworks that threaten to unleash. "I understand." It's nothing more than a strangled whisper from my mouth as I flee past him.

Violet calls after me just as I close my door and press my back against it. Her little feet come running and her voice croons through the door.

"Mama, okay."

I slide to the floor, frantically wiping my face.

"I'm okay. Just a minute."

"Mama cry," she says.

If she'd heard me, Chase must have too.

I clear my throat and say with more strength than I possess, "I'm okay, Violet." My voice is a little too bright. Luckily, it will take her years to figure out the falsehood in my tone. "I'll be right out."

"Let's go watch Dede," Chase says, confirming my suspicion he's nearby.

"Dora, silly," Violet corrects. "And Boots."

"And Boots," he says, sounding a little farther away.

Not wanting to lie to my daughter, I get to my feet and go into the bathroom to splash water onto my face. Then with my big girl pants on, I go back out to the living room to accept my punishment in the form of him freezing me out. I stiffly sit on the sofa, and when Violet spots me, she crawls onto my lap.

She takes my hands and claps them together as she sings

along to the songs on the show. When it's over, Chase shifts in his seat.

"I guess I should be going," he announces.

Violet shoots out of my lap, a cannonball of ringlet curls. "No go," she begs. Her little arms circle around his neck and she buries her face in his chest.

I have to cover my mouth, choking on emotion. His eyes meet mine, full of pain. I take several deep breaths before I feel strong enough to speak.

"Daddy has to go and Mama has to go to work. You're going to stay with Owen and Holly for the night."

"I'll do it," Chase says out of nowhere.

My jaw practically flaps in the breeze of my shock.

"Dada stay," Violet says, lifting her head off his chest to plead with me. "Dada stay. Pleze."

"Chase—" I stop myself from saying more in front of Violet.

"We'll be fine. How hard can it be?"

There are a number of things I could say, like point out he's never babysat in his life. But he's made it clear we need to co-parent.

"Are you sure?"

"Nothing like the present to make up for lost time."

That jab hits me squarely in the chest. I give him a tight nod. "Owen is just down the hall if anything comes up."

His glacial glare could give anyone frostbite. "I'm sure I can handle it. I was two once."

Violet lies back on his chest.

"Usually she's had a nap by now."

He nods and starts to rub her back. In seconds, her eyes are closed.

I whisper, "She shouldn't nap too long or she won't sleep any tonight."

"It's fine, Andi. She and I will figure this out. Besides, I can always call my brother or Cassie if I need any advice."

I close my mouth. Clearly, he doesn't want my help or Owen's. Can I blame him? Owen's spent more time with *his* daughter.

When my emotions flare again, I remember my period should show up in a day or so. No wonder I'm so teary-eyed. I go into the kitchen and make a plate for his dinner. I don't tell him what I've done, only put a sticky note with his name on it on the foil covering. I pass by him watching PBS with Violet fast asleep still nestled against him.

I ease my phone out of my pocket and silence it. Quickly, I get two snapshots of them from behind. I can see Violet clearly. Chase is in profile. When he turns, I spin on my heel and head to Violet's room. I clean up her toys and I'm in the process of laying out her pajamas when Chase walks in.

"I should lay her down. She's probably not comfortable."

"I think she's more than comfortable. But go ahead and put her down. I'm sure you have other things you'd like to do before I leave."

He doesn't do that. Instead, he stretches out on her bed, his feet almost hanging off the end. It was a good thing I'd opted for a twin instead of a toddler bed.

"There's nothing more important than her."

Another slash at my heart. I finish refolding her PJs and place them on the dresser. I'm ready to bolt. It's way too much. I haven't had time to prepare for this moment. Chase's animosity toward me is like being rained on and then struck by lightning.

"She looks like you. But I see now, she has my eyes."

I don't turn to face him or respond to his comment. I can't. I won't. Though fair is fair and I had this coming, it doesn't make it any easier. So I nod and walk out of the room.

Like clockwork, I let routine take over so I don't have to think. I do the usual and rush my shower while Violet is napping. What I've forgotten is the man in my house. I squeak when I enter my bedroom from the attached bath and he stands there watching me. The towel is in the process of falling to the floor when I clutch it tightly to my chest.

"You shouldn't be in here."

That is the extent of what I can say.

"We need to talk."

I'm not sure how much more of his hatred I can take in one day.

"What is there left to say?"

I hold my breath, wondering if he will threaten me again with taking Violet away.

"Your job? How often do you leave her with *that* man?"

I grind my teeth together, wanting to defend Owen. He's been nothing but kind. And I hadn't pawned our daughter off on him after casually meeting him. It had taken time for me to trust him enough to leave Violet with him. Still, I understand Chase's questions.

"Only when I have an overnight shift. I had a babysitter that we both used. It's only been recently when Violet could talk for herself that I let her stay with him."

"And how often is that?"

"Every few weeks."

We both turn when Violet screeches out, "Dada."

The panic in her voice makes Chase's expression harden. A second later, he's gone and is by her side because I hear him convincing her that he hasn't left and he's staying the night.

I still stand in nothing but a towel with the door wide open as Chase walks by with Violet in his arms.

"Drink?" Violet asks.

"Sippy cups are in the ..." My voice trails off, as Chase doesn't seem to need or want my help.

I think about finding him this morning. He'd taken care of her just fine. Though he hadn't cleaned up the present she left in the bathroom.

Trust, I tell myself as I get dressed for my shift. As I step into the living room, a knock comes at the door and I open it to find Owen.

"Is Violet ready?"

Owen's eyes shift over my shoulder to where Chase and Violet stack blocks.

"Chase is going to stay with her tonight." I lower my voice when Chase's attention is firmly on our daughter. "If you could just check on them later."

Owen nods. "Is everything okay?"

I offer him a false grin. "I'll call you later."

When I close the door, I call to Violet, "Mama has to go to work. Can I get a kiss before I leave?"

She runs over and I hug her so tight she giggles. The way Chase's cold stare meets mine, I feel like I should never let her go or it might be the last time.

"I love you," I choke out.

"Luv too."

I give her a smile I don't completely feel as my heart continues to break.

"What time should we expect you?" Chase asks.

It's a twelve-hour shift, but I don't say that. "I should be home sometime after seven."

He nods. Violet takes his hand and they go back to their blocks. Neither notices me as I leave.

FOURTEEN

Chase

_____

THAT WENT BETTER THAN EXPECTED. At least from my point of view. I'm pretty damn sure Andi doesn't see it the same way. Having Violet want me to stay is the greatest feeling … like nothing I've ever known before. When those little arms of hers wrap around my neck, I seriously want to melt. I'm a grown man. How can such a little mite make me feel this way?

Seeing the hurt in Andi's eyes was like feeling it reflected in my soul. But I'm not stepping back. She caused all of this with her ridiculous actions. I never would've done something like this had the shoe been on the other foot. Furthermore, when you love someone, don't you want to share this kind of shit? I'm not sure I can ever trust her again.

"Dada, drink."

"Thirsty, Little One?" Her head bobs up and down. "Come on. Let's get some water." I hand her a sippy cup and chuckle when I hear her slurping the liquid. When she finishes, I set the cup down and pick her up, lifting her high in the air. I'm oddly thrilled by her squeals of laughter. Then I look at her, really pay attention to her features, and notice more bits of me in her. It's definitely the eyes—steel gray—that are identical to mine. I missed it the first time, but I'm looking into a mirror. Maybe her mouth, too, the way it tilts up on one corner. I've observed that in pictures and it always annoyed me, but on her it's adorable. Her pointer finger takes aim and goes straight for my nose. This time my reflexes are quick and I intercept it before she makes contact.

"Dada funny nose."

"Yeah, Dada has a funny nose. But you kissed it and made it better."

She puckers up her lips to kiss it again. Then she grabs her nose and lets out a serious giggle. My mind churns and I wonder if she picked up any of the Wilde athletic genes. Maybe it's too early to tell. I set her down and ask, "Do you like to run?"

She nods super fast and then takes off around the house like a dart on feet. Little One can definitely run. I end up chasing her and her bubbles of laughter are infectious. This kid is too cute for words. I tackle her and we roll around on the floor, but I have to be careful of that damn finger of hers. She uses it as a sword, stabbing and pointing. She even finds a place between my ribs, just like Fletcher does. Damn, how does she do that? Her favorite phrase is, "Wa dis?" Most everything else is a garbled mess to me, though I'm sure Andi knows what she says.

Suddenly, she stops and pinches my cheek. That's not too comfortable either. "Dada like?"

"Yes, Dada likes." Not gonna lie. Violet is burrowing into my heart faster than anything. By the time Andi gets home, I'm afraid she's going to have a fight on her hands bigger than anything she's ever known.

"Story?"

"Story?" I ask. Does this mean she wants me to read her something? "Show me."

She takes my hand and tugs me up to a sitting position. I pretend she has to pull me to my feet. It's funny seeing this tiny toddler trying to do it. Finally, I stand and she grins. Her little teeth crack me up. Then she walks me to her room and picks out a book. It's the old classic called *Goodnight Moon* about a bunny in his bed saying goodnight to all the things in his room. I remember my mom reading it to me when I was young. I didn't know it was still popular.

"Is this your favorite?" I ask.

"Favrit." Her head bobs. She loves to nod her head.

When I'm done, she dashes out of the room like a streak of lightning. If she's this fast now, I wonder what she'll be like when she's older. Maybe I need to get her a little football and start working on her foot skills. Okay, that's probably a little aggressive. I'll bet she's more into dolls or something. That is an area I have no clue about. As if she reads my mind, she scoots over to a basket in the corner of the living room and picks up a fuzzy-haired doll. The poor thing appears to have seen better days. Her dress is fairly tattered and her shoes are about gone.

Violet shakes her in the air and yells, "Ishabew."

No wonder the damn thing is falling apart. Then she squeezes the thing until I'm sure the seams are going to pop. I'm sitting on the couch when Violet flies at me, coming to a stop as she barrels into my stomach. Christ, this kid is strong. "Ishabew."

"Ishabew?"

"ISHABEW."

Holy crap, she has a set of lungs on her too. "Okay, okay. Ishabew." She shakes her head and stuffs the doll into my hands. Then runs away. What the fuck. Ishabew. Ishabew. I feel like I'm in a foreign country here. And then I get it. The baby's name must be Ishabew. Or maybe Isabelle. Chasing after Violet is a full-time job. No one ever tells you about that part. I've always heard about the lack of sleep, but this kid wears me out. She's like that damn rabbit on the battery ad. She keeps going, and going, and going. And I have a lot of stamina. I can't imagine if someone doesn't.

"Dada. Pway."

"Okay. But what do you want to play?"

"Pony."

What the hell is Pony? "Why don't you show me?"

She hops off the couch and points to the TV. Ah, it's a show. I turn it on and she gives me the word. "No."

Then she points to a DVD. She must have a collection or something, so I have to hunt for Pony—whatever that is. "Show me, Violet." She scrambles around on her hands and knees to where I am and starts rooting through the pile of DVDs. When she pulls one out and grins, I notice it's *My Little Pony*. This occupies her for a while and it gives me a break. Now I get why parents love them so much. I check the time and am shocked to see it's almost seven. This kid is probably starving.

"Violet, are you hungry?"

"Hungy." She pats my stomach.

Heading into the kitchen, I try to figure out what to make. When I open the refrigerator, I see there are a couple of things in there. One is a plate with my name on it, and another is for Violet. Andi was forward-thinking on this dinner. I'll have to remember to thank her.

Violet is my first priority, so I get her seated and strapped into her high chair. Last time I used a towel. There has to be a bib around here. Maybe she can help.

"Violet, bib?"

That handy pointer finger sends me off in the direction of where I hope they'll be. I open a drawer and, sure enough, there is a stack of them. She claps her hands as I come and snap it around her neck. I have to wonder if she's always this agreeable.

I warm up her dinner, which includes chicken, mashed potatoes, and some green beans. Andi put it in one of those little divider plates and the meat is cut in nice little pieces. I hope this is better than the Cheerios.

Making sure the food isn't too hot to eat, I set it down in front of her, along with a plastic cup of milk and a spoon. I'm not sure how safe forks are for kids. Violet digs in while I heat up my plate. It's the same food, only a larger amount.

When I sit down next to Violet, I want to laugh. She has potatoes smeared all over her cheeks.

"Violet, is it good?"

"Good." She grins with her mouth full, and ordinarily I would be grossed out. But not now. I could kiss her she's so cute.

"Chew your food real good for Dada." The last thing I need is for her to choke. I wouldn't know what the fuck to do. "And don't put too much in your mouth at once, sweetie pie."

"Sweetie pie," she repeats. She does much better with this meal than with the cereal. Green beans, however, are a source of entertainment for her. I find her making little designs on her tray with them, or at least that's what it seems like.

"Eat your green beans, please."

"Beans. Pleeeez." Then she makes a scrunched-up face. Guess they're not her favorite.

I take a bite of mine and say, "Yummmm."

She takes a bite and says the same, but that face goes all crazied up and then she shudders. It's so comical I laugh. So does she. We do this several more times until she won't take any more bites. I give her a pass. She really must hate the things.

When we're both done, I wipe her down, making sure there's no residual food anywhere. Then there's a knock on the door. I have an idea who it is. Grabbing Little One out of her chair, I go and answer it. Owen stands there with his daughter.

I invite him in and the girls start playing when I set Violet down.

"Andi asked me to check in on you … to see if you might need anything."

In a terse voice, I answer, "You can report back to her that everything is under control."

"Oh, I don't think that's—"

I'm not interested in anything he has to say. "No, I'm sure it isn't. I'm not exactly excited about getting checked up on. By you or anyone. I'm fully capable of handling my own daughter."

His mouth sags open, then it clicks shut. "I see. Well, I'm happy to see you've decided to take part in Violet's life. A child needs her father."

This time it's my jaw hanging open. "I'm not sure what Andi's told you, but clearly you have the wrong information. Now, is there anything else?"

He suddenly squares his shoulders and pulls himself up to his full height, which doesn't come close to my six-three frame. "As a matter of fact, there is. Andi is important to me. I care about her. If you've come back to cause her problems, maybe you should rethink that. She and Violet were fine before you came to town."

Crossing my arms, I stare him down, just as I would an opponent on the field during a timeout or a foul. "Is that a fact? All I can say is, Owen, my man, you are in the dark. You know absolutely nothing about this situation, or me. And if I were you, I'd keep my nose out of this business."

The puzzled expression lets me know that Andi has told him nothing about us or this. He thinks she's an angel. Let him. He'll find out soon enough on his own.

Suddenly, he blurts, "Holly, come on, honey. We have to leave." His daughter skips over to him and they head out the door with Violet yelling, "Bye bye."

I do feel a bit guilty, because he's been good to my daughter. Plus, Violet and Holly are friends. But he's another one who believes I'm a deadbeat dad. Andi is going to set the record straight with everyone.

Violet and I watch more TV until she starts to nod off on my lap. I make her brush her teeth before I take her to bed. After I read her another story, she begs me to get into bed with her. I accommodate her wishes, with the intentions of getting up and sleeping on the couch. But that never happens. The next time I wake up, the sun is shining in the room and it's almost eight in the morning.

Looking up, I see Violet staring at me.

"Dada. Potty."

Great. I hope she doesn't leave me a surprise again like she did yesterday morning.

"Okie dokie. Let's get up."

I walk her to the bathroom, where she goes. It's quick and it's only pee-pee, as she tells me. I wash her hands afterward and have her wait outside so I can do the same. Then when I'm done, she brushes her teeth. I borrow her toothbrush and brush mine. She zips out of the bathroom like someone zapped her butt with a cattle prod, and the zooming begins.

"Mama."

Andi's bedroom door is closed.

"Ssh. I think Mama's sleeping."

"Look." She runs to Andi's room, and before I can stop her, she's inside and almost waking her up. Andi must've been tired, because she's asleep on top of the covers. I fold the blanket over to cover her up and take Violet out of there so she can sleep. Then I hunt for some breakfast to make.

When I check the freezer, I find frozen waffles. After suggesting them to Violet, she starts repeating the word over and over, so I'm sure they'll be a win.

Feeding her waffles is considerably easier than cereal. I'm learning more and more every day. After I clean up the dishes, Violet wants me to count her toes. We play all sorts of games, from hide-and-seek, to the tickle game, to story time. We're on the couch and she's snuggled on my chest when Andi finally wakes up.

"Sorry, I didn't intend to sleep this late. I saw you spent the night in her bed."

"Yeah, I didn't plan on that either. I lay down and fell asleep."

"I know how that goes," she says, rubbing her eyes.

Better to get what needs to be said off my chest now. "Look, Owen came by last night. I want you to clarify something with him. He seems to think I have now just decided to become involved in Violet's life. That's the last straw, Andi. I don't deserve that. From now on, it's nothing but the truth."

FIFTEEN

Andi

I STARE AT HIM A MOMENT.

"Let me set the record straight. I asked Owen to check on you because you might have had a concussion the other night and I was worried about you. And yes, I also wanted him to see if you needed help with Violet because I knew you wouldn't ask. But I didn't have him come over because I was somehow worried you couldn't handle our daughter." I take a cleansing breath before moving on. "Furthermore, I didn't tell Owen anything about you. Whatever he said to you, he came to those conclusions on his own, because my personal life isn't something I share easily. You of all people know this about me."

The animosity between us is palpable, and his humorless chuckle reflects that.

"I thought I knew you."

"Mama." I glance down at Violet tugging on the hem of my shirt. "Poopie."

Everything I'm about to say, I swallow and smile at my daughter. "Let's go." To Chase I say in a softer tone than I feel, "Thank you for staying, but you are more than welcome to leave."

I stand in the doorway with a pasted smile on my face as my daughter goes potty.

"Fineesh," she proudly announces.

I'm grateful she's quick because Chase has almost made his way over to me. I don't want to talk to him anymore. It hurts too damn much. She and I make fast work of cleaning up and washing her hands before I hand her a treat. The candy had been Owen's idea, and it has worked so far.

"So that's how it's done," he mutters.

With Violet nearby, I don't chance a response and nod. Violet rushes to him, explaining her potty success in a mix of words and gibberish. I feel like a dead man walking, so I go to the kitchen to tackle lunch while I still have the energy to do it.

Just as I put everything back in the fridge, Chase comes in. I glance over to see Violet is busy with one of her shows, so I prepare myself for another verbal beating.

"Yes?" I hiss.

He takes a second before answering.

"You look tired, Andi. Why don't you take a nap?"

"I can handle this," I snap, more out of weariness than anything else.

He reaches over and turns my shoulder so I face him. It takes monumental effort not to lean into his touch.

"As much as I hate that you kept Violet a secret from me, I can admit you've done an admirable job taking care of her. I'm sure you have another overnight shift and that Owen normally helps you out." His jaw muscles grind together, but he forces the words. "I'm here. Go get some sleep."

I turn away because I can't take his consideration. It only reminds me of the man I fell in love with.

"I'm fine. I can sleep when Violet does. I'm sure you have things to do, like your career. Don't you have to get back to Italy or something?"

He spins me around to face him. Before I know what's

happening, he's wiping a tear that's spilled down my cheek. I hadn't realized it. My body feels numbs from everything.

"I'm not going back yet. You let me worry about that. We need to take Violet home to Waynesville." Panic wells in my chest. "Andi, it's going to happen. You'll have some time off in a couple of days, won't you?" I nod. "We can go then, unless you can arrange time off sooner."

"Chase," I plead.

He shakes his head. "You can't hide her anymore. I won't lie to my parents. And it won't be fair to yours if they hear about our daughter from mine."

I cover my mouth. If I'd thought it had been rough dealing with Chase, my brother and parents are going to be devastated.

"We're going to get through this."

I can't handle the distance between us, and finally I dart past him, saying, "I just need a minute."

I quietly go to my room and close the door. I curl up on my bed for a good soaking-your-sheets kind of cry. At some point, I drift off. When I wake, the clock reads well past lunch. I shoot out of bed in search of my daughter. I breathe when I find her dancing around singing to herself in the living room with her poor seen-better-days doll. I've tried replacing it, but she'll have nothing to do with the new one. When I look, Chase is cleaning up the kitchen. *Lunch!*

I walk over to him. "I didn't mean to fall asleep."

"It's okay." He's being way too nice. I wait for the other shoe to drop. "Hungry?"

I think about it. "Yes, actually. Is there any chicken left?"

It's almost odd how normal our conversation is.

"I saved you some." He places a sandwich in front of me. And then normal is gone. "There is something else we should discuss." I bite into my food, knowing I'll probably lose my appetite at some point during this conversation. "I can't go to Italy without Violet." I nearly choke. "If you think about it, Andi, it's only fair."

I vehemently shake my head. "I can't go to Italy."

His expression cools. "I wasn't asking you."

My jaw drops. "You expect me to just hand her over?"

He gives me a *duh* face.

"It won't be forever. Just until the season's over, and we'll come back."

Every reason why this can never work pops in my head.

"And who will watch her when you're at practice or games all over the world?"

This is my *gotcha* moment. Only he has a reasonable answer.

"I'm sure I can find a temporary live-in nanny that you can approve of."

The idea of someone else taking care of my daughter kills me.

"And you think a nanny is better than her mother?"

He snaps back, "Do you think Owen is better than her father?"

I close my eyes, the fire in me extinguished because he's right, and let go of my next retort. "And what am I supposed to do?"

"You can play house with Owen for all I care, Andi. You owe me this time."

I sputter my next words. "Chase, she's my world. I know you need to bond with her, but I just can't imagine living one day without her."

"Welcome to my world," he says.

We glare at each other. But truthfully, I have no other reasonable argument. So I play my final card.

"And if I don't allow it?"

"I'll fight you."

He has the financial means to take her completely away from me.

"And no doubt you'll win," I spit out. He tilts his head toward one shoulder in a half-shrug. "And you want to take her now?"

"Yes."

Food forgotten, I press my lips together and stare at the ceiling before glancing back at Violet. "How can I live without her?"

"There is one other option."

Hope blooms in my chest. "What's that?"

"Instead of me hiring a nanny, you can come with Violet and stay in my spare bedroom. If anything Fletcher said to me makes total sense, it's that she needs you as much as she needs me."

Spare bedroom? Clearly, this isn't an invitation to be a true family.

"What about my job?"

"It's your job or your daughter. Maybe you could take a leave of absence? What's more important, Andi? I'm not going to leave Chicago without her."

SIXTEEN

Chase

ANDI STARES AT ME, foot tapping the floor. She's angry, that I know. "So, my job can be sacrificed, but yours can't."

"Come on, Andi. That's not the real reason."

"No? Sounds like it to me. Why don't you stay here in Chicago then?"

Grinding my teeth at her suggestion, I say, "I already answered that. You've had her for two years. I've been denied that by your choice not to tell me I had a daughter."

"I love my job," she says. "I can't just give it up."

"Why not?"

"It's not every day you find one like mine."

"You're a nurse, Andi. You could be a nurse in Italy if you want."

She laughs. "It's not that easy, and I'm not just a nurse. I'm a neonatal nurse. I work with prematurely born or post-surgical babies in intensive care. Some of them weigh only three pounds and are so sick. Imagine how tiny that is."

Three pounds. That's barely anything.

"How did you get into that?"

She shrugs. "I was pregnant and wanted nothing but a healthy baby, I guess."

"So what do you do?"

"Some of them are born with addiction problems, and we have to get them through that; some of them are multiples and born early. Some have heart defects and have to have surgery. There are so many things that can go wrong, and when I look at Violet and see how healthy and happy she is, I thank God it all went okay."

"Hmm." I never thought about all of that. "With all your experience, couldn't you get hired in Italy? Seems to me you'd be of great value to any hospital." And I mean that in all sincerity.

"I'm not licensed in Italy. I don't speak the language or even know how to go about doing that."

For the first time in the last hour, I smile. "That's easy. Max could tell us."

"Max?"

"He's my agent, and the knower of all. I could have him look into it."

"Oh." Andi frowns.

"Andi, I'm serious about having her with me. And I'm also serious about taking her back to North Carolina to meet our families. This secret shit is over."

She hangs her head, but I have zero sympathy for her. I can't even imagine what her parents will say … or mine.

"My mom is going to shit," she says.

"So is mine. But we're adults and can handle it. Besides, Violet has a right to know them too. Look at what she's missing out on. My God, she would be so spoiled."

Andi huffs. "That's what I'm afraid of."

Speaking of Violet, I glance over at the sofa and she's sound asleep. "Looks like we missed nap time."

"Yeah."

"I think I'll head home."

"Chase, I don't want things to be rocky between us."

A bitter laugh escapes me. How can it not be?

"Andi, how can you expect anything else?"

"What I meant was, it would be nice if we could work things out. Without having to go to court."

She's absolutely right. I would hate to drag this out. It wouldn't be the best thing for Violet, either.

"I agree, but I'm not backing down on this."

"I know. Do you want to come back for dinner?"

Her invitation surprises me. I've thrown a ton of shit her way, but she hasn't backed away from it. Yes, she's not happy about it, but I can't blame her.

"Sure. Can I bring something?"

"If you want anything alcoholic, you may want to bring that. I don't keep that stuff around. I don't drink much ever since I had Violet."

"Okay. What time?"

"Is six okay?"

"You tell me. You're the one who's cooking."

"Six then," she says.

I wave as I quietly leave, careful not to wake up Violet.

The walk home does me good. I'm able to clear my head away from Andi's apartment. But the farther away I get, the more convinced I am of my plan. This is the perfect time for the move. Violet is young. We wouldn't have to worry about school. If Andi wanted to work, Max could find her information on getting licensed. She would also need a work visa. We were so great together once. I would've done *anything* for her. And the reality is, I still would. Why did she do this? The betrayal is like nothing I've ever experienced. The deep ache in my heart is bone deep and so unexpected because I still love her so damn much.

A call to Fletcher is in order. He's my compass and my barometer.

"How's it going?" he asks.

"Okay. Violet is so fucking cute, man. You wouldn't believe."

"Told ya. They're something, aren't they?"

"I told Andi I was taking her to Italy, with or without her."

"Excuse me?"

"You heard me, Fletch."

"But you asked Andi, right?"

"Yep, but even if she doesn't go, Violet will. I won't be stopped. I can't leave that kid behind."

"Will Andi come?"

A rough chuckle leaves me. "I don't know. We're not exactly what you'd call best friends right now."

"Try to work it out. If not for the two of you, do it for Violet."

Changing the subject, I say, "I'm going to have Max check into how Andi could get a nursing license in Italy."

"Good idea," Fletcher says. "Hey, I gotta run. Cassie is calling for me. Keep me in the know."

I'm punching in Max's number when I decide to hang back. I'm not going to bring him into the mix until this is all a sure thing. I can hear him now, giving me shit about it. But I do call the charter service and charter a flight home to North Carolina for the day after tomorrow. Thank God the weather's finally cleared and planes are flying again. Andi can take a couple of days off. She will explain to our families about our daughter, whether she wants to or not.

After I take a badly needed shower, I dress and head down to the corner to pick up a six-pack of beer. Then I take a leisurely walk back to Andi's, which is pretty crazy since it's still freezing out. When I get there, her forehead is knotted with worry lines. It's understandable because I've put a shit ton on her plate. Even though I'd like to feel sorry for her, I don't. I'm generally not an asshole, but I'll never get those two years back with Violet and it's all because of Andi's foolish actions.

"Mind if I put this in the fridge?" I ask.

"Go ahead." I do and grab one. When I turn around, Andi is directly behind me, wringing her hands.

"Are you okay?" I ask.

"Violet has a fever. It's not very high, but I tend to get a little overly concerned about this stuff. It comes with the occupation, I suppose."

"When did she get sick?"

"When she woke up, she was a bit crabby, which is unlike her. That's when I noticed."

Not being very familiar with this, I'm not sure what to say or do. I know I don't want to look like a moron and have Andi hold it against me, so I say, "I suppose you gave her Tylenol already."

"Yes. She's in her room lying down."

"I'll check on her."

When I get to her room, I notice her eyes look slightly glassy. "Hey, Little One. What's up?"

"Hot."

I touch her forehead and she is warm. "Dada will kiss it and make it better, okay?"

"Okay."

I wish it were that easy, because I don't like seeing this little girl sick. "Do you want Dada to read to you?"

"Yeah."

She must feel like crap because usually this kid would be flying around the room with her feet on fire. I pick out a book and read it to her. When I'm finished, she asks for another. Her round cheeks have bright spots of pink on them, and her face is flushed. I guess that's what kids usually look like when they're feverish.

"Violet, does your throat hurt?"

"Throat hurt."

I wonder if she might have inflamed tonsils. I used to get that as a kid and had to have them removed. "How about watching a movie?"

Her head bobs, but slow and not the usual quick motion. I

pick her up and carry her into the living room. Then I cover her up after I lay her on the couch and put in a movie.

I find Andi in the kitchen fixing dinner. "Andi, she said her throat hurts."

"How did you ask her?"

"If her throat hurt."

"She probably just repeated you."

"You think this will pass?"

"If it doesn't, I'll take her in to see the doctor tomorrow."

Leaning on the counter, I think about how to tell her this. I might as well just get it out. "I chartered us a flight to go to North Carolina."

The weather has cleared and I was able to get one.

She stops stirring the pan of whatever it is she's cooking. "You what?"

"I chartered a flight for the day after tomorrow. We need to take care of this, Andi."

"What if Violet is sick?"

"Then I'll cancel it. When I made the reservation, I was unaware."

"I have—"

"I know, work. But you have vacation days, I'm sure."

"Yes, but I have to get someone to fill in for me. It's not that easy."

I take a swig of my beer, then walk over to check on Violet. Let Andi figure her shit out. We're going and that's that.

"Dada."

"Hmm?"

"Thirsty."

I head to the kitchen for a sippy cup, but Andi is ready for me, holding one in her hand. I nod my thanks.

"Here you go."

Violet grabs the cup and slurps it greedily. The Tylenol must be kicking in because her cheeks don't look quite as pink. I press the back of my hand against her forehead, like my mother used to do to me, and find it's still warm.

"Dada." I look at Violet and the sippy cup is jabbed back in my hand.

"More?" I ask.

She shakes her head. "Hungy."

That must be a good sign. "Okay. Mommy is making dinner now."

When I check back with Andi, I see she's on the phone. I'm not sure who she would be talking to, but I don't want to eavesdrop, so I go back and sit with Violet. But she's gotten off the couch and left the room. Soon she is back and dragging a scrapbook behind her.

"What do you have there, Little One?"

"Dada."

"Dada?"

"Dada."

I'm not sure why she keeps calling my name, but I help her pick up the large book and put her back on the couch. When she opens it up, it all becomes glaringly apparent. Now I know why Violet was dead set on me being her dad. This is a photo album filled with pictures of Andi, me, and our families. Violet flips through the pages, and every time she sees my picture, she says, "Dada." I glance up and catch Andi staring at us.

"That was a way for me to introduce her to you," Andi explains.

There are so many things I want to say, but I keep my mouth shut. Violet doesn't need to hear any of them. I'm glad she saw the face of her father, but it still doesn't make up for the two years I've lost.

SEVENTEEN

Andi
———

HIS NON-REPLY IS evidence he isn't impressed with the lengths I went through to make sure Violet knows who her family is even if none of them know about her.

"Excuse me," I say, walking away. "I need to have someone cover my shift."

"Why?"

I stop and turn around. With Violet staring at me, I force a sweet smile, but it's easy for Chase to see it's an artificial one.

"I need to stay home with Violet. She isn't feeling well."

"I can stay with her."

The embers of an argument kindle in my throat.

"I couldn't possibly ask you to do that."

"You don't have to. I'm her father." His smile is even more plastic than mine. "You can tell me what to do and we'll be fine."

The idea of leaving her makes me faintly ill. I've always been there for her when she isn't well. She burrows her head in the crook of his neck with her eyes still on me.

"Dada stay."

How can I say no to that?

"Okay," I croak, turning away. It feels like I'm already losing her. The way she clings to him, it's as if she wants him more than me. Isn't this what I've wanted—to be happy with having them united as father and daughter? But it hurts like hell that maybe she would be fine going to Italy without me.

When I find some paper, I channel my frustration into writing notes for Chase about when and if he should give her more Tylenol. I also leave Owen's cell phone number at the bottom.

Later, when it's time for me to go, I plead with him to call me if her fever spikes.

"I'll come home right away," I add.

By the time I get to work, I consider asking one of my doctor friends to prescribe me some anti-anxiety medication to ease my frayed nerves.

"What's going on?" Beth asks.

It feels like days since our Doc McDreamy conversation. For once, I really need a friend. The time for secrets has passed.

"Chase," I say by way of explanation.

"The guy from the emergency room the other night?" I silently agree. "He's hot."

"He's Violet's father," I blurt.

Her jaw drops.

"It's a long story, but he's threatened to take her from me."

"What an asshole," she says in true friend solidarity.

I shake my head. "He's not. It's complicated. But I have to talk to Peggy about getting time off."

She hugs me. "I won't ask why right now. But know that my brother's best friend's sister is a lawyer if you need one."

"Thanks. I'll let you know. We're trying to work this out outside of court." I spot Peggy. "I have to go."

She points at me. "We are so talking about this later. I want the whole story."

Later, on the way home, I'm grateful I found someone who can take my shift the next day. The problem will be giving a notice if I decide to just quit, as Chase seems to think I can. If I have a prayer at ever coming back to work here in the future or getting a decent reference, I will have to stay at least two weeks. Will Chase give me that time? Or will he demand to take Violet and have me join them later?

Lost in my thoughts, I run smack into Owen.

"Andi."

The man has the kindest face, one just as beautiful as the man on the inside.

"Sorry."

I take a step back, feeling for the first time like we are strangers. He tips my chin up so I can stare into his earnest eyes.

"Is everything okay?"

They don't make men like him anymore.

"No. But I'll get through it."

"I don't want to pry, but is it true? Did Chase not know he was a father?" I nod. "Wow."

"Owen, please don't judge. I didn't do it to hurt him. As crummy as this sounds, I thought I was helping."

"I guess I can't blame him for being pissed off at me, then."

"And me too. He's threatening to take Violet from me."

"Shit." The man doesn't curse often.

I shake my head. "I should have expected it, right? Worse, he has all the resources in the world to do it."

"I can help you. I get he's pissed, but it's not a reason enough for you to lose your daughter. I couldn't live without Holly."

"Why would you do that? Don't you think I'm a bad mother too?"

A smile grows on his face.

"Andi, I don't know your reasons for keeping him from her, but I trust and admire you. You have to know how much I care about you too. Our lives are already so entwined, I'd hoped—"

"Don't." I can't possibly bear to hear the words and have

even more guilt on my conscience. "The only choice he's given me to keep her is to move to Italy with him."

"So you can be together," he says resolutely.

I let out a bitter laugh. "No. But he'll let me live in his house so we can share our daughter."

"And that's it."

"For us, yes. But he says we can come back when his season is over."

"Season? Wait. What's his last name?"

I doubt he would know, so I say, "He's Chase Wilde. He plays soccer in Italy."

"He's *The* Chase *Wilde*. The leading striker in the Italian soccer league and brother of Fletcher Wilde, the top NFL quarterback?" The amazement would be funny if the situation were different. I bob my head. He blinks.

"That Chase Wilde has more money than I can dream of to take Violet away if I don't concede to his demands. That Chase Wilde who wants nothing to do with me."

"He's a fool, which works in my favor. Once you get back, maybe you and I …"

Why couldn't my heart accept this man?

"Owen, you're a really great guy. But I don't want you waiting on me. Even though Chase has written me off, the truth is, I'm still in love with him."

Hope doesn't leave his expression. "I'll see you when you get back, and we can talk about it then."

My apartment door opens just as Owen leans in for a hug. All I can think about is the building's paper-thin walls. How much of our conversation has Chase heard?

Chase doesn't speak when I step inside. I go directly to Violet's room to check on her. She's not warm, but I leave, closing the door to let her sleep. Chase is waiting for me.

"How was she last night?" I ask.

The distance he keeps between us is palpable.

"Everything was fine. I didn't have any problems or have to

give her any medicine." He holds up a hand. "I checked her temperature every hour with that scanner you left." It is a machine that you swipe over the forehead to get a reading.

"You didn't have to do it every hour." No wonder he looks tired.

After two-plus years of not being able to touch him, I ache to brush my fingers over the shadow that covers his chin. He's damn sexy with stubble on his face. But that isn't possible, so I dive into the next topic.

"I got the next two days off. So we have through the weekend to go to Waynesville."

"Good. I'll go back to my place and square things away. We can leave first thing in the morning."

I'm not sure he'll get why I say it, but I do anyway. "Thank you."

He barely tips his head at me and he's gone. The next time I see him, we're on the plane headed home.

I'd spent the previous day with Violet. Thankfully, her fever hadn't returned. Owen had come over for lunch with Holly. Things have been different between us. Oh, how one little act has such wide-ranging consequences.

"Dada. Color." Violet runs to Chase when she spots him on the small plane.

I'm left to sit alone on the flight. No matter how I play it in my head, I have no words to say to my family and his. They already know something's up. Chase had Fletcher gather everyone at his house.

Violet has definitely recovered. She continues to chatter nonstop during the car ride. Chase has rented an SUV, probably more for me because I'm sure his brother offered to pick us up.

As the scenery goes by, everything is different and the same when we arrive in Waynesville. The town is the same with a few new shops along the way. Fletcher's robin's egg blue house is trimmed in white and looks like a modern-day farmhouse. When I get out of the car, I just stare at how beautiful the place is. I'm reminded of how much I've missed home.

"I'll go in and give you a minute."

I nod, clutching Violet's hand and not just because she started after her father. I need her to ground me and remind me why I did what I did.

After a deep breath, I walk up the steps and through the front door. Chase hasn't softened the blow, considering the gasps that come from our parents. Cassidy, Fletcher's wife, gives me a sympathetic glance.

"Gamma, Gampa," Violet says, pointing out my parents. Then her finger lands on Chase's folks. "Nana, Papa."

I kneel down to her level and point at my brother. "Yes, and Uncle Mark—" Then I point at Chase's brother and wife. "And Uncle Fletcher and Aunt Cassidy."

I get to my feet for the rest. "Everyone, this is our daughter, Violet Chase Wilde …" Chase's head snaps in my direction. We haven't talked about her full name, so I add, "James."

"Andi," Mom whispers with tears in her eyes.

Cassidy steps forward. "How about I take Violet to get some cookies?" I nod as she holds out a hand to Violet while shifting her baby in her other arm. "Would you like a cookie and some milk?"

Violet glances at me and I give my approval. She takes her hand, and after they leave, all eyes are on me.

"This is why you haven't come home." Mark is furious. He points at Chase. "You got my sister pregnant and kept her hidden away?"

I hold up a hand. "Chase didn't know. I …" I suck in air for purchase. "I didn't tell him. I thought it was for the best. By the time I realized I was pregnant, he was already in Italy and I had school to finish and a future job in Chicago. I didn't want him to have to come back here or hold him back. His career was already in full swing by then."

Thankfully, Chase doesn't say anything. But my brother isn't done with his interrogation. I've never seen him so mad, considering he's one of the nicest guys you'd ever meet.

"What other secrets are you keeping? Are the two of you married?"

"No," Chase is quick to answer. His one word is so final, I have to glance away.

"Andi, I wish you hadn't thought you needed to keep this from us," Mom chimes in.

"I …" How I hate defending myself again because I know I'm in the wrong. "I thought if Chase didn't know, I couldn't very well tell the rest of you."

Mom blows out a breath and I'm afraid to look at everyone else's disappointed faces.

"I for one want to meet my granddaughter. She called me Nana," Chase's mom proudly says.

Our parents agree and leave me in the room with three angry guys, though Fletcher doesn't appear to be as mad at me as the rest.

Mark barrels forward, snagging my hand. "Let's talk outside."

Chase doesn't even give me a second thought before following our parents. Fletcher gives me a half-smile before following his brother. I bite the inside of my cheek and go with Mark willingly.

Tongue-in-cheek, I glance anywhere but my brother's face.

"I knew something was up. But I never thought … How could you hurt our parents this way?"

I'd been too chicken to meet my father's eyes.

"I didn't mean to."

"You expect me to buy that? Hiding a kid. Mom already thinks that you don't see us as your real family."

"What?" I glare at him.

"What do you expect? Since graduating high school, you've barely come home. And when you do, you spend most of your time out of the house. Now we know why."

If he's slut-shaming me for getting knocked up, I'm not going to take it.

"You either. Hell, when you didn't have your nose up Gina's skirt, you were at Fletcher's. Don't put this all on me."

Gina had been his best friend outside of Fletcher, and he'd wanted more. Now she's getting married to Ryder and he's with Riley.

"I wasn't the one Mom was worried about. It was always poor Andi."

"Mark." We turn to find Mom heading our way. "Stop it."

My brother, always the good son, does as asked.

She comes over and wraps me in a hug. "She's beautiful," she murmurs in my ear.

That's when the waterworks start. "I'm sorry, Mom. I love you and Dad. You have to know that. I was wrong. I made a mistake."

"Shhh," she says, rubbing my back. "You're a mom now. You of all people must know your children do no wrong." She pats my cheek. "I'm sad I wasn't with you. I always pictured being there."

I cling to her again. "I'm so sorry."

When I finally let her go, she shocks me.

"I always saw the two of you together." My jaw goes slack. "That's right. That boy has had moon eyes for you for as long as I can remember."

I ignore the moon comment.

"You knew?"

She gives me an indulgent smile. "Denise and I both knew."

I can't help but set the record straight.

"He hates me now."

"Do you blame him?" Mark interjects.

Mom glares at him, but her expression softens on me. "Give him time. Love like that doesn't die easy. If I'm right, he came to Chicago looking for you."

I can't answer because Chase comes out with Violet in his

arms, his mom, Denise, in tow talking with her. When they reach us, his mom says, "Her curls remind me of Chase's. When he was little and his hair was still sun-kissed, I would let it grow. He had the most beautiful curls."

When Violet reaches for me, I take her and give her a kiss on the cheek.

I'm grateful it's not bitter cold as Fletcher, the dads, and Cassie come outside too. Denise continues. "But then Fletcher and Mark got the bright idea to dress Chase up in a skirt."

Mom laughs. "I remember that."

"Don't remind me," Chase's dad says.

His mom continues. "When Fletcher introduced his sister to our dinner guest, Henry made me promise to keep Chase's hair cut."

Fletcher bellows with laughter. "I got in so much trouble."

"Me too," Mark mutters, almost cracking a smile.

Chase glowers, not liking the memory.

"I think I have a picture somewhere," Denise announces.

"You won't be showing that to anyone," Chase says.

His dad pats his shoulder. "I've got the grill going. Don't want lunch spoiled. Are you coming, George?"

My dad nods.

"It's pretty cold out here. Why don't we go make hot cocoa, Violet?" Cassie offers. "And, Fletcher, I think someone needs to be changed."

She hands over the baby. Chase watches his brother take the baby without comment. I take it in, all sad I won't have that.

"I'm going to check on Dad," Mark says before stomping off.

"Well," Chase's mom says. "I want to say thank you."

I look around because surely she's not talking to me.

"Yes, you, Andi."

"Why would you thank her?" Chase admonishes.

"Because, my dear son, I was a young mother once. I can only imagine the struggle she went through in making her decision." She holds up a hand to stop him. His jaw snaps shut. "We won't get into the merits of her choice. The point is, she was alone and decided to bring our granddaughter into the world. And from what I can tell, she did a wonderful job."

"She kept her from me. You'd think you'd be on my side," Chase grumbles.

"There are no sides, honey. I believe her when she said she thought she was doing the right thing. I might have done the same if I'd been in her shoes. Granted, I don't know what happened between the two of you. But Pamela and I knew the two of you were together." Chase stares at his mother. She shrugs. "Besides, if she planned to keep this a secret forever, why does Violet know who we are?"

"She has a book with our pictures," he says.

"Exactly. I know this isn't ideal, but you have to see that she didn't plan to keep Violet from you."

"That doesn't give me the two years I've missed back."

"I have lots of pictures and videos," I add.

Chase could have killed me with the glare he turns my way.

"Where are you all staying?" Denise asks, continuing to play peacemaker.

I turn to my mother. "I thought Violet and I would stay with you, Mom, if that's okay?"

Mom eyes Chase a second before saying, "Why don't you and Chase discuss what's best for Violet?"

Our moms leave and I bite my lip, taking the hint.

"I'm sorry. She's right. It's just going to take a little bit of time to get used to not making decisions on my own."

"Yeah, well, I'm not sleeping away from my daughter."

Patience, I tell myself.

"So what, you want her to stay with you at your parents'?"

He holds my stare like that's the obvious answer.

"My parents deserve time too. Maybe we should stay at a hotel so it's fair."

"Fair. Let's not talk about what's fair."

"Fine, Chase. Whatever. We'll do it your way so you can keep punishing me."

"Hey." Cassie suddenly appears with a baby on her hip. Violet isn't with her. "Okay, Mama Bear—" She meets my eyes. "—your daughter is chatting it up with the granddads. She's fine."

"Cassie, could you give us a minute? We are trying to work through something," Chase says.

"As if the neighbors couldn't hear," she admonishes. "I have a solution."

"And what is that?" Chase snaps.

"You can stay here: neutral ground. Besides, our house is completely baby-proof. We have the room and spare toys that are too old for our baby yet." She shrugs. "Everyone is spoiling our kiddo. But they would be perfect for my niece."

Fletcher and Cassie don't seem to play on the *Hate Andi* team, so I say, "I'm fine if Chase is."

I don't bother to look at him, only wait for his answer.

EIGHTEEN

Chase

B OTH WOMEN STARE AT ME, waiting for an answer. This is the best solution. Neutral ground to be fair to us both. But quite honestly, I feel betrayed by my parents. I would've thought Mom would've taken my side. It looks like everyone is Team Andi, other than Mark. At least he sees things my way.

"Fine, we'll stay here. Thanks, Cassie, for looking out for us." Then I stalk inside.

Fletcher approaches me. "Dude, she's a cutie. And you've taken to her like a fish to water. I'm proud of you."

Even throughout all of this, I have to grin. And it's a feeling of pride that I wear in my smile. "Yeah, I really have. It's an unbelievable feeling to hold your child in your arms, isn't it?"

"The greatest there is. So, I know this isn't the best topic, but are you and Andi working on things?"

"No." This is not up for discussion.

"Then what are you going to do about your daughter?"

"She's coming back to Italy with me. If Andi wants to fight me, she can bring it on. I'll put together the strongest legal team I can find. She was in the wrong and she fucking knows it."

"Yeah, I agree, but what I don't agree with is putting Violet in the middle of the battle."

"I'll keep her out of it as much as I can. She's the last one I want to hurt, believe me. She's been hurt enough as it is."

Fletcher nods. "And there's no way to work this out amicably?"

"I'd like to, but think about it in her terms. Would you want Harrison, your son, removed from you?"

He shakes his head. "Guess not. I do know this. If I tried to do that to Cassie, she'd go for blood."

"Yeah, but Cassie wasn't deceitful either. I think Andi does have somewhat of a conscience."

"You weren't looking at her face when you all walked in. She looked abso-fucking-lutely destroyed."

"Good. As bad as it sounds, that's what I felt like when I found out I'd lost two years of Violet's life … two years I'll never get back. Imagine losing two years of your kid's life, Fletch. It sucks so bad, I can't even explain it."

He pats my back and then squeezes my shoulder. "I don't know what I'd do, to be honest. Mark was pissed as hell too. He's still giving her hell over it."

I glance out the window and spot the two of them out on the deck. Andi has her arms crossed, either from the cool January air or from Mark's chilling words. Her crestfallen expression has me almost feeling sympathy toward her … almost. But I'm still too angry for that.

"You'd better get over that pissed-off feeling or those damn creases in your forehead are going to turn into a crevasse," Fletcher teases.

"Shut up. It's not that easy."

"Right. But you'll have to give it up someday. You can't carry that anger forever."

"Says he who was pissed off at his wife for what? Years?"

He slashes his arm through the air. "That was ages ago and

I was young, dumb, and stupid. Don't follow my footsteps. We wasted too much time. You two have already wasted years."

I look out the window again and think about why I went to Chicago in the first place. What a crazy ass trip that turned out to be.

Fletcher breaks into my thoughts and asks, "By the way, what the hell happened to your nose? Did Andi punch you or something?"

I explain that whole deal and he cracks up so hard, all heads turn. Then I have to tell everyone else. Dad says, "I was going to ask you about that, but then Violet stole all the attention."

Violet suddenly calls out, "Dada. Dada." Then she barrels full force into me.

"Good Lord, that kid is fast," Dad says. "She's faster than you were at her age, Chase. Maybe she's inherited the Wilde athletic genes."

Mom yells, "Not already. You men. Just give the child a chance, will you?"

Fletcher and I laugh.

Seeing Mom sitting there reminds me that I want a word with her. Dad's always been an outlier on these things. He'd never say a word, but I want Mom to know exactly how betrayed and hurt I felt when I found out about Violet.

Violet is still running circles around my legs and then grabbing onto me.

Lifting her high in the air, I say, "Little One, give me a smooch." She does and it makes a resounding smack. The grandparents laugh and so does she. "Hey, can you go and play with your papa?" She zooms toward my dad and he snatches her up like a "sack of taters," as he always says.

That gives me the opportunity I need to grab Mom's hand and take her into one of the bedrooms.

Not one to waste words with her, I jump right in and say, "I can't believe you sided with Andi."

"Whoa, whoa, whoa, son. I did not side with anyone, other than my granddaughter."

"Yes, you did. You said she did a wonderful job."

Mom grins at me. I'm incredulous. And pissed. The heat of my anger nearly explodes out of me. Then she has the nerve to say, "Why don't you just tell that girl how much you still love her?"

"What?"

She points at the bed and says, "Sit down," using her mom tone.

It's not in me to refuse. After I'm seated, she says, "Why are men so blind and stubborn? Can you not hear yourself? If you didn't care a thing in the world about her, why are you so angry?"

I nearly spit my reply, "Because she never told me about Violet, that's why!"

"And she didn't tell you, why? If she had, what would you have done?"

"I would've made her come to Italy with me." I sit and cross my arms in satisfaction, then grin.

Mom laughs. She fucking laughs at me.

"*Made her come*. You don't *make* anyone do anything, Chase."

"What's that supposed to mean?"

Mom laughs again. "Son, you have a lot to learn where women are concerned."

"So, you think Andi was right in not telling me?"

"Did I say that?"

"No, but you seem to think everything I do is wrong."

"Because you act like a dictator."

I scratch my cheek and think for a second. Maybe she's right.

"Chase, honey, think about what it was like being in Andi's shoes. And think how it takes two to tango. She got pregnant. You were partly responsible for that, you know. She was young. You were established in Italy already. She didn't want to ruin your career. She loved you. She didn't want you to resent her. What would you have done?"

"I didn't think about it that way. I only thought how I'd missed out on seeing my daughter's birth and the subsequent two years of her life. But Mom, I would've come back if I'd known."

"What's done is done. You were both in the wrong. And two wrongs never ever make a right. Stop all this ridiculous acting out and start behaving like adults. Move forward in your daughter's best interests," Mom says, grabbing my hands. "That's what's important."

"Yeah, you're right, as usual."

"Now sit here and come up with a plan. I'm going out there to play with my granddaughter."

I watch her leave and think about whether or not my plans to take them back to Italy are the right ones. Realistically, it's the only way I can spend time with Violet. If they stay here, there isn't any way to do that. My season is about to kick back up into high gear and there will be no way for me to travel back and forth. I could ask Andi to do that, but I'm not sure how much vacation time she has.

My mind made up, I head out to find her. When I do, she's still talking with Mark. I don't care if I interrupt. I grab her wrist, saying, "We need to talk." Then I take her into the room where Mom and I just were.

"Please sit." She eyes me with uncertainty, but does as I say.

"I just had a chat with my mom and she pointed some things out to me. Made me see things in a different light. I need to apologize for being overbearing. I won't apologize for being angry with you though, because I wish you had come to me about your pregnancy. Moving on, I would like to ask you to come to Italy. It's not a demand, and it's not an ultimatum. Here's the thing. I have a contract that I can't get out of, so the only way I can see Violet is if you were to come with her. I really don't relish the thought of separating the two of you. Flying back and forth isn't an option either, because my schedule is too demanding, with practices and games. Plus, I have to travel often for games. I'm not sure if you have enough vacation time with your job to do it either. So, I'm asking, Andi. I don't want to be separated from Violet either. Will you do it? Can you take a leave of absence or something? Will you come to Italy with me?"

NINETEEN

Andi
———

THE FACT that Chase is trying is more than I could have asked for. Given everything I took from him, how can I say no?

"Yes, I'll go to Italy with you."

"Great." He turns to leave when I stop him.

"You do realize we have to get a passport for Violet." I've already read up on it. "If we expedite it, we can possibly get it in less than a week. But it could take up to two. Can you wait to go back? Just to be sure things go okay?"

His perfect lips flatten. "I would stay, but I can't. I have a contract to fulfill."

"Can you at least stay to get her passport? Otherwise, even you can't get her there. There's one other thing." I hesitate. "I can't just leave my job if I ever want to come back or get a reference. I need to give notice."

Although his anger isn't at the surface, the distance between us is palpable. In his eyes, I can see the mistrust is still there.

"I can stay another day or two in Chicago when we get back to take care of the passport. Maybe my mom and yours can come along. Once you get Violet's passport, our moms can fly Violet over and you can come when you can."

I swallow my protest and nod stiffly because it's only fair to him.

"Good," is his one-word answer. "I'd also like to be added to her birth certificate as her father."

"You have to know I would've done it, if I could have. It wasn't possible without your signature. But it's a simple matter of you filling out a form, and then having my name dropped from hers."

"Thank you, Andi."

When he leaves, I let my forced smile drop. I wait thirty seconds before exiting the room to find my daughter. She's with the granddads chattering away. It feels so good to see her with them.

It's not long before Violet notices that Cassie and Fletcher have a swing.

"Mama, swing."

Though it's nippy out, I give in and take her out there for about ten minutes before tempting her to come back inside to get some more hot cocoa.

Later when my brother starts watching videos with her, I duck upstairs to the room Cassidy assigned to me. Mom finds me staring at my lap. She walks in and closes the door behind her.

"I thought we could talk."

It had been too good to be true to think that Mom had been okay with everything. I knot my hands on my lap when she sits next to me.

"You know I love you no matter what." I nod silently. She takes my hand in hers. "But the truth is, I'm really hurt. Dad is too. We just want to understand why you thought you couldn't talk to me or your dad about this."

"It wouldn't have been fair to tell you and not Chase," I reiterate.

"I get that. But what about when you found out you were

pregnant? It's upsetting to think that you felt you had to go through that decision alone."

It guts me inside knowing how badly I've hurt her. It hadn't been my intention.

"I was afraid to disappoint you and Dad. Mark always did everything right. He's your son."

Her eyes spark with anger. "You're as much my daughter as he is my son. It doesn't matter if you don't have my DNA. You're mine. Do you understand that?"

Although Mom is gentle by nature, she can be fierce when she needs to be.

"I do. And you and Dad are my parents. I feel awful that I've messed everything up."

She strokes a hand down the back of my head before pulling me in a fierce hug. "We forgive you."

"Not Mark."

"He'll come around." She smiles. "Just don't do it again."

My smile is filled with pain.

"I won't. I promise."

"I have to say this again. She's so beautiful. I'm in love with being a grandmother. I've missed kids in the house. I can't wait to spoil her." We embrace again before she gets to her feet. "Now I should go check on your father. The food should be ready."

"I'm not very hungry."

Mom knows why I'm hiding up in the room and doesn't call me on it.

"You take some time. There's plenty of food."

After she leaves, I start to unpack, giving myself something to do. Then I shrug on a sweater and leave the room. Noise comes from the kitchen where everyone is congregated. I bypass that and go for the front door. It's gotten colder, but I need a walk. I don't get far. At the sidewalk, a cruiser comes to a stop.

"Andi? Is that you?"

I give a small wave. "It's me, Ray."

He gets out wearing the full cop uniform, takes off his hat, and embraces me. "It's been a while. I didn't know you were back in town."

"Just visiting," I admit.

His eyes drift over me even though I'm covered head to toe. "You're looking good."

Ray had a crush on me in school. I'd never given him the time of day because my heart had been set on Chase.

He didn't have a shaved head then, but he hasn't changed much beyond that.

"You look good too."

He points to the house.

"Fletcher and Cassidy did really good with this place."

"They did."

"If you are staying awhile, you should come by for dinner."

I hadn't heard his approach. So when the hand lands on my shoulder, I jump.

"We won't be in town long."

Glancing up, I see Chase staring daggers at Ray. As much as I want to believe it's some show of possession over me, the two guys have hated each other for as long as I remember.

"Chase Wilde," Ray says, not at all sounding surprised to see him next to me.

"Ray Todd."

"I'd heard you were in town, but left."

"I'm back."

"Too bad." Ray turns his attention back to me. "Andi, you're welcome to come over for dinner. I married Marla, and she'd be pissed if I didn't give you an invite." I nod. "Well, it was good seeing you."

He puts his hat back on, tipping his head at me before getting back in his cruiser and driving away.

"Checking on me to make sure I haven't flown the coop?" I say, with a little bitterness in my tone.

"No, Violet's asking for you. When I couldn't find you, I checked outside."

"Is she okay?" I ask, losing all bravado in favor of panic.

"She's fine. She just wants her mom. I think she's tired."

I head for the front door. "I'm sure she's ready for a nap, but too excited."

"Yeah, you're probably right."

When I find her, she's fighting sleep.

"Hey, my darling girl, why don't we get a nap?" She shakes her head. "It's okay," I whisper in her ear. "Everyone will be here when you wake up."

Even with a nap, by the time my parents and his leave, Violet is wiped out. Chase offers to take her up to bed. After I shower and do my nighttime rituals, I find them curled up asleep together in his designated room. It's so cute, I snap another picture of them before heading downstairs where I find Cassidy in the kitchen with the baby.

"Sorry, I thought everyone had gone to bed," I say.

"It's okay. The baby is restless." She paces the floor, rocking her arms. "Besides, we are practically sisters-in-law."

"Not quite. Chase and I aren't together and never will be."

"Pfft. I saw the way he left here to go to Chicago to find you."

I'd heard that before from his mouth.

"Even if that were true, it isn't like that for him anymore."

"And you?"

As much as I want to dodge the truth, I've done enough of that for a lifetime. "I'll always love him. But it's time for me to let go of the idea of an us."

"Don't give up on him. I gave up on Fletcher and married a useless asshole because I needed something or someone to help me move on. In the end, it's always been Fletcher for me."

"Everyone saw that," I joke. "It's different for me. We might have had a chance. But the way Chase looks at me now, you'd tell me yourself to move on."

A sound and smell that should only come from an adult wafts over from the baby.

"Oops, I guess I've got to go change my kiddo," she says.

We say our goodnights. The rest of the time goes by fast. When it's time to head back to Chicago, I realize how short our time was and am grateful when our moms come with us.

With so many helping hands the next few days, I finally get some great uninterrupted sleep. The lot of us goes to the main passport office in Chicago to apply for Violet's passport. Where I'd been solitary, I'm constantly surrounded by people. It's all happening so fast, something I haven't told Chase. With the buffer of my mom and his, we barely speak to each other. He doesn't know of my growing panic, not that he'd care.

"I've sorted out the clothes that are too small for her. What do you want me to do next?" Mom asks.

Denise is in the living room with Violet as I make lunch for all of us.

"Pack what's left. There's no point in leaving any of it, as she'll probably grow out of it while we're there."

Mom agrees when a knock sounds.

"It's probably Chase," I say.

He's leaving for Italy today and had left for the hotel to pack up. Only it's not him. Owen stands on the other side of the door.

"Hey, I wondered if Holly could hang out here. I need to make a quick grocery run."

"Yeah, sure," I say, opening the door wider, and Holly darts in. Immediately, she and Violet start dancing around together.

Denise and my mom stare at Owen. So I wave him inside and make introductions.

"Denise and Mom, this is my neighbor, Owen, and his daughter, Holly. Owen, this is my mom, Pamela, and Chase's mom, Denise."

"Very nice to meet you," Owen says.

"Nice to meet you too," Mom says before arching an

eyebrow in my direction. I discreetly shake my head. Still, the awkwardness grows.

"Owen is running out," I say. "Holly is going to hang with us. Has she eaten?"

He nods. "Can I talk to you for a second?"

"Sure."

I lead him out in the hall and beat him to the punch.

"I'm sorry I haven't called. It's been a little crazy."

His eyes search mine.

"You have a deer in headlights look."

I want to sag in relief that someone notices and cares.

"Yeah, it's great to have help, but it feels like everything is happening so fast."

He nods. "Should I take Denise being here to mean that you and Chase have worked everything out?"

I blow out a breath. "No. That ship has sailed."

"Good."

Then before I know what he's doing, his lips are on mine. Gently, I push him back.

"Owen …"

"I can't have you leaving and not knowing what could be."

He's still so close. A part of me wants to wrap myself in his arms, just to feel steady. The other part yearns for Chase even as futile as that is. He rests his forehead against mine.

I bite my lip before speaking. "I can't ask you to wait for me. My heart is still …"

Rapid footsteps sound on the stairs as if the person is taking them two at a time. Owen takes his time stepping back, not caring who it might be.

His eyes hold mine before taking a step back. "I'll pick up Holly later."

I nod and stare at my nails because the steps stop nearby. I'm not yet ready to see Chase's face. Finally, I glance up and find his penetrating gaze on me.

"It's not what you think."

He shrugs. "It's not really any of my business," he says before he enters the apartment.

I brush a hand through my hair, already used to his rejection, and follow in behind him. Violet's gibbering away to Holly doing her version of introductions. I go back to finishing up lunch. When I offer Chase some, he declines.

"I really need to head out."

He's told Violet he's leaving and she continues to cling to him.

"Dada, no go."

He scoops her up and I watch as huge tears fall from her eyes.

TWENTY

Chase

———

THE ATTACHMENT I've developed toward Violet is already so strong, leaving her is extremely difficult. I'm not sure which one of us is the saddest. And then there's that Andi-Owen situation I interrupted. Just when I thought things might be improving between us, I run into that little huggie-fest on my way back here. Talk about a bucket of ice to cool things down. Mom walks me outside as my ride to the airport arrives.

"Chase, honey. A word, please."

"Yeah, Mom."

"Don't close yourself off to Andi."

This is not what I want to hear right now. "Mom," I huff.

"Honey, I know how angry and frustrated you are. But give her time."

"Time? She had over two years. How much more does she need?"

"That's not what I meant and you know it."

I blow out a lung full of frustrations. "Look, Mom, I've got a plane to catch."

"Yes, I know. And a lot on your plate. I only want you to think about the decisions she made. You were at the center of them. And look at what she's doing now. This can't be easy for her."

"And it is for me?"

"No. But you've been in Italy, have friends there. She's walking into a completely new world filled with strangers. People who she thinks will be against her. Go easy on her."

"Yeah, yeah, I get it."

"If not for her, do it for Violet. It won't do anyone any good if your daughter isn't happy with this transition." Then Mom hugs me and I climb in the car for the ride to the airport.

The flight back to Italy is uneventful. I actually sleep most of the way, exhausted from the entire trip to Chicago. I suppose it's emotional burnout. The roller coaster I've been riding has finally taken its toll. My body is out of shape—physically, that is. Coach is going to bust my ass when I get on the field.

When I walk into my apartment, it registers that this place is not going to work at all. What the hell was I thinking? For me, it was perfect, but it's not just me any longer. There isn't a chance our moms, Violet, and Andi will all cram into a two-bedroom home, not to mention, what if Andi wants to date someone? We aren't committed to each other, and I have no hold or say on what she does with her love life. That little interlude I witnessed with Owen was enough to make me realize Andi has her own life to live and I don't fit in. I have two weeks to find a new place and move, so I'd better scramble.

The first call I make is to Max.

"You finally back?" he asks.

"Yeah, just walked in. I need a new place to live." I go on to explain why.

"You don't need an apartment, my friend. You need a damn palace with all those people."

"That's an exaggeration, but I do need something drastically bigger than this. Can you help?"

"Let me make some calls. I can't help, but I may know of someone who can."

"Great. Thanks. Have you talked to the people in Germany?"

He laughs. "What do you think? They've been badgering my ass for weeks now. The real question is, what are you going to do? You need to make a decision, and soon."

"So what? I need to take a trip to Berlin then?"

"Not unless you want to turn them down or sign without meeting them in person. They've already agreed to a transfer fee with your club and are willing to offer you a new contract for more money—a lot more money. It's a win-win for you, Chase. It can't possibly get any better than this."

Would this be good or bad for Violet and Andi? They're both moving, so I guess it wouldn't matter. I should probably discuss this with Andi, though, before I do anything.

"Is it possible to delay them any longer?" I ask.

"You know how it works. If they can't make a deal before January 31st, you're looking at summer between July and August. Who knows if they'll be feeling so charitable then."

"And what are the chances of getting an offer back in the U.S.?"

"Is this some kind of a joke?"

"No joke, Max. I have a child to think of."

"You have a career and a bank account to think of too, Chase."

"Money isn't everything," I grumble.

"Excuse me?" he asks. "Is this the same person who made me beat down the Italian league for a few hundred thousand euros?"

"Right, I know, but I didn't have a daughter back then."

"Which is exactly why you should be more concerned with money now."

He does have a good point. But I'm a great investor. My brother has guided me well, along with Andi's brother, Mark. My money has grown because I'm not out spending it foolishly like some athletes do. I have enough to live off of for years to come, even if I were to quit playing tomorrow. On the other hand, if I did the Germany contract and played for a couple of years, I could put all that away and we could move back to the States before Violet was ready to start school. I would be set for life and I could play or even coach somewhere if I wanted to.

"Check my schedule and let's make a quick trip up there. I'll talk to my family right away."

"Great choice. I'll check in with you later, and by then I'll have a name for you for some temporary living quarters until your move to Berlin."

"Thanks, Max."

When I check the time, I notice my window is opening on Violet waking up. So I pick up the phone so we can FaceTime. Andi answers and she's smiling. I'm glad she's in a happy mood. I ask to speak with Violet and the Little One's grinning face appears before me.

"Dada, miss you."

"I miss you too. But I'll be seeing you soon. You and Nana, Gamma, and Mama will all be here soon."

"Holly too?"

"No, sweetie, not Holly. But maybe she can come to visit sometime." I hate the lie, but it's the only thing I can think to say. There's no way Owen will ever be invited to my home—at least not for a while.

"Okay. Can I bring toys?"

"Of course you can bring your toys. Every single one of them."

That crazy crooked grin of hers melts me on the spot and I know when she gets older I'll never be able to say no to anything she asks of me. I'll be putty in this girl's hands. I am so fucked.

"Dada, love you."

"I love you too, Little One. Now let me talk to your nana."

Mom gets on, asks how the flight was, and we chat a bit, then she hands the phone off to Andi. I decide to be the chicken shit and not mention anything about Berlin to her. It can wait until they're all here. What will it matter anyway? At least that's my justification. We end the call on a fairly good note, although things are a bit stilted. I promise to call the following day.

The next day I show up for practice and have a lot of explaining to do. After a very long meeting with the coaching staff, I finally persuade them to let me back on the field. I'm to report to practice first thing in the morning. I'm not even sure why. If I go to Berlin and sign with them, what difference will it make? If this doesn't happen before the end of the month, we have to wait until summer. Who the hell knows? Talk about turmoil.

On the way home, I get a call from an agent who leases homes. He has a few he can show me this afternoon. Since I'm already out, I agree to meet him at his office. The first place he takes me to is so ostentatious, I immediately say no. I can't see any of us spending one night there. The second one looks unlived in. I want somewhere that's comfortable, a place where we can all kick up our feet and feel okay doing it. The final place we visit is perfect. It's a villa on the outskirts of town, yet closer to the soccer complex. It has a heated pool, which Violet will love, and the furnishings are cushy and the ultimate in comfort. There are five large bedrooms all with their own private bath, a huge kitchen, two living areas, a room upstairs that Violet could use as a playroom if she'd want, and room for Andi and me to spread out and not get in each other's way.

"I'll take this, as long as it's month to month."

"The owner would prefer a six-month contracted lease, but let me see what I can negotiate."

"I'll pay extra in rent, if necessary. I really want this house." If we go to Berlin, Max will have to locate something similar for us. This affords us everything we need.

The real estate agent wanders off for a few minutes and returns with a smiling face. "I'm pleased to announce you have yourself a house, Mr. Wilde. The owner, who is out of the country for the year, is happy to let you have this place."

"Excellent. When can I move in?"

"Today, if you'd like."

I mentally tick off what needs to be done. Packing, selling my furniture because there's no use keeping it, hiring movers, and then settling in before the rest of the group arrives.

"Mr. Wilde, do you need assistance? Our company offers relocation services."

"Yes, that would be wonderful."

He makes a few calls and says someone will be coming around later this afternoon. I head home and experience a real sense of being overwhelmed. I can delegate a lot of this stuff, but I want everything to be in its place when everyone arrives.

I'm walking in the door when the phone rings. It's Max. "Can you fly to Berlin this weekend?"

"Yeah, I'm free. Are you? I'm not going without representation."

"I would not have asked if I couldn't go. I'll make the arrangements."

I'm just about to kick up my feet when there's a knock on the door. Fuck, not a moment's rest around here. I'm still worn out from the trip, and I need to sleep because if I'm not on my game, I'll receive an ass chewing for sure. It's going to be bad as it is because I'm out of shape, having not worked out in almost two weeks.

Not bothering to check who it is, I sling the door open to a frenzy of cameras, the paparazzi, and reporters asking a million questions. But the number one answer they are hounding me for is, "Mr. Wilde, what did you think when you found out you were a father?"

TWENTY-ONE

Andi

—————

IT HAD BEEN SO hard to say goodbye to my little monkey bear. After her passport arrived, Chase had a plane ready for her and the moms to go. At the airport, Violet clung to me and I had to make promises upon promises to get her to leave without me. I'd held back my tears until after they disappeared behind the gate. Then, I'd dissolved in a river of my own making.

"Earth to Andi."

Beth stares at me as if she's waiting for me to answer some question. I push away the scene so fresh in my mind.

"What?"

"You were going to tell me about Chase. But you're barely here and I haven't talked to you in over a week."

I shake my head to try to clear away the pain.

"I'm sorry. It's been so crazy. Chase arrived and now Violet's gone." She lays a hand on mine.

"I can't imagine. But he's the father?" she asks, trying to put me back on track.

I nod. "He's the father." I unload the entire story from start to finish.

"And he didn't know?"

My head slowly drifts side to side as if I don't believe it myself.

"Wow, Andi. That's pretty messed up."

"Don't start on me too." I press my palms to my eyes before raking my fingers through my hair. "I can't take back what I did."

"I'm not judging you. It's just I don't know who to feel bad for. It's a tough situation. When do you plan to give notice to Peggy?"

Groaning, I say, "That's the thing. My landlord won't let me out of my lease."

I'd been spending my breaks the last few days contacting him and reading through my lease as if it would change.

"Why not let Chase handle it?"

A bark of humorless laughter escapes me.

"I can't ask him to pay my rent. Besides, he wants nothing to do with me. He'll probably be happy I can't come."

Her earnest eyes hold mine.

"So what will you do?"

"I don't know. I can't afford to pay rent and not work." I close my eyes again. "His season is over in May …"

The idea of not seeing my daughter for nearly five months makes me physically ill.

"You should talk to him. Not doing that is what led to all of your current problems." She's right. My silent agreement is enough for her to abruptly change subjects. "When was the last time you got laid?"

I chortle. "How old is Violet?"

"You can't be serious. Two, almost three years?"

"Almost four if you consider my pregnancy. I didn't feel right about sleeping with another man while I was carrying Chase's child."

"And after? What about your hot neighbor? You two never did it? All that time you spend together."

Owen and I had only really gotten close to something more than friendship recently. I shake my head.

"There's your problem. You need to free the dragon."

"The dragon?"

"Come on. It's a stress-reducing activity."

I'm saved from answering when Beth gets paged, ending our break. The day only gets worse when one of our tiny patients passes away. It's hard when that happens. I'm so emotionally exhausted when I leave the hospital, I almost miss several people with cameras waiting just outside the exit. I stop at the security desk to ask what's going on.

"They are looking for an Andi James."

The hospital is huge and not everyone knows me. I cover my badge the officer hadn't bothered to look at.

"Wow, I wonder why," I say out loud before heading in the opposite direction.

From the rumors I've heard, they've used the basement morgue level exit for high-profile patients in the past. I make my way there and take the exit, keeping to the shadows. I don't bother with the trains and hail a cab home, an expense I can't afford.

By the time I get home, I'm rattled and dead tired. But if I want to talk to Violet, I have to call before I go to sleep. Luckily, I worked the night shift so it's seven in the morning here, which means my sweet child will be awake.

The video kicks in and her cherubic face fills the screen.

"Mama."

"Hey, baby."

I miss her like crazy. Already it seems she's grown and I'm missing it. It's a reminder of what I did to Chase.

"Mama, come now."

"Soon," I say, biting back tears.

Then she gibbers on about a pool. Questions fly in my head. We haven't started swim lessons yet. With my schedule, I couldn't swing it. After our conversation dies down, I can tell she's sitting on Chase's lap.

"Give kisses to Nana and Grammy and let me talk to your daddy."

Chase puts her down and she runs off.

The screen shifts to shine on his beautiful face.

"You need something."

His coldness almost has me clamming up. But I promised I wouldn't lie or keep secrets. I start with the easy question first.

"You have a pool?"

He nods. "I'm teaching her to swim." I must have grimaced because he adds, "Don't worry. Mom got her floaties and a suit. She's safe."

It's another thing I'm missing, but say nothing. Chase missed her first steps. I look down before I speak.

"There's one more thing. I'm not sure I can come." His perfect brow arches. "My landlord won't let me out of my lease. I can't afford to leave work and pay rent too."

He waves a dismissive hand. "Give me the details and I'll handle it."

"I refuse to be a burden. I'll figure it out somehow."

Though I haven't a clue how.

His face contorts into a frown. "This is your problem. You refuse to let anyone help you. Is your pride more important than our daughter?"

"No," I spit. "But you've made it very clear how little you think of me. I'm surprised you're not glad I can't come."

I exhale, reining in my temper.

His lips compress. "Jesus, Andi. I don't want to fight with you. I have the means to help you. Take it. As much as I think I can do this alone, our daughter needs you. She asks multiple times a day when her mama is coming."

That stills any further protest. I would move heaven and earth for my daughter.

"Fine, I'll pay you back," I promise. "Did your agent find out if it's possible to expedite a work visa?"

"He did and I can send you the details. It's just …"

"What?"

"He says most positions will require you to be able to speak Italian."

I'd thought that might be the case. "I'm not going to be able to find a job, am I?"

"I'll support whatever you want. Remember though, I'll be traveling a lot. If you can find a job, we'll have to get a nanny."

His words kick in.

"And Violet's already adjusting to a new place."

"Exactly," he agrees.

"So it's better if I just stay with her."

"Again, I'll support your decision. You'll have whatever you need no matter what."

"For Violet," I clarify.

"For the both of you."

I can see it in his eyes he means it.

"I can't expect you to take care of me," I say softly, trying not to hope that maybe …

"Taking care of you is like taking care of my daughter. Besides, I got a bigger place, so you can have your space and I can have mine."

It's as if the axe comes down on my fantasies. How can I possibly live with him and only be his roommate? Even staring at him through the screen, my body remembers every touch, caress, and kiss he's given me.

"Sounds good," I force myself to say and blow out a breath. "There's just one more thing."

"Yeah."

I'd almost forgotten.

"Reporters were waiting for me at work."

He doesn't seem surprised.

"Somebody found out about us. Did you tell anyone?"

I glare at his accusation. "Me? Tell anyone? I've only told my best friend the story today. And I can trust her."

"What about Owen?"

"Owen wouldn't do that to me," I say emphatically.

"How well do you know the guy?"

"Well enough to know he cares too much about me."

Chase's lips thin. I decide turnabout is fair play.

"What about your girlfriend?" I ask.

"I don't have a girlfriend."

"I'm sorry. I meant fiancée." Though I try not to sound sarcastic, even I hear it in my voice.

His jaw tightens. "I'll handle it."

What will the hospital administration say tomorrow when I show up after the press has been hunting for me?

"What am I going to do if they come knocking on my door? I don't have a doorman. It's likely just a matter of time before they find out where I live."

As if on cue, a knock comes. I sigh.

"Don't answer it," he says.

"I won't live in fear."

I head to the door and Owen stands on the other side. Chase asks who it is when I invite him inside.

"It's Owen."

Chase's expression darkens a fraction before Owen gets my attention. "I dropped Holly off at preschool to find a horde of people with cameras outside."

I face the screen and Chase is ready with an answer. "Like I said, I'll handle it."

"I can take care of Andi," Owen says and I spin around to face him. "You can stay at my place until they give up looking for you here."

At a loss for words, I angle my head back to the screen again.

"Chase, I'll talk to you later."

I don't wait for his reply, but end the call, deciding on the spot I'll call back to talk to Mom later. I already know she's having the time of her life sightseeing. When the screen goes black, I give Owen my full attention.

"I mean that. You're welcome to stay however long you need."

"Thanks. Depending on how things go, I may take you up on that."

"I have to ask. Have you been avoiding me?"

I have been. He's everything I should want. Yet, my heart yearns for Chase.

"I've been busy trying to pack everything." Which is true, but an excuse.

He steps way too close and I smell his woodsy cologne.

"Did my kiss scare you off?"

I think of my conversation with Beth. Here is a man willing to take care of me in ways that any woman would want, and he's not doing it just out of duty. Add that to the fact that I haven't been touched or even kissed in years before that quick one between us. Maybe it's time I move on, because Owen kisses like a man who knows what to do in bed. I glance up into his golden eyes and try to forget Chase, which feels monumentally impossible. Maybe my heart can move on if I let my body do the same.

I step back. "I can't." Owen's disappointment is evident. "I'm sorry." I feel like a broken record. "I just need time."

When he leaves, I wonder if I'm making a huge mistake. A man like him doesn't come around often.

Only a day has passed when Chase's handling things has me on a plane to a dream trip to Italy. The hospital was more than happy to grant me leave with all the disruptions from the paparazzi.

Chase made good on arrangements to pay for my Chicago apartment while I'm overseas. Though we haven't discussed what will happen when we return to the States after his season is over, I think it will be good for Violet to come home to a place she remembers.

It's so surreal when the plane lands. It hits me that I'm in Italy. However, the dream of leaving the country doesn't come close to how anxious I am to see my daughter again. As soon as I clear customs, I rush through the exit to find Violet waiting for me. She runs into my arms.

"Mama, Mama."

I scoop her up and she feels like she's gained weight. I hold on tightly, vowing to never let her go. I want not to be disappointed that Chase isn't with them, but I am. Mom, who can read me like a book, whispers during our embrace that he had practice.

"Happy Bitday," Violet says.

"No, not today, Monkey Bear. In a couple of days."

Chase's mom comes over and gives me a hug. Then she whispers to Violet, "Don't tell Mama about the surprise."

They grin at each other conspiratorially.

"How about we go see this house I keep hearing about?"

"Swim?" Violet's eyes brighten.

"The house is pretty amazing, Andi. And the views," Mom adds.

But it isn't the view out of the window that stills my heart when we arrive. It's the sight of Chase. He obviously didn't expect us as he only wears a towel slung on his hips as water droplets cover his golden skin.

TWENTY-TWO

Chase

————

I DON'T HAVE to turn around to know Andi's eyes are on me. I feel them burning through the towel that's wrapped around my waist. She still has that effect on me, even though I've done everything in my power to suppress those emotions. My fucking heart betrays me each time I look at her, even through my anger, and even though I know it's that little runt Owen she wants.

Glancing over my shoulder, I catch her eye. A blossom of color spreads from her neck up to her cheeks. I almost laugh, but I don't because I wish it were real. I wish it were because she wants me exactly the way I want her.

"Dada, Mama's here."

My thoughts are broken by Violet as she teeters around Andi and heads straight for my legs. A chuckle breaks loose from me, as the Little One grabs my calves and then looks up at me with her goofy grin. I snatch her and toss her up in the air, threatening to dump her into the water. She screeches and giggles simultaneously as I see Andi's look of horror.

"Don't worry, Andi. I won't endanger our daughter. If she goes in, so do I."

She visibly relaxes, so I add, "If you're not too tired, why don't you put your suit on and join us?"

Mom walks out and says, "I'm making dinner, Andi, so there's plenty of time for you to relax if you want."

"Uh, okay," Andi says. She turns around and heads inside. Mom offers me a smile.

"Come on, Little One. Let's get in the pool." Violet claps and I lose the towel that's around my waist. She immediately splashes me in the face as soon as we get in, and I splash her back. Violet isn't one of those kids who hates to get her face wet, of which I'm happy.

"Under," she says.

"You know what to do," I say. She bobs her head as I blow in her face. Then I do a quick dunk. She comes up laughing. It's at that particular moment Andi walks out.

"What are you doing?" she asks, panicked.

"Teaching her to hold her breath," I answer calmly.

"You can't do that."

Violet smacks the surface of the water with her hands, grabbing our attention. "Dada, under again."

I shoot a pointed look at Andi and say, "Okay, remember to hold your breath." I blow in her face again and do another quick dunk, then pull her back up. She's laughing as soon as she clears the surface.

Andi watches in fascination. "Is that how they do it?"

"I'm not sure about they, but it's how I do it," I say.

Violet kicks her legs and says, "Swim." I put my hands under her back and help her float. She kicks and we move about the pool.

"Violet, what should you never ever do?"

"No swim lone."

"Right. Always be with Mama, Nana, Grammy, or me."

"Yeah."

The three of us swim for a while and I hand Violet off to Andi and observe the two of them together. Andi looks amazing in her too-tiny bikini. There's no evidence at all she ever had a child, and again I'm reminded of how I should've been there.

Mom's words come back to me, and if I'm honest, they even haunt me a little. In my anger, I didn't stop to think of what Andi must've gone through, being alone and on her own, caring for a newborn. She had to work and didn't have anyone to rely on for help. She must've been scared shitless. I know I would've been. Many women might have buckled under the pressure, but not Andi. She remained strong and did a great job with Violet, even taking the time to make sure she knew who her father was.

No, it wasn't ideal for me, but did she have to do that? She could've lied to me had she wanted to. She didn't have to tell me the truth. I never would've known. Maybe I would've figured it out, so nix that, but whatever. I can't totally hate her for what she did. People make mistakes. Yeah, I've made a shit ton myself. Maybe I need to rethink this whole thing with her. But then again, there's that Owen issue. Perhaps if I keep them apart long enough, she'll forget about him. But then that makes me an asshole, and I don't want to be that guy.

I need to clear the air with her once and for all. But dumping all this on her at once is entirely too much. I'll wait and do it a little at a time. If I take long enough, maybe she will have forgotten him by then.

"Dada. Airplane. Dada. Plane."

I've been so bogged down in my thoughts, I didn't hear Violet calling me.

"Coming." I swim over and grab her out of Andi's arms. Then I lift her high in the air and pretend to be an airplane, swooping low over the water, then back high again. Her arms and legs kick in excitement. She loves this.

Andi's voice comes to me from over my shoulder. "You're going to spoil her."

"I plan on it."

"Thanks. I can see it now. You're at practice and it'll be,

airplane, under, this or that. I won't be able to keep up. I'll be chasing her all over the place."

"Probably so, but tell me you won't love it."

"Yeah, you're right. I've never been a stay-at-home mom, so it'll be different." Then she picks up Violet's hand and says, "Monkey Bear, it's time to get out. You look like a raisin. Look at your fingers."

They're shriveled up as can be.

"Dada, look." She holds them out for me to see. Then I show her mine look the same, and she likes that.

"Come on, Little One. Time to get out and ready for dinner."

Andi wraps Violet in one of the many towels out here, and then wraps herself in one, while I do the same. Together, we walk inside.

"You didn't say, but I guess your flight went well?"

"Yeah, it was great. Thanks for handling everything for me. I really appreciate it. And the apartment too."

"It's good. I want you happy here."

She offers me a smile. "This house is amazing. I guess I need to unpack."

"Sure. Did one of the moms show you which room is yours?" I ask.

"Yeah. Are you sure you want me to have the master?"

"Actually, all the bedrooms are like that."

"Seriously?"

Laughing, I answer, "Yeah, unpack and when you're finished, let me know. I'll show you around. Violet's room is great. I had to buy her a few things for her toys and such, but everything else was furnished."

She goes to take Violet and I say, "I'll take her. You go take care of your things. Meet us downstairs when you're done."

"Thanks. Oh, Chase, your nose looks a lot better."

"Yeah, it's good. I had it checked here and I'm cleared to

play. I have to wear a face shield for six weeks, but other than that, I'm good."

I take Violet and change her into clothes and run her downstairs to her nana. Then I go back up to change. When I'm finished, I walk over to Andi's room and knock on the door.

"Come in."

"It looks like you've got a lot done."

"There's a whole other suitcase I haven't opened yet."

"Oh, I didn't see that one. You doing okay?"

She glances around and nods. "Yeah, I am. It'll be an adjustment, and there will be things I miss, but …"

I'm pretty sure she's referring to Owen.

"About your work. It's not going to be easy like we talked about. And with Violet, I thought it might be easier if you were here with her."

"I agree. Maybe when she's older or something. I'll cross that bridge, you know."

"Look, Andi, I do want you to be happy. And I want us to be … well, I want us to provide a wonderful home for our daughter. That's my number one priority."

"Sure, yeah, me too."

There are so many things I want to say to her, but it's awkward and I can't get the words to form on my tongue. Instead, I find myself offering her a smile and then walking out the door. It's not exactly what I had in mind, but then again, Rome wasn't built in a day either. Maybe somehow we can find a way to rebuild what we had. And if not, I'll be one miserable son of a bitch with her living under my roof.

TWENTY-THREE

Andi

———————

A WEEK FLIES by in no time. The moms and Violet surprised me with a birthday cake that Violet helped make. It was just the four of us because Chase had been away at a game. I'm sorry when it's time to say goodbye to our moms. After they are gone, the house seems empty, especially when Violet is sleeping as she is now. I go and check on her because she's usually up by now. When I brush her hair from her face, her skin is warm. Immediately, I find the thermometer and swipe it across her head.

"What's going on?"

Chase must have heard me frantically rooting through Violet's bathroom. When I glance back, I find him in the doorway with an arm resting on the frame.

"She's running a low-grade fever," I say, turning my attention back to my little one.

He scratches his head. "She had a slight one several days before you arrived."

I snap my head around.

"What?" I have to stop myself and lead him out of the room. I don't want to fight in front of her in case she wakes up. "You didn't tell me," I accuse.

"My mom and yours said it was fine. They gave her the Tylenol you packed and she was good."

He's clueless about how betrayed I feel.

"But you didn't tell me!" Anger boils in me.

"They thought with everything you had going on, they didn't want to worry you."

"But she's my daughter."

Chase's jaw ticks. "She's my daughter too. And I didn't know about her first word or when she took her first step."

It feels like a slap. I step back, reining in my temper. He's right. He's missed so much. What right do I have to call him out on not telling me something? I soften my tone.

"Can we just agree to share information like this? I am a nurse. I need to know when she's sick."

He nods and takes a second. "Is she going to be okay?"

Sighing, I say, "I think so. It's probably just a reaction to being in a new place with new germs. She'll be fine."

In the back of my head, I make a mental note of a possible pattern. If she gets another fever, we will take her to a doctor to get checked out.

Chase walks away and awkwardly, I head back to my room. I don't know what to do around this man anymore. We used to be friends and could talk about everything under the sun. Now, he feels like a stranger.

Then I remember his words and go find the things I brought for him. After I have them, I search for him in the house, but he's not anywhere. I knock on his room door.

He opens it, shirtless. For a second, I forget the entire English language. The man is perfection. His defined muscles beg to be touched. I swallow hard, gulping down air.

"Do you need me?"

That is such a loaded question. My body is on high alert, recognizing him as someone who could light it on fire. I clear my throat and hold out my hand.

"What's this?"

He takes the envelope and thumb drive I offer.

"It's the letter I meant to send you a thousand times. And the other has pictures and videos of Violet from her birth. You may not have been there, but I didn't want you to miss those important moments. It's not everything, because some things happen when you least expect them. But her first word was *dada*, by the way. There is a video of her saying it and me trying to get her to say mama. Anyway, it's all I have to give. It doesn't make up for the time you lost, but …"

My throat closes and I wave a hand, unable to speak, and walk away. Several seconds tick by before his door clicks shut.

Violet gets up not long after and Chase leaves for practice. He has an away game in two days. He'll be gone for a couple of days. That's the extent of most of our conversations, which are limited to anything to do with Violet, including his schedule.

With the moms not here to cook, I decide to make a special dinner. Though nothing could compare to their cooking, I try.

Chase has made sure to be home to spend time with Violet. I wonder when that will change. He has a social life, based on the tabloids. Still, he arrives predictably and dinner is almost ready.

"Dada," Violet says as he comes through the door.

He scoops her up and it's a sight to behold the two of them together. For a man who used to flee when little kids or babies were around, he's an amazing dad.

"Hi," he says by way of greeting to me, but immediately focuses on Violet before I can do anything but give a quick hi back. "Ready to fly?" he asks her.

"Fy, Fy!"

She's already in her bathing suit.

"Give me one minute to change."

He sets her back down and she nods. She waits by the glass doors that lead to the infinity pool. I keep an eye on her, but so

173

far she hasn't broken the rules of waiting for someone to go with her before she goes outside. It's not much longer than the minute he promised, and they are in the water.

I swallow back the loneliness. Although we live together in this big house, he and I might as well be on different continents. *Your fault.* I blow out a breath and set the table.

When they come in, Chase stares at the table spread.

"Wow, it looks like your mom made us dinner."

"Eat," Violet says.

He finally looks at me like he actually sees me here. "Is it ready?"

I nod. He puts Violet in the booster chair and gets her all strapped in. Again, I'm amazed how well he's adapted to being a father.

After we are all seated, I ask him about practice.

"Well, Coach was being an as—" He stops himself midsentence and I watch him try to find another word.

"As," Violet repeats.

"Asset," Chase corrects. "Coach was being an asset to everyone today."

I bite back a laugh, but can't stop the grin. "I guess he thought you were a liability."

"Exactly." Chase gestures with his fork in my direction.

The grin he gives me is so damn sexy I have to glance away. He has no idea of the effect he has on me.

"Mama makes good food." He smiles at Violet, who gives him a toothy one of her own.

As Chase inhales most of the meal, I just enjoy watching the two of them together. He's so patient with her as she talks a mile a minute. Over half of what she says doesn't make sense. Is this what it would have been like if I'd told him from the beginning that I was pregnant? My thoughts drift to the letter and thumb drive. Has he read it or viewed the pictures and videos? I don't dare ask. He has a right to do it on his own time, not mine.

Chase insists on doing bath time since he will be leaving first thing the day after next. I'm sitting in the living room watching the incredible sunset when he comes in.

"You guys must have had a busy day. She fell right asleep," he says as the cushions dip under his weight.

I wonder if he notices what little distance he put between us.

"We did. We took a long walk. It was such a pretty day."

I keep my gaze at the horizon, for fear he will see the longing in my eyes. The picturesque scene is too romantic for words. And if I turn, it won't be a stretch to lean over to his gorgeous mouth.

"Thanks for dinner, by the way."

I lick my lips and try to keep my breathing under control as he shifts, putting us closer together.

"No problem. It's the least I can do."

His next words fan through my hair as his heat warms my exposed skin.

"You don't have to. I don't expect it." I nod. "Andi …"

The way he says my name has me finally turning to look at him. His lips part. There is a second where I swear he's thinking about kissing me. I dare hope, but then his phone chimes. When he checks the screen, he apologizes. "I'm sorry. I have to take this."

He moves away, taking his heat with him. On his feet, he drifts out through the wall-to-ceiling doors to the pool area, cutting me off from hearing his conversation. Is it his fiancée? From the way he's at home, there hasn't been a lot of time for him to see her, unless he's lying about his schedule. And I don't believe that for a second. We aren't together. He has no reason to lie about something like that.

As I watch him, I become envious of the shorts he wears on this unseasonably warm night. They cup his ass in such a way that I find myself guzzling my glass of wine. My body buzzes with excitement. It's been far too long since I've been touched. I can't stay here lest I not be responsible for what I do next. So I take the glass to the kitchen and wash it. Chase's conversation is so intense, he doesn't even know I leave. I close myself in my room after a quick check on Violet. Her fever has passed, just as fast as it came yesterday, but now I burn with something so very different.

The next day, Chase is gone early because the team is leaving the next morning. That much I'd gotten from our previous night's dinner. I spend the afternoon trying another recipe. Cooking has become my pastime with nothing else to do. It feels weird not to work. So I fill it with YouTube cooking videos.

When he gets home, like clockwork they are in the pool. Violet's not going to be happy when he's gone. I'll have to think of some activities to distract her.

The doorbell rings, startling me. I glance over to see Chase tossing Violet in the air. We haven't had visitors and he hadn't said he was having company. So I answer it.

A stunning brunette is on the other side. I recognize her immediately as Lucia, Chase's fiancée.

Her voice is beautiful, much like the woman herself. Only her rapid Italian is more than my self-teaching Duolingo app can handle.

"English?" I ask.

"Who are you?" she asks in a thick accent.

How do I answer that question? If she's Chase's fiancée, doesn't she have a right to know?

"Why are you here?" The question comes from behind me.

I glance over my shoulder to see Chase towering there, glowering at her as he holds Violet in his arms.

"I came to talk to you," she says.

I reach for our daughter, who leans toward me. "Come on, Violet. Daddy has company."

Chase doesn't stop me. As I walk away, I can't make out

their hushed tones. The only thing I feel is extreme jealousy. But there is no way I can compete with a woman who looks like her. She's gorgeous in a Hollywood movie star kind of way. No wonder he never once tried to get me back in the years after he left. How can I blame him?

TWENTY-FOUR

Chase

IF LUCIA WERE A MAN, I'm pretty fucking sure my fist would be making contact with her jaw right now. The fact that she had the nerve to stalk me after practice, and by her admission, sit and wait outside my house for an hour pisses me off even more.

"How long have you been following me?" I ask, trying to rein in my anger.

"Only a few days."

"Only a few days," I repeat. "And to what end, Lucia? We're through. We've been over. You and I are no more. We haven't been together for months."

"But, Chase, I still love you."

"Stop it," I grit out. What more does she want from me? She can't need money. She earns enough in her own right. "There isn't now, nor has there ever been any love between us. In fact, I was never in love with you, and you knew that from the start. I never lied about it or made false promises to you."

"No, Chase. I do love you."

"Fine, but there's a huge problem with that. I. Don't. Love. You. I don't know what it's going to take to get it through your head, other than to be this blunt."

"Why didn't you tell me about your daughter?" She makes a point to look teary-eyed. I've seen her act this way, and it does nothing to me. In fact, all it does is make me even more pissed off.

"Because it's none of your fucking business. Nothing I do is your business, Lucia."

And she starts to sob. She sounds absolutely ridiculous too. So much so I want to laugh.

"Give it up, Lucia. None of your tactics are going to work."

She sniffs loudly a few times, then stares at me. How could I ever have thought she was beautiful? Andi is the girl of my dreams, not the gaudy Lucia. Her eyelashes are heavy with mascara and her face carries a ton of makeup. Andi needs none of that. She's perfect without it.

"I'm pregnant, Chase."

The words tear through my brain like a speeding rocket. Did I hear her correctly?

"What did you say?"

She grins and suddenly she looks like a serpent. "I said I'm pregnant, si? That's how you say it?"

"Pregnant." My mind races. We never once had sex without a condom. I made damn sure of that. My eyes instantly drop to her stomach. Lucia is fond of dressing provocatively. She wears tight jeans and short shirts that show off a wide strip of skin. If she's pregnant and it's mine, she has to be at least several months by my calculations. Her stomach can't be that flat. "Are you sure it's mine?"

Her mouth compresses into one thin line. "Yes, it is yours."

"Fine. I want to go to the doctor with you. For proof and DNA testing that I'm the father. Who's your doctor? Give me his name."

"Um ..."

She stumbles around for words.

"Unless you're making this up."

"No, I am not."

"Fine. I want your doctor's name. Anyone I know would be able to rattle their doctor's name off in a snap. Why can't you?"

"B-because I have not yet gone."

"Better yet. I'll make the appointment and we'll go together. Expect a call from me. Now go home." I watch as she gets into her car and leaves. I don't trust her one bit. Why wait to tell me only after she finds out about Violet? She's not pregnant. This is just a ploy to try to get me back, and it's not going to work.

I open the door to walk back inside and practically knock Andi over as I do. She must've been listening on the other side. Her expression is so comical at getting caught that I want to crack up. She stumbles as I grab her arm. That's when I notice the wine glass in her hand.

"Sorry, I was coming to fill my glass," she says.

"Uh, Andi?"

"Yeah?"

"The wine is in the kitchen over there." I point in the direction of the kitchen, which is on the other side of the house.

"Oh, yeah." She giggles. "I must've gotten turned around."

"Yeah, you must've."

I ogle her tight little ass as she sashays toward the refrigerator. Then I have to question how much of our conversation she heard. If that damn Lucia screws anything up for me, I swear I'll … just what will I do? And what if she is pregnant? I will not leave her alone like I did Andi. Jesus, wouldn't that be fucked up? Knowing Lucia, she probably poked holes in all the condoms just to ensure she got pregnant. She's crazy enough to do something like that. I ask myself for the hundredth time, *what did I ever see in that woman?*

Andi has disappeared into another room, so I go to find her. She and Violet are watching TV and eating dinner at the coffee table. It looks like a meal of pizza tonight.

"Is there any left?" I ask.

"Oh, yes, there's a bunch left warming in the oven. I made it myself. Well, I cheated. It's store-bought crust, but it's really good."

I fill my plate and rejoin them. Violet is done and Andi is close. Violet rubs her eyes so Andi takes her off for a bath. I finish up my pizza and join them in the bathroom. Violet splashes in the tub so I offer to finish and give Andi a break.

"I can put her to bed, if you'd like. I leave in the morning, so I'd really like this time with her."

Andi smiles, leaving me alone with Violet. The kid loves the water, so she splashes around until the water cools and then I pull her out of the tub and wrap a towel around her. She's so small, I joke about losing her in it until she pokes her head out so I can find her. I put her jammies on and let her pick out a book for me to read. I don't even get halfway through before she falls asleep. Every minute I spend with her, I am more amazed at this beautiful child. She's truly perfect in every way.

When I get back downstairs, Andi is gone. I head back into the kitchen and eat the rest of the pizza, then go to my room to pack for the trip. I'm in my room when I hear Andi's, or at least I think it's Andi's, door banging, so I go down the hall to see what the problem is.

"Andi, is everything okay in there?"

"Yeah." She giggles. "I think so. Only I can't get the door open."

"What do you mean?"

"I think I locked myself in." She full-on cracks up.

"You can't unlock the door?"

"I'm not sure how."

"Uh, Andi, have you been drinking?"

"Well, yeah."

"How much wine have you had?"

"A few glasses."

"Okay, turn the lock," I say.

"There isn't one."

"Hang on." I run into the guest room across the hall so I can check out the door. I haven't paid attention to the locks. The lever is sort of tricky. So I head back and tell her, "Andi, push it down, then back up."

I hear her doing it and the door opens. "That was easy."

She holds an empty glass in her hand. "A few glasses, huh?"

"Yeah. This is the best wine I've ever had."

"I'll have to remember that." Her mouth is so close and as sexy as ever. All I want to do is taste the wine on her lips and tongue.

"Thanks for rescuing me."

"You're welcome. Just don't lock yourself in when I'm gone."

Her hand flies to her chest and she nearly turns ashen. "Oh, God, I won't."

"You'll be fine."

"I have to admit, I'm a little scared to be here alone."

I lean on the door frame and say, "Max, my agent, will be checking in on you."

"Oh. That's nice. Thanks."

"So, I'll leave you be, then."

"Yeah. Okay. And, Chase?"

"Yeah?"

"I, uh, hope you win."

I slowly nod because I get the impression she wants to say more. "Oh, I had the chance to look at the video and pictures on the flash drive. Thanks for doing that. You didn't have to. That birth, it was … it was really something. I think I would've been scared, Andi."

"I was." She takes a step closer to me, then stops. "I was afraid she wouldn't be normal or healthy. And then I was afraid I would be a shitty mother. But mostly, I was really afraid of telling you. Of what it would do to your career. So I just didn't. And I so fucked it all up. I don't think I can ever say sorry enough."

"Maybe you already have." I head back to my room,

thinking about everything she just said and about the birth video I watched. How can anyone go through something like that alone? But Andi did. And then she came home from the hospital with a newborn alone too. I don't know how she pulled it off, but she did.

When I'm back in my room, I get ready for bed. My suitcase is packed, but then I realize I need a few Ziploc bags. I like to carry them to put my liquid items in to prevent spills, so I head back down to the kitchen and to make sure the place is locked up. I make the rounds, and when I get to the kitchen, I find a little surprise in there.

Andi is rummaging through the drawers like a cat burglar.

"Can I help you?"

"Eep!" She practically jumps out of her skin at the sound of my voice.

"Jesus, Chase. You scared me to death."

"What in the hell are you doing?"

"I'm looking for batteries."

"For what?"

"For this." She holds up a vibrator. I almost die laughing, but I hold it back. "Oh, what's that?"

"It's my fake boyfriend. Look, I'm not gonna lie. It's been a while. Too damn long if you wanna know the truth. Like, well since I got pregnant with Violet. I'm super horny and my damn batteries are dead. So I'm on the hunt."

What the hell is she saying? Since she got pregnant? That would make it the last time *we* had sex. What about Owen? Wasn't he banging her? If it's been that long, evidently not.

"On the hunt, huh?" I walk up behind her. If she's on the hunt, I can certainly help in that category—if she's willing, that is. Because I most definitely am.

"Yeah. I need some, you know?" She finally looks my way. "Holy shit. I just ran my mouth to you like ..."

I don't give her another minute ... second ... to think before I spin her around and my mouth is on hers. I don't want to kiss

Andi. I want to devour her. I want to own her. I want all of her at once. I've waited years just for this moment. My balls tighten to the point where my knees almost buckle. But I don't give a fuck. She's not pushing back. So in one swift move, I pick her up and carry her to my room. It all happens so fast, I don't give her time to back out. She kisses me back as eagerly as I'd dreamed of. The oceans that existed between us are gone in an instant, and the only thing that remains is us—two people who desperately want and need each other.

We both frantically tear each other's clothes off, and when we're both bare to each other's gazes, I can only stare at her perfection. She's better than I remembered. Softer and curvier instead of straight. More womanly and sexy. My hands seek what they've missed: her face, neck, breasts, nipples, and following all with my lips and tongue. I drop to my knees before her and kiss her belly, the same one that carried our child. Then I move lower until I bury my tongue in her pussy. She's already wet—drenched, in fact. My hand seeks her sex, and her moans are the best sounds I've heard in ages. After she climaxes, I look up at her and ask, "Was this better than batteries or not? Because I have a lot more tricks up my sleeve."

TWENTY-FIVE

Andi

———————

BREATHLESS, I can barely move, let alone answer him. My head swims as the alcohol courses through me; it's hard to discern the difference between fantasy and reality. It had been so long, I let myself go. No matter the truth of it, it's better than my vibrator.

I manage to nod, responding to his question. His answering grin is priceless. I can barely breathe as the tremors pass for what feels like hours rather than minutes.

When he lifts up to stand before me, his eyes blaze like he plans to murder my pussy with his cock. As I remember, his dick has a way of filling me like nothing else.

The dream shatters when he asks, "Are you on the pill?"

I narrow my eyes on him, trying to focus. "That's not very sexy of you to ask."

"If you want me to get you off again, you'll answer."

My body craves more of him. "No. I haven't seen any action since you."

"Shit, I don't have any condoms with me."

I want him so bad, I blurt out, "Have you been safe?"

"Always, except with you, and I've been tested."

"Okay, I trust you."

He licks his sexy lips as if tasting me again. I moan as he frees himself. His cock is hard and thick, making my mouth water.

"None of that. I want to be inside of you."

He spreads my legs and hooks his arms under my knees before he lines his cock up with my entrance. His invasion has me bending my head back. I suck in air, feeling full for the first time in years as he pushes inside me.

He curses, his neck muscles straining as if he's holding back.

"Damn, baby, I've missed this."

His words warm my breasts before he sucks them.

If I could speak, I would agree with him. But then he moves and I let the sensations take over.

Electric impulses dance across my skin as his lips kiss their way to my other nipple.

His tongue is hot and I'm wet. I reach for his head and scrape my nails over his scalp through his thick hair.

"Fuck me harder," I say, all bold and confidently.

When he does, it only makes things ten times hotter.

"Damn, Andi, you feel so fucking good."

He loses himself in me as I lose myself in him.

When he comes, it's with a roar as my whole body quivers with another release.

He collapses beside me before cocooning me in his arms. I treasure his heat and close my eyes against all the emotions that run through me. It isn't long before sleep claims me.

Sunlight spills into the room and I blink against the light. My body feels cozy, like I'm wrapped in a blanket. It's then I see the arm draped over my hip. *Chase* lies beside me, and I remember how his mouth had done delicious things to me.

I thought for sure he'd be gone when I woke. Instead, he's here when a tiny ball of energy bursts through the room door.

"Mama, Dada."

It would have been comical for how fast we pull the sheets up to cover our nakedness.

"Violet," I say.

"Hungy."

I glance at Chase before answering, "I'll be right there. Why don't you get a book to color?"

She nods and bounds out of the room.

"Andi."

"Chase," I say at the same time.

I still clutch the blanket to my chest, unsure about what happened last night.

"We should talk," he says.

"I get it. It was a mistake."

"No, not that. I have to get ready to leave. But I only think it's fair that I'm honest with you."

"About what?"

I fear his next words. Does he think it was a mistake anyway? Is he going to tell me it changed nothing?

"Lucia claims she's pregnant." So that's why she was here. "I'm not sure I believe her, but if she is and it's my kid, I'm not going to miss all the things I missed with Violet."

Another slap in the face. Will he ever get past what I've done?

"What are you saying?"

He runs a hand roughly through his hair. "I don't know. Other than I don't want any lies between us."

With that, he gets up. For only a second, I get a perfect view of his gorgeous ass before he covers it with his shorts.

I bite my lip as lust flares in me. He turns and smirks as if he can read my thoughts. Had I made an audible noise?

"I'll see you in a few days."

I nod, at a loss for words. I have no idea where we stand. But the ache between my legs is real. And the feelings I have for him are too. What the hell am I going to do?

I echo that through the phone when I call Beth while Violet takes a nap.

"Hold up, girl—what happened?"

"I slept with Chase." Her yawn is loud. "I can call you later. I'm sorry for waking you."

"No, it's fine. I'm on break. This conversation will keep me up for sure."

"So what am I going to do?"

"The Macarena."

"Funny," I say.

"Serious, girl. You got laid. I'm so proud of you."

"What if I told you his fiancée is pregnant?"

"Shit."

"Yeah." I tell her what I know.

"So he doesn't believe her."

"He says he's not sure. But what if it's true? He makes it seem like he'll marry her or something. Where does that leave Violet and me?"

"There's always Owen."

"Beth," I admonish. "I love him. I gave him up once. I don't think I can do it again."

"Then fight for him."

"Yeah, I don't think he'll appreciate if I beat up his pregnant girlfriend."

"So he's really with her."

"No. He says he's not. But what do I call her?"

"The bitch that's in the way. Even if she's carrying his child, that doesn't make you irrelevant. I have a feeling he didn't sleep with you only to end up with her."

I might have thought the same thing a long time ago. But Chase has changed and so have I. When he gets back, I need to just ask him the question. What does he want from me?

TWENTY-SIX

Chase

FUNNY how I never minded being away from home before, but now … the short time I've been gone seems like forever. The worst part of all is I miss not only Violet, but Andi too. I want her lips on mine and her sweet pussy wrapped around my—

"Wilde, you with us?"

"What?"

"I was just saying that you played a great game today."

"Oh, thanks." One of my teammates pounds my back as we leave the locker room.

"You must be ready to get back to Italy," he says, laughing.

"Yeah. I'm tired."

"You should be with the way you ran and fielded the ball. Nice work. Wish I had those double-footed skills of yours."

"Thanks."

We're headed out to the bus when my phone rings. It's Andi, and I'm a little more than surprised. She's never called me since she's moved here. Not once.

"Hey," I answer, smiling. Maybe she's missing me as much as I'm missing her.

"Chase." I immediately detect the concern in her tone. A chill races down my spine.

"What's wrong?"

"It's Violet."

"Is she okay?"

"I'm not really sure yet."

"What the hell is that supposed to mean?" My voice levels up several notches.

"Okay, calm down, tiger." That's a name she hasn't used in years. It makes me pause and take a deep breath.

"Right. So, why the call?"

"She spiked another fever last night so I took her to the doctor today. You know … the one we agreed on."

"And?" I prompt.

"He wants to run some tests. With as many of these fevers she keeps getting, I concur."

The team is loading up on the bus that will take us to the airport to fly home. This isn't a conversation I want to have in front of everyone, so I amble off to the side where I can speak freely.

"Is this serious?" My brain doesn't want to go anywhere that might spell devastating illness. I won't accept it.

"We won't know unless they run tests to find out."

"Andi." Her name rips from my throat as I feel the burn of possibilities I don't dare think of.

"Chase, don't go down that road."

"Right. Right." That's what I say, but my mind is moving in the opposite direction. How can this be? I just found my daughter, and now this? Someone calls my name and I glance up to see the team has boarded the bus, except for me.

"Listen, I've got to go. I'll call when I get to the airport."

"No, it's fine. She doesn't have the tests scheduled for a few weeks."

"What the hell do you mean? This needs to be done now." Again, I'm practically yelling.

"Chase, call me from the airport. You can't do anything from there. We'll talk in a little while."

How can she be so calm? I'm ready to tear heads off of some people. I stomp up the steps of the bus and flop down on the first available seat.

"Wow. Who stole your ..."

"Shut up. I don't need any sarcasm right now." I pin my closest friend and teammate with a glare that would wither a pit bull.

"Hey, you okay?" he asks.

"Won't know until I get home. And, Leo, I don't want to talk about it."

"Okay, I got it."

We get to the airport rather quickly, and I collect my bags and head to check in. It doesn't take long before I'm at the gate calling Andi.

When she tells me the reason for how long until Violet can get the tests run, I tell her I will make some calls when I get home. Violet will have those tests before several weeks pass. Andi says they are only blood tests and she needs to see a specialist. But her pediatrician wants the tests run first.

The flight, which is only an hour and a half, seems to take forever. I thought my issue with Lucia was bad, but Violet's potential health problem just pounded that into the ground. I had already decided to hire a private investigator and find out whether or not Lucia is telling the truth. My attempts at accompanying her to the doctor will not be pushed aside. If she is indeed pregnant, I will be with her to find out. But I have my suspicions about that. Lucia is the type of woman to use any means to get what she wants. I can see her pretending to be pregnant and then saying she lost the baby. But I will ferret out the truth in this situation.

Exhaustion nails me by the time the house comes into view. All I want to do is sleep, but then again, when I think about Violet, sleep is the last thing on my mind.

It's late—past Violet's bedtime—by the time I get here. Andi greets me at the door, and it's not hard to see the worry etched around her eyes.

After I drop my bags, I open my arms and she walks straight into them. This isn't about sex. It's about comforting each other. I feel her body trembling, and it lets me know how hard this has been on her.

"She's sleeping?" I ask.

"Yeah. Her fever is gone now, but it zaps her energy."

I grab her hand and pull her toward the living area so we can sit.

She asks me, "Have you eaten?"

"No. I lost my appetite after our conversation."

"Yeah, I haven't had much of one, either."

"So tell me everything."

Violet has had way too many fevers for this to be a coincidence. There must be something else brewing. Andi knows more than she's telling me, considering her medical background.

"Spill it. I can take it."

"It's not a matter of that. There are a ton of things it could be, and then it could be something that could burn itself out. The doctor was telling me about a patient he had about ten years ago that came in with fevers of unknown origin—which is what they're calling it right now—and they never could find out what was wrong with her. Suddenly, they went away as quickly as they came. It was a mystery to everyone."

"Hmm. Sure is weird." I scratch my head because it sounds super fishy.

"I know, but weird, unexplainable things happen in medicine all the time."

I look her dead in the eye. "Andi, what else could it be?"

She squirms, so I know it's not good. "Things you don't need to hear about."

"Yeah, I do, because if I know now and she has one of them, I won't be caught by surprise."

"Leukemia."

A knot the size of Mount Everest forms in my gut. Fuck. I don't break eye contact. I have to be strong for all of us.

"Go on."

"Rheumatoid arthritis or other illnesses like it—what they call autoimmune diseases."

"And?"

"Aplastic anemia."

"What's that?"

"An incurable form of anemia."

"So, what? Would she just take vitamins or something?"

Andi slowly shakes her head. "No, Chase. She would undergo treatment with medication."

"I see. Anything else?"

"Those are what they look for initially, then other types of cancer if all comes back normal."

"Ohhhkayyy." Another gut punch that leaves me gasping. I can't imagine that little ball of energy with an illness such as any of those. Filling my lungs with air, I say, "She doesn't have any of that. Violet is good. She's fine."

"Yeah. She's fine."

We sit in silence for a couple of minutes, then out of the blue, Andi says, "That woman came by."

"Woman?"

"The one who says she's pregnant." She twists her fingers together and won't look me in the eye. This has to be awkward for her, and me as well.

"What? She came here?" It pisses me off because I told Lucia to stay away from here.

"Yesterday."

A long puff of air blows out of me. "Andi, I broke it off with her a while back. I don't believe she's telling the truth, but I want all doors open between us. I'm hiring a private investigator to dig into things, and I told her I wanted to be at her doctor's appointments." I head to the refrigerator to grab a beer. I'm thirsty, but now I need something to calm my pissed-off nerves.

"She doesn't look at it that way."

Andi had followed me into the kitchen, but I didn't hear her. Spinning around, I say, "I don't give a fuck what she thinks. I never lied to her or kept the truth from her. She knew from the beginning we were never going to be together. She's delusional." I can't believe I'm discussing this with Andi.

In a soft voice, she asks, "Can I ask you something?"

"Anything."

"Is it possible? That she could be pregnant, that is."

How the fuck do I answer this? I can't lie, even though I know it will hurt her.

"Yeah, I suppose so, but," I rub the back of my aching neck, "we haven't been together like that in months. So she would have to be really pregnant. And I always used protection with her. I never trusted her."

Andi opens and closes her mouth a couple of times, then blurts out, "Why ever would you be with a woman you couldn't trust?"

Fuck me. Has this conversation ever gone deep? Dare I tell her the truth and bare my stupid soul? I'm not sure I have the fucking nerve to do it.

The coward in me rules and I answer, "I don't know. She was always there, showing up at the right time, saying the right things. And I was stupid."

"I'll say."

"You don't have to rub it in. I've already learned my lesson. Max has done damage control way too many times with her. I thought after that fake engagement announcement she did I was through. I made it perfectly clear to her we were done countless times. But the damn woman won't stop."

"Chase, she's a stalker. You realize that, don't you?"

Having someone else say it makes it so much clearer to me.

"She could be a danger to our daughter."

My head snaps up. "Do you honestly think so?"

"How the hell do I know? You're the one who knows her, not me."

"True." I think about Lucia and everything she's pulled and wonder about that.

"She seems pretty desperate," Andi says.

"I'll talk to Max and see what he thinks. Maybe I need to hire a security team."

Andi glares at me.

"What?"

She doesn't speak, but walks away.

"Hey, don't do this. I don't want any walls between us."

She stops and turns. "You've put our daughter in a precarious situation with that woman, Chase. I don't know what she'll do. You're not here very much. I'm alone in a foreign country with Violet, who is now ill, and I'm left to deal with this … this shit."

"You won't be alone. I promise. I'll get someone here tomorrow. You won't have to deal with her again. If she shows up here, I'll have her escorted off the property and arrested."

"You can't have her arrested unless there are super strict laws here or unless you have a restraining order of some kind."

"Then I'll get one."

"I swear to God, if anything happens to Violet because of her …"

She doesn't finish, but walks away, leaving me in the kitchen alone. I immediately call Max. He'll know what to do. When I explain the situation, he says he knows someone who can help. Max seems to know everyone. I'm not sure how, but he does.

"I'll have someone out there tomorrow. And your Violet will have her tests run by the end of the week."

"And, Max, I want a private investigator on Lucia. She's lying. I know she is."

"I think so too. I'll get you the best, Chase."

That night, I get zero sleep because all I can think of is

Violet. The what-ifs haunt my thoughts and erase any chances of rest. By the time my room shows signs of daybreak, I'm the caged animal, ready to run free.

Thankfully, there is no practice today, only a team meeting to review our game and go over what we did right and where we fucked up. That'll last all morning, which will suck. My concentration won't be on anything discussed. I'm sure of that. I head to the kitchen for some coffee to find Andi already beat me to the pot.

"You couldn't sleep either?" I ask.

"Yes and no. Violet woke me. She spiked another fever last night."

The cup in my hand hits the floor and shatters, sending pieces of ceramic all over the place. It's somehow fitting, because it's the exact same way my heart feels.

TWENTY-SEVEN

Andi

———

OUR HEADS BUMP as we both kneel to pick up the broken pieces. As I stare at the shards of ceramic littering the floor, tears well up in my eyes. I've tried to be strong in front of Chase, but the truth is, I'm cracking on the inside.

"I'm sorry," we both say at the same time.

I give him my best smile, which is brittle.

"She's going to be fine." My determination fuels my words, but isn't a reflection of the fear inside me.

"Can you be sure?"

"I can't be sure of anything."

"Does cancer run in your family?" The reminder that I'm adopted flattens any pretense of a smile. "Shit, I'm sorry." His hands rub at his eyes. He must be every bit as weary as I am.

"You don't have to be sorry. It's a valid question. Just one I can't answer. And believe me, I've been thinking a lot more about who my parents are than ever before."

He cups my chin between his thumb and forefinger. "We'll get through this … together."

Before I know what I'm doing, I lean in, needing his warmth more than ever. Our lips collide and the softness of his has me sighing inside. His tongue sweeps over mine and the power of his kiss is the balm I need.

"Mama."

I pull back to see Violet standing there. Her flushed skin and tired eyes send panic through me. Since I'm on my knees already, I crawl over to her and place a hand over her feverish head.

"Feel bad," she adds.

On instinct, I scoop her up in my arms just before she throws up all over my shirt. I rush into one of the palatial bathrooms and make it to the toilet just before she vomits again.

When I'm pretty sure we are in the clear, I take off her soiled clothes and my shirt. I turn on the water and get a cool cloth to clean her off.

"Do you feel better?"

She shakes her head. I'd been expecting that answer, but hoped that maybe I was wrong.

Chase stands in the doorway wearing a lost expression.

"How can I help?"

"Can you get her some clean clothes while I go get the Tylenol to bring down the fever?"

He nods. "Should we call the doctor?"

"Yes, let's get," I nod to Violet, "taken care of first."

I dash out of my room in my bra, but not caring. I wash my hands and get the correct dose before going back to our daughter. I find her in her room with a smile on her face. Chase sports a goofy expression that has her captivated.

Though I hate to break them up, I want to get the medication in her so it can start working.

"Here, why don't you get this to Violet and I'll make the call?"

His eyes look up at me. I mouth, *you're doing great.*

I leave them and go in my room. Closing the door, I make the call. They can see her at two in the afternoon. Chase nearly goes ballistic when I tell him.

"Calm down. If she has strep, they'll run a rapid test and we'll know right away. It's fine. You have practice this morning anyway. You can go, then come back, and pick us up."

After he calms down, he sees the logic in what I say.

That afternoon, we are headed to the doctor to have him run tests.

Violet babbles to Chase while we sit in the waiting room. She points to pictures as he makes the sounds of the animal to make her giggle. The medicine I dosed her with has her feeling better, but I know something is brewing inside her.

"Violet Wilde James."

I stand and Violet reaches out to me. I pick her up as we are herded into a room. When the doctor comes in, Chase is first to speak.

"What's wrong with my daughter?"

I jump in and give him a rundown of her symptoms, including the fever, tiredness, and vomiting.

His English is perfect. "It could be a number of things, maybe the flu or strep. We can run a couple of tests."

"What about her fevers? They've been happening too often to be random."

"As we discussed, it could be the normal. Your daughter is very young. She's in a new place and exposed to different germs." When I start to cut in, he adds, "Or it could be an autoimmune disease."

"What about leukemia?" Chase asks.

"That could be a possibility, but let's not go down that road yet. I want to run some blood tests before we start jumping to conclusions. However, my nurse will be back in to do the rapid strep and influenza test. And she will take a blood sample as well."

Chase looks as though he has a million questions. I reach out and take his hand. When he glances over, I squeeze our joined hands.

Violet, sensing Chase's distress, crawls between us onto his lap. She wraps her tiny arms around his neck.

"'K, Dada." She gives him a kiss on the cheek.

Violet does well for the strep test, which the nurse explains as a little tickle on the back of the throat. The flu test is a little easier up her nose. But it's the blood sample that makes our daughter cry out and cause Chase to give the nurse a dirty look.

"It's her job," I whisper while rubbing soothing circles on Violet's back to calm her down after the nurse leaves.

"She could be a better one," Chase grumbles.

"There is only so much she can do. I'm a nurse and sometimes babies cry after the things I have to do. Does that make me a bad nurse?"

He shakes his head. "It's just, she's my—"

"—Daughter, and you want to protect her."

He nods. Thankfully, it's only been about five minutes when the doc comes in and tells us the bad news.

"The strep test came back positive. I'll prescribe her a course of antibiotics."

"What about the flu test?"

"It takes a little longer. It's doubtful she'd test positive for both. Even still, there aren't antibiotics for the flu. If for some odd reason it does come back, I can call in an antiviral for you."

Chase isn't mollified. "You're still going to run other blood tests?"

"Yes. I'll give you a call with the results."

When the doctor glances at me, I nod and he leaves. Once we get home, Chase carries our sleeping daughter to her room. I wait in the living room.

"Do you think that's it?"

As much as I want to say yes, I can't.

"I don't know. But once the CBC panel comes back, we'll know a lot more," I say.

"What's a CBC?"

"The blood test the doc ran."

"Oh, yeah. What will it tell us?"

"A lot, actually. It will help him diagnose conditions, such as anemia, or infections. It can also indicate whether she has leukemia, an autoimmune issue, and many other disorders. But then they will have to run more in-depth tests to determine exactly what's going on."

"Why can't he run them all now? I can pay for it."

I reach out and lay my hand on his arm.

"I know you can. But they probably follow a diagnostic protocol here. You know, look for the most common things first and then if they come back negative, they keep searching for answers."

He runs a rough hand through his hair.

"It's just that I want to know. I don't think I'll get a good night's sleep until I know she's okay."

I wrap my arms around him and he pulls me in tighter. I glance up at him.

"She needs you not to be tired. So why don't you get some sleep? I'm not sure how things work over here in Italy. It might be another day or two before we hear anything back."

When I step out of his embrace, he takes my wrist and pulls me back.

"Thank you," he says.

"For what?"

"For being a great mother."

I give him my best smile before walking away. It's as if I can feel his eyes on my back. Selfishly, I want him to call me again. I need a distraction. I need him: his touch, his kiss, his mouth devouring mine. But when I make it to my door, I resolve to spend a restless night alone.

TWENTY-EIGHT

Chase

———————

THE CEILING IS MY FRIEND—OR enemy—I don't know which, for approximately thirty-nine minutes. I push the covers back and walk down the hall to Andi's room. I don't bother with knocking. Maybe I should. When I push the door open, I hear her soft sobs and it only takes me a few seconds to climb in behind her and pull her against my chest.

"This isn't a time for us to be alone. I need you and I'm pretty fucking sure you need me too. Which brings me to another point. I still love you. Haven't stopped loving you since … well since. I think you know what I'm saying here, Andi." I breathe in deeply because my lungs are screaming right now. "You don't have to say anything. There are other pressing things at the moment. But I wanted you to know."

She rolls over and pushes her face into my neck. I feel the dampness of her tears as she holds on tight. Then her words, the words I never thought I'd hear again, heat my neck as she breathes them. "I love you too. Always have, always will." Her body trembles with sobs and she lets her sadness flow. I'm not gonna lie. My face isn't exactly dry either.

"Whatever happens, good or bad, we're going to get through this. We have a tough little girl. She's not going to take this, Andi. She's sassy and will fight whatever's at war in that tiny body of hers."

Andi's head bobs against mine. She's holding on to me tighter than ever, but for once I feel secure. This is what we need—the two of us working as a team.

"Hey."

She raises her head.

"We're Team Wilde. And Wildes don't give up. You got that?"

A watery smile spreads across her face. "I got it, tiger."

"Now put your lips here." I point to mine so she can see.

"Are you hitting on me?"

"I might be."

"And here I thought you were helping out a damsel in distress."

"I'm the damsel and I'm in distress. That's why I need your lips."

She rolls on top of me and presses her salty tasting lips on mine. "Thatta girl. Now put your head on my chest and close your eyes." I massage her silky hair and she hums. Before long, the sun's streaking through the shutters and I'm shocked we both slept like logs.

Andi lifts her head and smiles. "This is nice."

"Yes, it is. Thanks for saving this damsel."

She giggles. Until she hears Violet cry out, and she's out of bed in a flash with me on her heels.

"Mama, Dada."

Violet is feverish, not super hot, but she doesn't look so good. The bad news is she threw up in her bed. And it's disgusting. I can handle a lot of shit, but puke isn't one of them.

I cover my mouth and gag. Andi looks at me and rolls her eyes. Then she says, "You weren't kidding about the damsel thing." She pulls Violet out of bed and takes her into the bathroom to get cleaned up.

"Bath?" Violet asks.

"Yes, honey. We have to get you cleaned up." She looks at me and says, "You're on sheet duty."

"Great," I say with false cheeriness. Poor Violet. She can't help throwing up. I hold my breath and tear off the offending sheets, then run them over to the washer. Thankfully, it's on the second floor. By the time I'm done, so is Andi. Naked Violet is wrapped in a towel and Andi is hunting for some clean pajamas. I open a drawer and grab some for her.

"Thanks." She dresses Violet while I head to the linen closet to find clean sheets. I quickly make up the bed and Andi watches with a smirk.

"What?"

"You don't do this very often, do you?"

"When I have to." She's right. The maids do it. The bed looks ridiculous, but it'll do. "I'll take her while you shower. Take your time."

She gives me one of those *yeah, right* looks. Violet and I head down to watch some TV. Andi joins us a few minutes later with wet hair.

"I'm not going to practice today."

"Yes, you are." Andi stands with her hand on her hip.

"Dada sick too?"

Andi frowns. "No, he's lazy." Then she motions to the kitchen with her head. When I get there, she blasts me with, "We have to be as normal as we can. You staying here isn't going to get us answers any sooner. Go. You know I'll call if something happens."

"Okay! I'll go." I grab some things to make breakfast and sit at the island to eat.

"Mama, hungy."

"Shit. I'm afraid to feed her. I really don't want her to keep throwing up."

I don't know what to say to that. "When my stomach is upset, I don't want to eat. Maybe this is a good sign."

Andi frowns. "It could be the antibiotics too."

"Yeah. Those things have upset my stomach before."

She ends up making Violet a half of a waffle. "Cross your fingers on this."

On the way up to my room, I call Max to remind him about the security I want out here. I also need someone available for Andi in case she needs to go to the doctor. He says someone is coming at nine.

"Can you be here for that?" I ask him.

"Yes, I will. How is your Violet today?"

I bring him up-to-date. He still wants to get her into a specialist. But I explain we don't exactly know what for yet. "I need to hit the road or I'll be late. I'll let Andi know someone will be here at nine. And please make sure the security keeps Lucia away from here."

Practice is hell. My mind isn't on the field and I miss way too many passes and opportunities to score. I turn over the ball, don't steal it, and basically it's a disaster.

Coach pulls me over and wants to know if I'm ill. At his question, I practically break down. So I explain what's going on with Violet. He walks me off the field and sits me down in his office.

"You can do a couple of things. You know we need you out here. Until you find out what's going on, you can keep playing and take your frustrations out on the field. Or you can give up."

"What? Why would I give up?"

He shrugs. "Your attitude is that she's already lost the battle, and you don't even know what she has."

Fuck! Is that what I'm doing?

"Chase, take your game face and use it to fight this thing. Your daughter and her mother need that part of you now. You are one of the strongest opponents I've ever had the opportunity to work with. You are undefeatable. Use that tactic to your advantage. Teach it to your daughter. It could save her life. But whatever you do, don't lie down in defeat."

Why haven't I thought of that? The fear of the unknown is what kills athletes. They let it fuck with their heads. I can't let it fuck with mine when it comes to dealing with this ... whatever it is. And Andi and Violet have to learn this too. We can all face this thing together, with two feet planted firmly on the ground. And we can fight it with everything we've got.

Standing, I look Coach in the eye and thank him. This was the greatest thing he could've done for me. We return to the field, my mind focused, and I have the best practice I can remember.

That afternoon after I get home, the doctor's office calls with the results of the blood tests.

"Your daughter's iron levels are very low. She has severe anemia. It could be nothing but your average garden variety easily treated with supplements. But with everything else she's been experiencing, I want to be cautious and send her to a doctor who specializes in the study of blood-related diseases."

Andi has her phone set on speaker so I can hear too. "A hematologist?" she asks.

"Yes, a hematologist. I have taken the liberty of making that appointment for you. It's for next week, if that is okay."

That's not okay by me. So I say, "Can't we get in any sooner?"

"Not with Dr. Esposito. He, in my opinion, will be the best for your daughter."

"Okay, then next week it is."

Andi jots down the time and place, and I put it in my calendar as well.

"Please make sure to allot at least three hours for your visit there, because they will want to do more tests."

"Yes, doctor, thank you."

"And best of luck to you."

When she hangs up, she has a pained look on her face.

"What?"

"It doesn't sound good, Chase."

"We'll deal with it. But at least we'll have something to fight."

"At least we'll have something to fight," she murmurs. "But we may not have anything to fight it with."

TWENTY-NINE

Andi

LATER THAT NIGHT, I lie alone in my bed, unable to sleep. Though Violet's doctor tried to put us at ease, he had to be worried enough he felt it necessary to send her to a specialist. I rest my forearm over my eyes, as tears spill onto my pillow.

I'm so engrossed in my thoughts, I don't hear Chase enter.

He pulls my arm free and his beautiful face turns to concern.

"What's wrong?"

All the hurt and anger I feel toward myself pours out in a sobbing mess.

"I've screwed everything up."

I try to turn away, ashamed of my many mistakes. He doesn't let me.

"What have you screwed up?"

I almost glare at him, because he knows. That's why up until recently he could barely stand to look at me. Still, I have no right to be mad at him.

"You, for one." I don't state the obvious that I've ruined any sort of relationship between us. I make no allusions to our nights together. That was born out of need and grief. "What if? I mean, I took time with Violet away from you that you'll never get back."

He stares at me. "You're already assuming the worst. What do you know that I don't?"

It's true that I've held back my fears. After Violet had gone down for the night, I'd researched until my eyes crossed.

I shake my head. "It could be nothing, like the doctor said."

"But…?" he prods.

"But, the anemia coupled with unexplained fevers can be bad."

I hate the worry I've created in him.

"What are you saying?" His eyes hold mine. "Lay it out, Andi. I want … know I need to be prepared."

I lift my shoulders before letting them sag like a deflated balloon. I'd searched and found things that really scared me.

"It could be that blood disease I told you about before. Aplastic anemia."

His hand comes up and wipes the tears I hadn't known were still falling.

"We're not going to think that way. This is our daughter. She's a fighter like us."

Unable to bear looking into his hopeful eyes, I bury my face in his chest and admit everything.

"I've already lost you. I can't bear to lose her too. She's the best of me."

He strokes a hand over my hair before settling his hand on my back.

"We're not going to lose her. I refuse to let that happen."

My sob comes out choked, and it's selfish. He hadn't mentioned us. I suck in air and push the tears back. I wipe the back of my hand over my face and pull away from him.

"We're not. And thank you. I'll be fine. You can go back to your room. I need to check on Violet."

He snags my hand, and that simple touch has a way of undoing me. Another cry escapes my throat.

"Violet's fine. I checked on her before …" Had he heard me cry and come in? "She's good. No fever. You need to get some sleep, Andi. You're no good to her if you're tired."

Though I silently agree with a bob of my head, I know there is no way I'm sleeping anytime soon.

"You're not going to sleep."

I shake my head. "How can you be so calm?"

"I'm not calm. Inside, I'm fighting a battle with an invisible enemy. I'm armored up, ready to do whatever Violet needs me to do so she'll be okay. But that's the point. Right now, there's nothing I can do but be there for her. Me being pissed off isn't going to solve anything."

I want to be brave like him, but everything I read continues to swirl in my brain.

"I can't seem to shut off my brain."

He leans in and murmurs, "Let me help you," before he dives in for a kiss.

His fingers skim under my nightshirt before he palms my breast. His touch sends butterflies into flight beneath my skin. I arch into his hand, enjoying the flick of his thumb over the peaks of my nipples.

"Can I have you?"

His question could mean for the night or forever. It doesn't matter, because my answer would be the same.

"Yes, it's only ever been you."

He'd lowered himself as I'd answered and now hovers over my breast.

"What are you saying?"

"You've always had me, no one else."

His eyes widen. I bite my lower lip. "It was you in high school. Then when we got together that Christmas, I got pregnant, and I've dated no one else."

While I talked, he'd been positioning his other hand. I gasp as he slips two fingers inside me. Once again, my back leaves the bed. He sucks in a bud to take things higher.

"You'll always be mine, Andi."

I can't ask him if I heard him right, as his mouth is back on mine while he moves to lie on top of me, wedging himself between my legs. I spread them, giving him room. I want him there. No, I need him inside me. For just these moments, I want to lose myself in sensations.

He trails his fingers down until he finds the fabric that covers my entrance. My heartbeat kicks up several notches as his head follows. Slowly, he uncovers me until the fabric is only a memory. Then his mouth is on me. I bite a finger to hold back from crying out. Masterfully, he switches between tongue and fingers, moving in and out of me to take me to a place only he can.

"Please," I beg.

"Hold on, baby."

I do as he asks and fist my hands in his hair, needing just a bit more before I go tumbling over the edge. I ride out my pleasure, grinding against his face as it takes me higher and higher.

Coming down, a part of me is so limp I can't move. But the idea of tasting him rejuvenates me. As he gets up, takes off his pants and briefs, poised to crawl back over me, I slide down, hooking an arm around to grab on his ass and taking hold of his straining cock with the other.

I swallow him whole as best I can, my eyes tearing with the effort.

His curses of pleasure spur me on. I work him in and out, deeper and deeper.

"Stop," he says. "I need to be inside you."

He crawls off the bed and lifts my legs from where they hang off the side. Then he maneuvers a hand to aim himself at my opening before driving in. My world narrows down to just him. I claw at his chest, needing him to be closer. Our skin becomes slick with the effort as we are both greedy for one another. He pushes himself a little farther each time, thrusting with the force of the desperation we both feel.

I give as good as he gets, rolling my hips, enjoying the brush of his cock against that magic button, sending me to the moon and back.

"Dammit, Andi, if you don't stop, I'm not going to last."

"I want you to come, because I need to come too."

That spurs him on. The slaps of our flesh become erratic until I arch as my core squeezes the ever-living life out of his cock. He jerks once, twice, pumping into me like a man possessed until I feel him pulsing inside me.

His fingers dig into my hips as he pours every drop of his seed inside me. Then his weight is there, crushing me. I find I don't mind that at all. There's comfort in his body covering mine. I wrap my arms around him and pretend he's mine forever.

This man, who'd been my first in every way, will be my last no matter what happens between us. And that thought forces moisture from my eyes.

Not too long after, he pulls back and then he crawls back on the bed and pulls me to cradle against his chest.

"I love you," he whispers.

"What?" Because I'm so not sure I've heard him right.

"I'm still a little mad at you. But I've had enough time to see that you didn't do what you did to hurt either of us. I just wish you trusted me enough to tell me the truth."

I rush to put the record straight. "The problem was, I did trust you. I knew you'd give up your dreams to take care of me."

"I would have with no regrets."

"But I would have regretted it."

"You could have come to Italy with me."

I shift my head to peer up into his eyes. "And what? Lived with you as your pregnant girlfriend?"

"As my wife."

I pull away and rest my head on my hand. "And that's why. My parents, my brother, you, have been taking care of me my whole life. I needed to stand on my own and go to school too.

Though I regret not telling you. It wasn't fair, but I couldn't go to school in Italy and you couldn't have played soccer here."

"Football, but let's not talk about that. Get some sleep, Andi. Our daughter is our priority. And she needs us at our best."

I lie back down and listen to his heartbeat as he plays with my hair. At some point I drift off. Still, I'm not sure where we stand. If he says he loves me, I believe him. But he hasn't said where we would go from here.

THIRTY

Chase

———————

THE NEXT WEEK DRAGS. In fact, time seems to halt completely as we wait for our upcoming appointment with the hematologist. Violet runs intermittent fevers, but never complains. Ignorance is bliss. Andi and I do our best to act as though everything is perfectly normal.

I say, "Violet, let's watch *Frozen*," one evening. Even though she'll fall asleep long before it's over, her grin of excitement is worth the thirty minutes she'll see. She claps her hands and says, "Owaf." Olaf is her favorite.

She snuggles into the curve of my body as the movie begins. Andi's watching us instead of the TV. Her eyes droop along with the rest of her body. She's already weary from all the stress. I can't begin to think of the weeks ahead.

But the words of my coach come back to me and I refuse to let this unknown opponent let defeat coat me in fear.

"Hey, you over there." Andi's focus sharpens on me. "We're Team Wilde, remember?"

Andi says, "Team Wilde."

Violet glances at us. "Teem Wilde."

That gets a chuckle out of Andi. "You got it, firecracker."

"Not a firecracker. I snowman," Violet insists.

I rumble with laughter. "You can be whoever you want. But I'm calling you my snow cone."

"What a snow cone?" Violet asks, her tiny brows drawn together in curiosity.

I ruffle her curls and answer, "It's like an ice cream cone, only made with snow."

Her mouth twists up as though she just swallowed a lemon. "Icky, Dada. I wanna be ice cream cone."

"Okay." With a peck to the tip of her nose, I say, "Then you're my ice cream cone."

That satisfies her and she switches her gaze back to the movie.

Not much after that, her head droops and she's sound asleep. I carry her to bed, tucking her in, and stand there staring at this beautiful child. There is no way in fucking hell anything serious is wrong. Only a bump in the road, and they'll patch her up and send her on the way.

Andi stands in the doorway observing. When I turn, she backs out of the room.

"She's good. You'll see." I'm not sure if I say that for her benefit or mine.

A couple of days later, Max calls.

"Chase, I've gotten word from the PI we hired to tail Lucia. In the past several weeks, she hasn't made any visits to an obstetrician, and as far as we can tell, isn't planning on it. They've gotten a list of her phone records going back several months and she hasn't made any calls to any doctors at all. I think she's scamming you."

This isn't a surprise. I say, "Just as I suspected."

Max isn't finished. "That's not all. She's going out and partying. We have pictures of her at clubs, drinking and dancing. If she's pregnant, she shouldn't be smoking either. But she is. I have the evidence. Also, she sure is thin for being pregnant. Not that every woman shows, but by my calculations, the last time you two were together was at least six months ago, so that would put her at least that far along."

"Yeah. I'm almost positive she's not pregnant. What do you recommend?"

"I think we should confront her, and I say we because you don't need to go in without a witness. I'll go with you when you show her the pictures and phone records. Then you tell her to leave you alone. If she persists, you end the rent on her lavish apartment. That should take care of things. If it doesn't, we move in with a restraining order to get her to stop stalking you."

After a moment of thought, I say, "I agree. With everything going on here, I don't need her around to add to the stress level for Andi. "When can we do this?"

I can hear Max shuffling some papers. Then he says, "Is tomorrow okay? I know it's Saturday, but if you can call her and ask to see her, we can get this over with."

"Sure. I want to check with Andi first. I promised to keep her in the loop."

Max and I end our call and I immediately find Andi to explain everything to her.

Andi pulls in a long breath. "Wow, I can't believe she lied about something like that. Actually, I take that back. Am I being selfish that I'm actually relieved? I can only hope she doesn't continue to just show up."

"Believe me, I'm just happy to have the truth. And don't worry about her. You have the extra security too. Max and I are planning to go over to her place tomorrow and confront her about this. I hope that doesn't bother you."

"No. You should go and get it over with."

Leaning into the woman I love with all my heart, I wrap my arm around her and hug her. Then I find her lips, pressing mine to hers. "Thank you for being so patient with me."

Now I have to call that lunatic. Fortunately, she answers and agrees to see me the next day, so I call Max to let him know.

Then I look at Andi. "I'm relieved too. But more importantly, I'm in love with you. I hope you realize that."

Though I'd said it the night before, she looks speechless. I slide my arm around her. "Team Wilde, right?"

"Yes. Team Wilde."

I remember the words of wisdom my coach shared with me.

"My coach told me something the other day, and you need to hear this. The fear of the unknown is what kills athletes. They let it fuck with their heads. We're not going to let fear fuck with ours when it comes to dealing with whatever is going on with Violet. We're going to face it head-on with two feet planted firmly on the ground, and fight it with everything we've got. You got that? Because you and me ... we are a team."

She stands on her tiptoes and winds her arms around my neck. "Thank you, Chase. I don't know what I'd do without you." Then she plants her lips on mine. When she pulls away, I lighten the mood and slap her on the ass.

"Okay, tiger, you can talk to me like a player, but none of that locker room stuff."

"Hmm. And here all this time I thought you liked an ass slap here and there."

We're interrupted by a two-year-old as she halfway runs into us, yelling, "Hungy, Mama."

The following morning, Max and I show up at Lucia's. Her eyes betray her shock when she opens the door to see the two of us standing there.

"Max. I didn't know you'd be coming too."

That's obvious. She's wearing a silk nightgown you can see her nipples through. Evidently, she had different ideas about this meeting.

Max, God love him, doesn't break stride. He walks in and briskly says, "Buongiorno, Lucia." He doesn't stop until he gets to her table in the kitchen, which can be seen from the entryway.

I follow, keeping an eye on her and hiding my grin. She's in for a shock.

She's my problem. I figure I'll start this painful conversation. "Lucia, we came here to discuss the issue of your pregnancy."

Her hands immediately fly to her belly, which is a mistake, because that silk gown only emphasizes how flat it is.

"Oh, yes, Chase, I've been meaning to tell you when my next appointment is."

Max doesn't wait for me to comment. He gets right to it. "Stop with the lies, Lucia. There is no appointment because there is no baby." He commences to pull everything out of his folder that he carried in. First, he pulls out the phone records, then the pictures. "I believe if you were pregnant, one of these calls would've been made to an obstetrician, which they weren't. Also, these are pictures of you. You can see the dates on them. You're smoking and drinking. It doesn't look like the behavior of a pregnant woman." Finally, he pulls out a pregnancy test and hands it to her. "Here, go take this now to prove you're pregnant."

She starts bawling her eyes out and begging me to come back.

"Stop it, Lucia. I'm not coming back now, or ever. If you don't stop with this ridiculous behavior, I'll get a restraining order on you. This is the last time I want to deal with you."

Max pulls out a piece of paper. It states that Lucia admits she's not pregnant. Technically, it's not a legal document, but at least it's her admission she's not pregnant. She signs it along with the two of us. Then we leave.

"You think that'll work?"

"She's not pregnant. She can't create a baby out of thin air. She has no legal binding on you."

Shaking my head, I say, "That's not what I meant. I was thinking more on the stalking level."

Max pats my shoulder. "That's what the added security is for. Now go home and be with your family."

When I walk in the door, my smile fades. One look at Andi and my gut twists. She doesn't even have to tell me. I know my little one has another fever and I want to punch my hand through a wall. Instead, I take Andi's hand firmly and say, "Team Wilde, remember?"

THIRTY-ONE

Andi

EVERY FEVER, every night until the doctor's appointment, I worry. If not for Chase's comforting presence, I probably wouldn't have gotten one hour of sleep. As it is, I get a few hours a night.

"You have to tell Mom and Dad," Mark says. "You can't keep any more secrets."

It's the same thing Beth says when I call her and tell her about my fears for Violet. I miss her so much.

"I promise I'll tell them. Can you give me until after the doctor visit tomorrow?"

"Andi—"

"Mark, what if it's just basic anemia that an iron supplement can fix? Why worry them for nothing?"

He sighs. "Fine. But no matter what, promise me you'll tell them."

"I promise."

"So what's going on with you and Chase? Is he still pissed?"

He's told me he loved me twice. And I know he's committed to our family, but I don't say any of that to my brother.

"No. I think he's forgiven me."

"But?"

"But, I can't expect anything more."

"You deserve happiness."

"Do I?" I shoot back.

"I don't agree with how you went about things, but even I know you thought you were doing right."

"And I've made a mess of everything. If something's wrong with Violet, it's my fault."

"How can you say that?"

"I don't know if my biological parents have this type of problem in their DNA. Maybe if I'd known …"

"You'd what? You wouldn't have had Violet? Come on, Andi. You're better than this. You just need to get some sleep. Violet's going to be fine. Mom, Dad, and I can come to Italy if you want?"

"Mom was just here, and you've just started your own business. Maybe we can come home if Chase agrees."

"I think it's better if we come there."

What he doesn't say is that I shouldn't take any Violet time from Chase.

"You're right. I just miss home."

Italy is beautiful, but I miss Beth, Chicago, work …

"Hang in there."

"Thanks, Mark."

When we hang up, I sit looking at the four walls in my room and feel claustrophobic. I pull my hair into a messy bun on top of my head and head out into the darkened hallway. Faint light shimmers through the wall of windows. The sky is a dusky purple and calls to me. I pour a glass of wine and walk out into the chilly night. Violet had gone down early and Chase hasn't come home yet.

The view from the hilltop home is priceless.

When a warm body molds against me, I lean into it. Chase's scent is more familiar to me than my own.

He kisses the top of my head. "Everything's going to

be okay."

I turn in his arms and set my empty glass down. I press my cheek to his chest and listen to his heartbeat.

"I would give up my own life for her to be okay."

"I happen to love your life and intend to spend it with you, so I need you both safe."

I lift my head and search his eyes. "You want to spend your life with me?"

He seems more confused than I feel. "Team Wilde."

"Yes, but that's for Violet. I don't expect anything more after everything."

My emotions are on the cusp of bursting from my eyes in a torrent of tears. He tips my chin up.

"I have only ever loved one person. And that person is you. I want us to be a family in every way. You, me, and our daughter, we are going to make it through this."

"You mean that, don't you?"

"When have I ever lied to you?"

"Never."

He kisses me and it lingers as the sun dips, making the sky turn a midnight blue. We end up in his room, where he shows me just what love is. It ends with the most restful night I've had in a while. I would need it the next morning.

With Violet playing in a room with glass separating us, Chase holds my hand as we wait for the doctor. Salt-and-pepper hair crowns the very distinguished-looking man. But it's his gentle smile that puts me at ease.

As he speaks, his pristine English comes out in the loveliest accent. "I won't lie to you. Between your daughter's CBC panel and her continued fevers, some explained and others not, I suspect as your pediatrician has suggested that this is more than just basic anemia."

"Doc, just give it to us straight. What do you think it is?" Chase asks.

He sits up and flattens his hands together.

"If I were to venture a guess, I would say her symptoms line up with aplastic anemia."

I close my eyes, knowing the news can't be much worse.

"How will we know for sure?" Chase asks.

"We'll run some additional tests with the sample we've taken today."

Chase squeezes my hand as if he knows I'm going to shatter to pieces.

"Will we know for sure what it is?"

"We are ruling out other things. The only test to confirm an aplastic anemia diagnosis is a bone marrow test."

"Is there a cure?" Chase pipes up because my throat has seized.

My worst nightmare has been realized.

"I'm afraid not. Though we have great results with a bone marrow transplant."

"I'm willing to donate," we both offer, even though I know better.

The doctor lifts a hand. "We're getting ahead of ourselves. Let's run the test and see. Besides, it's unlikely either of you would be a match." When Chase looks as though he will argue, the doctor continues. "We will run the test if you like, assuming it comes to that. But parents are usually not matches. A sibling is more likely a match."

"We don't have any other kids."

The doctor nods. "Just something to consider. In the meantime, keep doing what you are doing. Children with this disease are more prone to catch viruses and other illness due to a compromised immune system. This can explain the fevers she's been having. If this is her diagnosis, there are many options afforded to us to manage the disease." Violet's laughter has us looking up, but her arms are raised and the delight on her face takes any fear from my heart. "You have a wonderful child. We are here for you every step of the way."

"Next steps," I finally say.

"I'll give you a call. If we need to run the bone marrow test, I'll get that scheduled."

He reaches out a hand and I shake it. Chase does it next before he practically has to lift me from my seat. The idea that Violet could be saddled with this disease kills something inside me.

Chase rubs my back and I nod at him. He heads into the other room to gather our daughter.

"Doc?"

He turns.

"You mentioned a sibling. What are the chances that if we had another kid, he or she could have the same thing?"

He bobs his head. "A valid question. There are no guarantees in life. However, this disease is rare. The likelihood is slim that another child would have it."

Chase comes back in with Violet, so I don't bring up that I read that this could be inherited or that I could have unwittingly passed this to our daughter. Guilt continues to eat at me on the ride home.

Violet is asleep when we arrive home. I cradle her in my arms and remember holding her like this after she was born. When I lay her down in her room, I kiss her head.

"Sleep well, my love," I whisper, even though she's too far in dreamland to hear me.

Chase is at the door and presses a hand to the small of my back.

"This is really a bad time, but I have to go to Germany for a few days. You guys are welcome to come, or maybe we can get our moms to come back. I don't want you to be alone here."

I stop in the middle of the hall. "You have a game in Germany?"

"Not exactly. It's something we should discuss, but a German club wants me. I've put off this visit too long. Max says Germany wants me to come check them out."

"But now?"

He sighs and runs a hand through his hair. "Time is quickly running out on a winter trade. But I can cancel."

I want to be selfish and agree, but I don't. "No, you should go."

"Do you want to come?"

The idea of being here alone isn't appealing. At the same time, if Violet really does have aplastic anemia, the last thing she needs is to come in contact with more germs most people could easily fight off.

"I should stay. You go. Maybe Beth could come."

Though that is a crazy idea. I don't know if she has a passport or time off available.

"That's great. You find out and I'll pay for all her travel arrangements."

This man, I'm not sure how I lived without him. I draw him down and kiss him deeply.

"I love you," I say, knowing it is more than love.

"There is nothing I won't do for you and Violet."

And his words arrow straight to my heart, because they are a statement more prophetic than the three I said.

"Me too."

He scoops me up and leads me to his huge suite. "Your room?"

"No, ours. If we're together, we share a bed together. From now and always." He pointedly waits for me to say something. "Agree?"

"Yes. Together and forever. You, me, and Violet."

THIRTY-TWO

Chase

GERMANY IS the last place I want to go right now, but if I don't get this taken care of, the trade time will expire. I've put this off for as long as I can. Leaving Andi and Violet is more painful than anything I've ever experienced—worse than when I walked away from her the first time. If Violet's diagnosis comes back as the worst-case scenario, I'll have to make some contingency plans. Andi can't be left alone with me gallivanting all over the damn place while she's left to care for Violet alone. That won't work at all.

Luckily, Andi's friend was able to come and stay with her while I'm away. If she hadn't, I'm not sure how I could've left them.

Max meets me at the airport in Rome and we board the chartered jet. I'm not fit company for anyone.

"Chase, you need to calm down."

"Easy for you to say. My daughter is sick, Max. What I need is to be staying in Rome and not be flying anywhere for this contract bullshit."

"Right. But this is your livelihood."

I take my seat and think for a minute. If the worst happens, and Violet truly has aplastic anemia, there's no way I'll be able to travel constantly. What the hell am I thinking? I cross my ankle over my thigh and huff.

"What is it?"

"I can't do this, Max." My head swings back and forth as I weigh out my options.

"What do you mean?"

My arms fly out as I begin to explain. "It's easy really, when you think about it. I can't be here when they're there. If Violet has to undergo treatments, I have to be there." My finger points in the direction of where I believe my house is.

"Slow down. Where's there?" Clearly, Max is confused.

"Home. Violet may have a really bad disease. We don't know yet."

He leans forward and pats my arm. "See there, you don't know yet. So there's no need to get all worried."

Shoving his hand away, I say, "No, we do know. We know she doesn't have the run-of-the-mill anemia. What we don't know is how serious it is. We're praying it's not aplastic anemia, but everything is pointing in that direction."

"Chase, how can I help?"

I spread my hands wide, saying, "I don't know. It's so frustrating, Max, not knowing anything."

He checks his watch. "Maybe I can come up with something once we get there."

"Like what? Pull a magic trick out of your hat?"

"No. But maybe we can get them to extend your contract here in Italy."

Then an idea strikes me. "I need to go back to the States."

The pilot announces we're taking off and we need to buckle up.

Once we're in the air, Max says, "You can't go back, Chase. It will end your career."

I mull this over and say, "It doesn't matter. The two most important things to me are Andi and Violet. I can't leave them anymore. And I can't leave Andi alone to shoulder this burden while I'm off playing in some football game and she's tending to a sick child. Besides, my head wouldn't be in it anyway. A leave of absence isn't possible. The only thing to do is go back home and have Violet get treatment. Maybe I can get a position with a team close to one of our families, so after this is over, Andi will have someone nearby who she can rely on. And if I do go out of town, she won't be alone."

"The career you've worked so hard to build will be over."

"Max, you're not listening. I don't give a damn about it."

"But the money," he insists.

"Is socked away in all kinds of investments. I've been wise with what I've earned. I can live a nice life on what I've made for a damn long time."

"I want you to think about it."

"I have. If they're willing to give me a leave of absence for six months, then I'll do it. If not, then I have to decline."

"You can't just walk. You'll have to finish out your year."

"I will. I only have a couple more months. Can you ask them to allow me to take leave?"

"This is highly unusual. They don't generally grant these when there isn't a known medical emergency."

"It's fine," I say. "I'll finish out my year and go back to the States."

Max pushes for me to ride it out in Europe. But I interrupt him.

"Max, I appreciate that, but we need to be closer to our families. If this is as bad as it's looking, we can't be on different continents without a support network nearby."

When we get to the meeting, at first they aren't pleased by my deferral, but when I explain, they become more accommodating.

The group we are speaking to clusters their heads together for a moment, and then one of them says, "May we have a moment, please?"

Max and I leave the room. When we get out in the hall, Max stares at me, his eyes telling me more than I need to know.

"You just killed your European football career. But I'm pretty sure I didn't have to tell you that."

"It doesn't matter. As I've said before, only two things matter and those are Andi and Violet."

He heaves a long sigh. "I hope you don't regret this decision."

"I won't."

Max paces the length of the hall until one of the men calls us back in. After we're seated, they detail their contract offer.

"However, considering everything, we are prepared to suspend negotiations until the summer trade period. You finish this season with Italy and take a few months. After that, we can offer you the contract as discussed."

"This sounds good. However, if my daughter is still undergoing therapy, it's likely I will decline the offer."

"We understand."

Everyone shakes hands, and then we go for a tour of the team's facilities. If I'm to accept a contract here, I have to be comfortable with everything. I have to admit, they are a step above where I currently am, and the stadium is fantastic. Afterward, they take me on a tour of the city and surrounding area where I could be possibly living. I inquire about schools for Violet and they assure me they are the best around.

When I get to the hotel, Max and I head out to dinner shortly after checking in. I try to call Andi, but there's no answer. I hope everything's okay. I text her and ask her to text me back when she gets this.

During dinner, I'm distracted, thinking about everything back in Italy.

"Chase, are you listening?"

"What?"

"I said, that's a sweet deal they offered you."

"It is. But it's all contingent on Violet's health. I hope it all works out for the best."

I check my phone again and there isn't anything from Andi.

Max is talking again, but I don't hear a word he's saying.

Next thing I know, he's clicking his fingers in front of my face.

"Hey, what's going on with you?"

"It's Andi. She hasn't responded to my call or text. That's not like her."

"Maybe her phone died."

"Uh, not Andi's."

My head swims with all kinds of horrible ideas when my phone finally buzzes. I snatch the thing and practically yell, "Is she okay?"

"Jeez, yes, she's fine. We were outside playing in this beautiful weather and I left my phone in the kitchen."

I breathe out, "Fuck." Then I sag in my chair with relief. "I've been worried sick."

"I'm so sorry. Beth is in love with this place and we took a walk around the area with Violet in the stroller. Let me tell you. She was not happy about that. She kept yelling, '*walk, walk.*' But I wouldn't let her. And then we sat out back for a while. It's at least seventy degrees today."

I honestly don't give a fuck about the damn weather. My heart is still beating out a rhythm that could rival Ringo Starr on the drums.

"Chase, are you there?"

"Yeah, Andi, I'm here. I only suffered a minor heart attack is all."

"I'm sorry."

"It's okay. I'll live. I have to say I was ready to jump on the plane though."

"Oh no. Really, we're good. Violet is getting spoiled. We're going to have a rotten child on our hands after Beth leaves."

"I think we can handle it. You go and have a good time with

233

your friend while I head to the emergency room to get shocked by the paddles."

Her bubbles of laughter put a grin on my face as we end the call.

"Better now?" Max asks.

"Yeah. I'm better."

"Good. Now eat."

I look at the plateful of food that stares at me. I haven't touched a single bit of it, and suddenly I'm starving.

"I think I will."

The next morning, Max and I have a meeting with the team manager and coaching staff. Afterward, we board the plane and head back to Italy. I'm more than ready to be back home, holding Andi and Violet.

When I walk in the door, a flurry of curls and arms and legs bulldoze me, yelling, "Dada!" Then two stubby arms wrap around my knees and squeeze me. "Pick up!" she demands.

I reach down and swing her high in the air to the sound of her squeals. Andi stands by watching. I walk over and kiss her, wanting more but knowing it'll have to wait.

"How was the trip?"

"It was good after I recovered from my heart issue."

She smacks my ass and laughs. "Violet, why don't you go and play with Aunt Beth?"

"No. I want Dada."

I swing her around and set her down. "We can play in a minute. Mama and I need to talk for a little bit. Go on." She wobble-runs into the large den where I imagine Beth is.

Grabbing Andi, I pull her tightly against me. "I missed you. It's not good being away from you."

"No, it isn't." Her pause catches my attention. "Chase, the doctor called this morning."

I look down into her eyes and don't like what I see.

"He wants to do a bone marrow test on Violet."

"Fuck."

THIRTY-THREE

Andi

I CLING to Chase as they wheel our baby through double doors. Chase kisses the top of my head.

"She's going to be fine."

I swivel in his embrace to face him.

"What if she doesn't have anemia but something worse?"

Chase's eyes are tired. He's been burning the candle at both ends. It's practice, a game, or spending time with us even after a long day.

"Let's not play the what-if game. Whatever this is, she'll beat it. And we should consider having another baby."

Butterflies race through my stomach. A world of happiness stirs at the thought he wants a family with me until my mind retracts to the reason behind his statement.

I shake my head. "Is that fair to another child? What if—"

His thumb silences me as he cups my chin. "No *what if*. Besides, I don't want Violet to grow up an only child. I want her to have what Fletcher and I have."

I half-smile, remembering how he and Fletcher fought, but Fletcher would still include him. That had meant Mark had to

235

bring me along. I can't begrudge it because that's how Chase and I had gotten so close.

"There's no guarantee our child would be a girl."

He shrugs. "That didn't stop us from being best friends."

"Best friends, huh? You just wanted to kiss me and play doctor."

A mischievous grin brightens his face. "It worked, right? You let me play doctor and I got to kiss you and—"

I play slap his arm. "Don't go there."

"What?" he teases. "I got the prettiest girl in school all to myself. I consider that a win-win."

"Yeah, and what about Becky Big Boobs?"

He laughs. "You're still jealous."

"Did she really give you a blow job in the boys' bathroom?"

His eyes twinkle. "Did you kiss Andrew under the bleachers and let him feel you up?"

We'd both been stupid, neither of us wanting to change our friendship to something more at first … until things changed.

"I'll answer if you do."

He chuckles and I realize he's been distracting me. I turn to glance at the doors again. He turns my face.

"Eyes here, princess. Our daughter will be fine. You have to tell me the truth."

I swallow and force myself not to think about the fact that they are putting our daughter under.

"We've got this. Team Wilde, remember?"

I lick my lips, noticing that his smile doesn't quite reach his eyes. He's worried too. It's my duty to help him get his mind off of things.

"Team Wilde."

His head dips and captures my mouth in a quick kiss. When he pulls back, I say, "Fine, I'll answer, but you first." His gray eyes dance in the light. "Was I really your first?"

There had been rumors that he'd bedded a ton of girls. Still,

I'd given him my virginity. It had been clumsy at best, but he'd done other things that had gotten me off.

"Yes," he says.

"It's so hard to believe. Every girl in school was after you. I always thought, I don't know."

He shrugs. His face alights with amusement.

"Everyone said—"

"I'll admit I did a whole lot of base rounding before you, but never got to home until you."

"And after me?"

It had been hard to maintain a true relationship when we were hiding it from everyone. I had been jealous, but so had he. Girls and guys had used our names as bragging rights for things we hadn't done. It had broken us up a couple of times.

He clears his throat. "Do you really want to know that?"

The more I think about it, I don't.

"No, never mind. I have you now and we don't have to hide it anymore."

He draws me close and we hold each other.

"Are you hungry?" I nod. "You wait here and I'll go grab us something."

I watch him walk off and marvel that he's mine, though I feel bad. He's missing a game. I'd heard him on the phone with his agent arguing about his need to be here. The owners of the club had been understanding, but they saw a biopsy as no big deal. Chase had told them in no uncertain terms he was going to be there for this daughter. The contract gave him family leave for emergencies. He said he'd argue with them all the way to a court to say that this was. He'd had no idea I'd heard.

When he comes back, we eat. It's not great, but it's something. The procedure isn't long and Violet is still pretty out of it when we head home.

Once we get home, Chase carries our sleeping daughter inside. I love seeing the two of them together.

I open a bottle of wine when he comes back.

"She's still out," he says.

"Doctor said she would want and need rest."

He moves closer to me. "And I need you."

His arm snakes around me and I let out a muted squeal as he hikes me up onto the counter, wedging himself in between my legs.

"What are you doing?" I ask, giggling as he gets to his knees and shoves up the skirt I'm wearing.

I glance back at the hall, listening for movement.

"I'm starving."

He shoves aside my panties and licks my slit from top to bottom and back again.

Breathlessly, I ask, "What if Violet wakes up?"

His tongue is inside me and I fall back, bracing my arms behind me.

"Listen out for her."

Then he's back and I keep my eyes peeled for as long as I can. I bite my tongue as I come hard with Chase's face buried in my pussy. I'm barely coherent when I hear his zipper go down.

"Chase," I whisper, trying to admonish him.

We are definitely taking things too far out in the open. Though the doctor had said she would probably sleep for a couple of hours.

Then he's inside me, muttering hushed curses and other words that have me on the verge of coming again.

"I'm going to get you pregnant."

He sounds like a caveman, which is a complete turn-on. I could tell him no. But the truth is, I want to have another child with him, and not just for Violet. I'd dreamed about having his kids once I realized boys weren't gross.

The only sound in the house is our flesh slapping together as he fills me.

"You know how much I love you, right?"

"Yes," I hiss.

He easily brings my lady parts back online. With every one of his thrusts, I'm catapulted closer to liftoff.

"You love me?"

"Yes," I agree, so easily because I'd never stopped loving him.

"Then we'll make this official and get married."

The orgasm that's been building bursts. In the back of my mind, a smile curls my lips as I wonder how in the future I'll answer the question *how did Daddy propose to you?*

Chase's heart beats wildly in his chest as he covers me.

"Are you going to get off me?" I jokingly ask.

"I'm going to keep you here until my swimmers can get to their final destination."

"I'm sure we'd have twins or more as hard as I came." I laugh.

"And are you going to ask me if I'm on board with your plan?"

"You have to know I'll do anything for my girls, including knocking you up. But we both know you want me to," he says with a cocky grin.

"Your ego knows no bounds."

"Maybe, but the same with my love. Violet is mine forever, but so are you. I was dumb enough for not forcing you to come to Italy with me. I've known all along you would be my wife. That was never a question. It just took me a while to pull my head out of my ass and admit it."

"You have wonderful timing," I say, full of sweet sarcasm.

"As long as I got you in the end, the means don't matter." He scoops me up. "Besides, I'm not done with you yet. You'll be lucky to walk when I finish."

"Promises, promises."

I giggle as he heads to his bedroom, where he makes good on his threat. We are playing around in his huge walk-in shower when Violet walks in, getting a clear view of her father's ass.

I groan, thinking we should have locked the door, when I

notice the flush on my baby's face. I grab a towel and practically run out of the shower, barely getting it around me when I kneel to touch my daughter.

"Mama, tummy hurt," she says, and then throws up all over me.

THIRTY-FOUR

Chase

It's terrible when your child is sick and there's not a damn thing you can do about it. I stand by helpless as Andi tends to Violet, cleaning her up.

"Chase, can you fill the tub?"

"Sure." I get the water going.

"And, Chase?"

"Yeah?"

"You might want to ..." Her finger motions up and down, so I glance to where she's pointing and realize I never got dressed. I'm running around naked in front of Violet. "It's okay," she assures me.

"I'll be right back." I quickly pull on a pair of shorts, and by the time I get back to the bathroom, the tub is ready.

"Hand her to me," I say.

Violet is limp and lethargic. I only hope she doesn't throw up again. I'm not like Andi in that regard. She's so tough when it comes to that stuff. I'm a pussy, though I would never admit it.

When I dip Violet into the warm water, she whines and I want to whine right along with her.

"Dada, don't feel good."

"I know, Little One. Your tummy hurts, doesn't it?" I ask her. "Let me rinse you off and we'll get you back in your jammies." I make short work of the bath and soon have her wrapped in a warm and fluffy towel. Andi has clean pajamas waiting, so we put those on her.

Once she's dressed, she wants her mama. Andi gathers her up and cradles her in her arms. I watch the two of them and my heart pinches at how it must be killing Andi to see Violet ill. We have to get her better. There is no other option.

"Let's get in the bed," I suggest. "She's so tired. Look at her eyes."

"It's probably the aftereffects of the anesthesia still. Maybe that's why she threw up. She doesn't feel warm to me. Does she to you?"

"No, but let's check her temperature, just to be on the safe side." I go to Violet's bathroom and grab the thermometer. Andi scans her forehead, and sure enough, it's normal.

Andi hands it back to me, saying, "I'm sure it's a side effect from all the meds they gave her."

"I hate to say it, but that makes me feel better."

"Me too."

I rub Violet's soft curls and ask her if she wants to sleep with us tonight. The only response I receive is a small nod.

Andi gives me a questioning stare.

"What?" I ask.

"Are you sure about this? She may throw up again."

"Then we'll move to the other bed. She's so pitiful, I can't bear to send her back alone to her room tonight."

"I know. Then let's all snuggle in for the night, shall we?"

Luckily, in the morning, Violet wakes up feeling much better after not having any more episodes during the night. Soon, she's slapping us both on our stomachs, telling us she's hungry.

Andi groans, "Well, that's a good sign."

"I'll get her breakfast," I offer.

"I'll get her dressed," Andi says.

By this time, Violet is half-jumping on the bed. She's not one hundred percent, though. I mention this to Andi.

"It's probably because she might be a bit sore from the test yesterday."

"Yeah, I didn't think of that."

"They said she'd act a little funny, remember?"

"I do now. And now starts the waiting game."

"The doctor said it may take up to a week, but it could be sooner."

"I hope sooner, Andi."

She grabs my hand. "So do I. Now let's go feed our daughter."

After breakfast, we watch movies and hang out with Violet. With each passing hour, she seems to feel better. I notice that Andi is less stressed as well. She even mentions that I should practice the next day.

"I will. But … if you get any calls, you must promise to call me immediately. Will you do that?"

"I will. I don't think we'll get a call that quickly, though."

The following two days we settle into somewhat of a lull. Andi fusses over Violet, as do I, and we play with her as much as possible. I go to practice every day, coming home exhausted. Luckily, I have two home games in a row. But I'll be on the road next week, which disturbs me. The truth is, my nights are sleepless because I lie in bed, hoping that bad news doesn't occur for our precious little girl.

It's a week later that Andi gets the call. It happens, of course, when I'm at practice. One of the coaches calls me off the field and I'm told to go home. It doesn't take any deduction on my part to figure out what the problem is. I don't even shower before I jump in the car and go.

When I storm through the door, she's standing there, waiting.

"Well?"

"He wants to see us. In the office."

"More waiting, dammit."

"No. He said to come as soon as we could and he would see us when we got there."

"I haven't showered."

"Go now. We'll go as soon as you're done."

My legs chew up the steps and I set a record for how many minutes it takes for me to bathe. I dress and get back downstairs in no time.

"Where's Violet?"

"Watching a DVD. Where else? She's oblivious. I wish I were."

"Me too," I answer. "Let's do this. And, Andi, remember: Team Wilde."

She gives me a shaky laugh. But I can't have that, so I pull her up to my chest. "We got this." I press my lips to hers for a brief kiss. "Have the faith. We can do anything, including beat the worst news. Now stiffen that steel spine of yours."

"Yes, sir."

I go into the living room and grab my daughter. "Come on, kiddo. We're going for a ride."

We arrive at the doctor's and they usher us straight back after Andi tells them who we are. We're given the red carpet treatment and I want to chuckle, only not with humor. I guess you have to have a dreaded disease before you're treated like this.

They escort us into the doctor's office instead of an exam room this time. We don't wait even five minutes before he comes in. He smiles, but it doesn't quite reach his eyes. I glance at Andi. She notices it too.

"Ms. James, Mr. Wilde, I was hoping for much better news than this. I'm afraid Violet has aplastic anemia. It's very puzzling to us. We don't usually see this in children her age. That's not to say it never happens. But it is quite rare, particularly since hers is the acquired type. We do have treatment for this, but the ultimate cure is a bone marrow transplant. I would like to try the treatment first."

Andi has done a lot of research already since she's a nurse, so she pipes in with questions. "For the bone marrow transplant, my understanding is that the best matches are siblings. Is that correct?"

"Yes, it is."

"Violet is an only child."

"I am aware. There are a few options. Although it's unlikely you both would be a match, we can still test both of you, if you choose. And if there are any relatives that would be willing to be tested, that would be a good option. There is also a bone marrow registry."

Andi looks at me. "We could ask Fletcher," I say. "And what about Mark?"

Her eyes tug down at the corners and appear pained. "I'm adopted, remember? Mark and I wouldn't share any genetic markers."

Shit. Why didn't I remember that? "It's okay, baby. We'll figure something out. Doctor, how much time do we have?"

"We may have years. That's a question I can't answer. But it's best to get this arranged now and not wait until you need it."

Andi nods. "I agree."

"We've been discussing having another baby."

Andi jumps into the conversation. "Chase. Not here."

"Actually, that's a good idea. That is, if you were planning it anyway. It's the best option for Violet," the doctor says. "The first thing I'd like to focus on, though, is getting Violet started on treatment that may bring her blood count up to normal. If that works, then the bone marrow transplant can be shelved for later."

"Is there a possibility she would never need it?" I ask.

"Yes, if she's controlled by the drugs. Some cases are."

"I have one last question, doctor. Would you recommend that we go back to the States to be close to our family?" I ask.

"That's something only you can decide. But I can say if it were my family and me, I probably would want to be close to them."

"Thank you. I think you gave me the answer."

Andi asks, "When can we start treatment?"

"Tomorrow, if you want."

"Are there side effects?"

"Possibly. But not any different from her being ill, and as soon as she begins to feel better, those side effects should dissipate. We'll be using bone marrow stimulants because we want her bone marrow to start producing new blood cells. We'd also like to give her transfusions if necessary."

"Is that safe?" I ask. I've always heard about the risk of disease transmission through blood transfusions.

"There are always risks associated with it, but we'll only do them if we think it's medically necessary."

Andi says, "Can we start with the marrow stimulants?"

"Yes. Can you bring her here tomorrow? These are given either by IV or injection. I want to discuss her treatment with another hematologist before I decide on which stimulant to begin. And after she receives it, I would prefer for her to remain here for a few hours to monitor her for side effects."

We leave with an appointment for eight o'clock the next morning. I'm sure Violet won't be happy, but we are both praying these drugs work. In the meantime, we have to make a decision on whether to stay or go home. I can't stand the idea of us being so far away from our families with no support structure in place.

And then there are all the phone calls that will have to be made. My head aches with the thought of them.

As we pull in the driveway of our house, Andi leans over and presses her lips to mine. Then she says, "What should we do, Chase? I don't want to pull you away from your career."

"I won't have a career if all I do is worry about this."

THIRTY-FIVE

Andi

VIOLET IS our priority and we spend time playing with her and reading her stories before her precious little eyes can't stay open any longer.

Chase carries her off to bed and I follow, watching him tuck her in. It doesn't get old seeing what a great father he is. I shouldn't be surprised. Even though he never saw himself as a dad, he had such a great role model in his father.

When he kisses her forehead, my heart breaks. The idea that we could lose her kills me inside.

Chase sweeps a hand down my back and to my waist. There is nothing sexual about the move, though my body gets hot every time he touches me. We pass the bedrooms and end up back in the living room.

"I'm very serious about getting you pregnant."

Though we've had the conversation, with the news from the doctor, this decision takes on a whole new meaning.

I meet his gorgeous gaze. "I wasn't sure at first. I didn't want to chance bringing another child into the world with this disease, not that we wouldn't love him or her."

He nods. "I get it."

"But the doctor doesn't seem to believe that she inherited this from us."

"Does that mean you're on board?"

"Yes," I breathe the word like I've held it in for weeks, and maybe I have.

He draws me close and kisses the life out of me. As much as I feel his amorous mood lift, there is more we need to do first. I gingerly step back.

"I do think we shouldn't delay treatment and start it here. If we go anywhere else, they will want to run their own tests and it will take precious time away from getting her well."

"I agree. No delay," he says.

"We should probably call our parents first before the time difference works against us."

He sighs. "Okay."

I point to the hall. "I'm going to call in my room." Then I head for it.

The space feels foreign since I've been spending all my time in Chase's bed. I have to push away thoughts of how little time we've spent sleeping as I dial Mom's number. Dad answers.

"Hi, Dad."

"Hey." He covers the phone, but I can hear him call out to Mom.

"Jane, Andi's on the phone." Then he speaks to me. "I'm glad you called. Your mother and I have something to tell you."

There is a hint of warning in his voice that suggests bad news.

"Hey, sweetie," Mom says.

A churning starts in my gut. Mom used her *I'm so sorry* voice. "What's going on?"

I'm not sure how much more of any bad news I can take.

Mom takes over. "Your dad and I felt like you needed to find your birth parents. We decided to hire another private investigator, and we have news."

Air takes up permanent residence in my lungs. My investigator had come up with nothing. Granted, I hadn't been able to afford to pay a really good one.

"What did you find out?"

Time stops, as I don't know what I want to hear. Are they fine? Together or separate? Do they have another family with kids they kept? Will any news be welcome? I'm on the verge of telling Mom I changed my mind and I don't want to know when she drops the bomb.

"Your father died in a military training accident before you were born. And your mother died last year of a heart attack."

Tears spill from my eyes for people I've never met.

"Do they have other kids or family?"

"No kids on either side. You do have an aunt on your mom's side. Your father was brought up in the foster care system. The investigator says your father had enlisted around the time you were conceived. He isn't sure he ever knew about you, though his name is listed on your birth certificate. They were barely eighteen."

Dad goes on to explain that there is a small amount of money from his job and military benefits sitting in a state unclaimed money account for me to claim. Mom adds they have pictures, but by then I've checked out. My vision is cloudy with tears and my heart breaks yet again.

"Andi?" Mom asks.

"I ..."

"I know, honey. It's a lot, and I wish I didn't have to do this over the phone."

"I—" But the word gets stuck in my throat.

Using the back of my hand, I wipe at my eyes.

"I need time to think about all of that. But I did have a reason for this call."

"Okay," Mom says hesitantly.

I picture my father wrapping an arm around my mother and long for his embrace. I miss my dad. And that's when it hits me. Though I may never know about my biological parents, I had great parents who loved me more than maybe I deserved at times.

"Thank you," I say.

"We never meant to keep them from you," Dad says.

"I know. I love you guys. And I appreciate you doing that. You didn't have to."

"We did," Dad says. "We should have done it a long time ago."

I shake my head as my tears resume. "No, you didn't. It was me. You guys have always been enough. I feel awful for making you feel like you had to do this."

"No, baby, it's only human to want to know who your parents are."

"That's the thing. I know who they are. They are you and Dad. And I'm the luckiest girl in the world to have been given to you."

Mom chokes. "No, we are lucky to have been blessed with you."

"We love you," Dad adds.

I walk to the bathroom for tissues. "I love you guys so much."

They return the sentiment. When a quiet moment comes, I hate to sour the mood. But there's no choice.

"Can you put me on speaker while I conference Mark in?"

"What's going on?" Dad asks.

"I know this isn't the best of times, but I'd like to say it only once."

Dad's easy and agrees without a fuss. I initiate a three-way call and bring Mark on the line.

"Andi," Mark says.

"Hey, is Riley there?" I ask about his girlfriend.

"No, she's on the practice green. I'm leaving shortly to meet her."

"Dad and Mom are on the phone as well. I have something to tell you all."

They all say hi and then Mark laughs. "Are you going to tell us Chase asked you to marry him?"

I think about all the things that Chase has said, but remember that time isn't on our side.

"I'll ask that you keep this to yourself. Chase would like to talk to his family and tell them."

They agree, though Mark chuckles, sure I'm going to announce our impending nuptials.

"Violet is sick. She has aplastic anemia, which basically means her bone marrow doesn't have what it takes to produce enough blood." They gasp. "There are many treatments, but the only cure is a bone marrow treatment."

"I'll be tested," my brother says without prompting. "I'm sure Riley will too."

"And we will," Mom and Dad agree.

"Thank you. I'm just so mad that I—"

The words are lost as I lose the battle to sobs.

"Let's not go there again, little sister. We will do whatever you need."

I tell them about staying in Italy at least for now. When I finally hang up, I leave the bedroom and hear Chase on the phone in the living room. My mind travels back to their news about my birth parents and I head to check on Violet. I don't want Chase worrying about me. He's got so much to think about himself with his career. His season ends in May, with only a little over a month or so to go. If all goes well with Violet's treatments, he won't have to choose between his little girl and his career. Though I know without a doubt what he'd choose.

THIRTY-SIX

Chase

––––––––––

MOM AND DAD are in shock.

"How sick is she?"

"Pretty sick, Mom. She's starting treatment tomorrow to make her blood count come up."

"Will it work?" Mom asks.

"We hope so. If not, there is another option."

"Like what?" Dad asks.

"Bone marrow transplant, but the donor has to be at least a fifty percent match."

"We'll get tested," they both chime in.

"Thank you. I'm going to ask Fletcher too."

"You know he'll say yes," Mom says.

"I still have to ask."

"Chase, can you come back to the States for this?"

"Mom, right now, the treatment is only an injection." I explain what it does. "It makes sense to stay here since her doctors have all the tests and everything right here."

"Do you want me to come? Dad and I are retired so it's not a problem for us to travel."

Mom always was hands-on. "Let's see how this goes. If Andi needs anything, I'll send for both you and her mom."

"Okay. But don't hesitate. I know Jane would want to come too."

"I won't."

"Son, if you need anything at all, just call."

"I will, Dad. And thanks."

After I hang up with them, I call Fletcher and Cassidy. My call with them is equally as shocking. Cassidy cries and says they'll all be tested, even the baby. "You never know. Any of us could be a match."

"Thanks, Cass. It only has to be fifty percent."

They also wonder about us coming back to the States. "The care here is good, and unless something happens, we'll stay here. My season ends in a month so we'll see."

After we end the call, Andi and I exchange stories.

"Between both of our families, hopefully we'll find a match," I say.

Then Andi surprises me with the news about her birth parents. She breaks down and cries, which tears me up. "Andi, it's going to be fine."

"But that could've been another chance for Violet."

"Don't worry. We'll have enough, and then if we get pregnant, that will be our other option."

"Oh, Chase. I'm so scared." My arms wind around her as her body trembles.

Tipping her chin up with my finger, I say, "Andi, everything is going to be fine. Remember, we're Team Wilde. We've got this."

Her eyes bore into mine and I wish I felt as positive as I sound.

"Right. Team Wilde."

We hug each other, and I'm not quite sure which one of us is stronger. "Let's go to bed. I have an early morning tomorrow.

I need to be on the field an hour before everyone else since I missed the last two days."

Andi gives me the nod and we head up to bed. The next morning, she's still asleep when I get up. I don't want to disturb my sleeping beauty, so I ease out from under the covers and tiptoe my way to the bathroom. I'm dressed and almost to the door when her voice catches me off guard.

"Trying to leave without a goodbye kiss?"

"No, I wanted to let you sleep." I go to the bed and let her outstretched arms wrap around me. "I wish I didn't have to go. You make it too hard on a guy."

"Those are my intentions. That way you'll miss me more."

"I always miss you. Now I really do have to go or I'll be late."

"Go get 'em, Wilde."

I give her nipple a quick pinch and she lets out a squeak. "See you tonight. Call me if you need me."

"I will."

Practice is long and difficult. Since I was gone, I go at it especially hard. Even one of the coaches takes note.

"Are you trying to kill yourself?" he asks.

I only want to work the demons out, but I don't tell him that. "No, just making up for lost time."

"Just make sure you don't injure yourself. That's the last thing we need." His sour expression tells me he's not exactly happy.

"Noted," I yell back to him.

When practice is over, the coach calls me into his office.

"Chase, fill me in on what's happening with your daughter."

It's only fair he knows, so I take the time to give him a rundown of what's happening.

"She started treatment today. If everything goes as planned, then she should be good. If it doesn't, then she'll need a bone marrow transplant."

"I see. And what does that entail?"

I glance at the ceiling. I don't want to open this can of worms yet. "We don't really know yet because we are being optimistic on this first round of treatment."

"I see. Then keep me posted on her progress. And if there's anything you need from us, please let us know."

"Thanks."

I head to the showers, and afterward I'm on the way home to find out how Violet's first day went. As I'm pulling into the driveway, the front door opens and Andi is on the porch holding the little tyke in her arms. I hope this is a good sign.

"Dada, here." Her tiny arms reach out for me. Dropping my bag on the porch, I take her from Andi.

"How's my girl today?"

She lays her head on my chest and holds out her arm. There's an elastic wrap on it where I imagine they gave her the injection.

"What's this?"

"Boo-boo."

Glancing at Andi, she shakes her head.

"A boo-boo?"

"Yah. Kiss."

I kiss her arm and ask, "Is it better?"

She bobs her head, which is still pressed against my chest. "Yah."

Andi grabs my bag and we walk inside the house. "It smells wonderful in here," I say.

"Lasagna."

"Mmm."

"Lazana," Violet murmurs.

"That's right. Daddy's favorite."

I walk into the living room where a video is playing and put Violet down on the couch, but she's not having any of that. So I sit down and pull her on top of me. That seems to make her happier.

Andi sits next to us and says, "This is how she's been all day. Much clingier than usual."

"She must not feel well."

"No fever, though, so she just must feel off."

"What are the side effects?"

"You don't even want to know. The list is endless."

"Great," I groan. I smooth Violet's curls as she snuggles against me.

"You thirsty?" Andi asks.

"Yeah, I could use some water, please." I don't add how starved I am.

She brings back a huge glass of ice water and adds, "We're going to eat in about fifteen minutes. Is that okay?"

"It's great because I could eat a horse."

"Dada eat horse." Violet giggles. In turn, we all laugh. That's a relief.

After I guzzle the water, I ask Andi about the day.

"The treatment only took about an hour. They did an infusion and Violet was pretty good. They said depending on how many she'll need, they may switch to the injection. But to start with, they did this kind. If she responds well, we may do another one next week, and then set up some kind of a schedule. They talked about putting in a port."

"What's that?"

"It's a surgical procedure where they put in a permanent line so they don't have to stick an IV into her every week. I would be in favor of this."

"Where would it be?" I ask.

"On her chest."

This horrifies me, and Andi can tell because she pats my arm and says, "It's barely noticeable and is so much better for the patient, Chase. This way, she wouldn't have to get stabbed by a needle every time she goes to the doctor. It was awful holding her today. I hated it."

"I hadn't thought of that. I hate you had to do that." My

eyes drop to her tiny arm and that bandage that's wrapped around it. No wonder she wanted me to kiss it.

"And she'll have to get this every week?"

"Maybe even more." Andi's face tells it all.

"Then there's no question about it. We'll do it."

"Tell me about practice."

After I fill her in, she checks on the lasagna and pulls it out of the oven to sit for a few. "It'll be ready to cut right away."

"I've been thinking. If Violet's treatment doesn't work out, I think we should go back to the States for the bone marrow transplant," I say.

"What about your career?"

"My season is over in a month. If she's getting better, we'll know by then, right?"

"I should think so."

"And if not, we'll know that too."

Andi nods.

"Then if it's what we don't want to hear, we can go back to where our families are. We can ask the doctors here which is the best place."

"Yeah, about that. I've already been researching just in case."

"And?"

"Everything points to the Children's Hospital in Nashville."

"Okay, then we could live there, and that isn't very far for either of our parents. Maybe what? Four hours?"

"Yeah, I think so. But that still doesn't answer what you'll do. You can't work from over there."

"I'll figure that out. I can take a year off, or I may not even need it if the timing is right. And if it's not, then I'll do what needs to be done. But never forget that she's my first priority."

"And I can always go back to work if need be."

"Andi, money won't ever be an issue. I've been very wise with what I've made, making some very good investments. We'll never have to worry about that, even if I don't ever work another day in my life. So put your mind at ease."

"How much ... never mind. It's not my business."

"Everything about me is your business. I'll show you later if you want. But don't worry about the money."

The three of us eat dinner and afterward we watch more TV with Violet until she drifts to sleep in my arms. I stare at my beautiful daughter and know it won't be possible for her not to beat this terrible affliction. She is a Wilde, and Wildes are strong and tough. We are made of hearty stock. I know without a doubt that Violet is going to win, hands down.

But for once in my life, I'm wrong—dead wrong. And this time, the stakes are much higher than a game or even a championship. This time it is winner takes all, and loser ... loser doesn't even have any air left to breathe.

THIRTY-SEVEN

Andi

WHEN CHASE SLIPS in beside me, I'm deliriously happy and not just because I feel the long, hard length of him pressed against my back. Violet is responding to the treatment. Her energy level is up and she hasn't had a fever since.

Chase spoons in behind me and nuzzles my neck as his hand glides up my thigh to my hip.

"Are you awake?" he whispers, his words fanning my hair.

Though I'd awoken to the sounds of him entering the bedroom, a silly giggle escapes me. It's late and I don't care as his fingers squeeze my side before traveling down and then up my sleep shirt to find my center. I suck in air.

"I need you. It's been a long day without you," he says.

I nod because I always need him. He lifts my leg and guides his cock to my entrance. I stifle a moan as he pushes inside me.

"Damn, you're always wet and ready for me."

I moan out an agreement. It's true. Just knowing he's near, my body responds.

His thrusts are fast and hard, taking me higher each time. He works his magic touch on my clit with precision. It won't be long as he pumps in and out of me.

"Touch yourself," he commands.

His hand disappears to glide up my stomach. I use my hand where his was to keep up the pressure.

"I'm close," I beg.

He cups my breast and pinches my nipple. I bite my tongue to hold back a cry. It would be loud and might wake the neighborhood.

His mouth is at my pulse point, sucking as he squeezes my tit and tweaks my nipple.

"I'm going to come so hard there's no way you're not going to get pregnant."

That's enough to send me over the edge and moaning out his name.

"Damn, baby, that's it. Your pussy is fisting me so tight right now, I can't hang on."

He rolls me toward him some to sink deeper as he pulses inside me. It spurs on my orgasm to last that much longer. Then he's still and we are both breathing hard.

"I shouldn't have woken you," he says.

I shake my head. "That's worth waking up for."

I don't ask why he's late. I trust him completely.

"How was Violet today?" he asks.

"Great. She's like a different child in a good way."

He nods as he moves us back to our sides, but doesn't pull out his softened cock. He's long and thick enough to not slip out. And I like the feeling of him there and enjoy these quiet moments. Soon, his breathing changes. He's fallen asleep and I have to smile. It's so damn wonderful to have him possessively wrapped around me even with his hand still holding one breast. Just as quickly, I follow him into dreamland. It's not a wonder, as I would follow him anywhere.

A tap on my nose wakes me. Chase is gone. Since Violet's gotten better, he's gone to practice early and comes home late. I don't complain because I know he'll be there for me in a second if I need him.

I open my eyes and find Violet with a pink substance all over her face. I sit up and bend down to examine it. It smells fruity.

Laughing, I say, "What have you gotten into?"

"Yogie," she says, all proud of herself.

I glance at the time. It's past nine in the morning and I groan. I've overslept. I should've set an alarm. Violet decided to get herself breakfast and had gotten a yogurt.

"Let's clean you up and fix you a proper breakfast. How about pancakes?"

She nods and we do, making a mess of the kitchen while we prepare. But I don't care. I love how happy she is. It's so great how fast kids bounce back from illnesses as if they were never there.

That afternoon, my bestie video calls.

"Hey," she says somberly.

I tell her all about Violet. I look over to where my baby sings and dances to the cartoon character on the TV.

"Everything's great. She's responding well."

"I'm still getting tested," Beth says.

"God, I miss you. I hope you can come out again for your vacation."

"Me too. But so many people have quit in the last month, you wouldn't believe."

I feel guilty. "I wish I could come back."

"No, you don't." She laughs. "You're in Italy for goodness' sake."

"How's Joshua?" I tease.

She may have pushed him toward me, but I know my friend secretly crushes on the guy. He is hot. I can't blame her.

A blush flames her face. "He asked me out. You're not mad, are you?"

I feign shock. "No way. He's all yours."

"Oh, I'm being paged. No rest for the weary. I'll call you later."

When we hang up, a pang of longing for Chicago hits me. I

dial another number to FaceTime. It's not long before Owen's face pops up on the screen.

"Hey, stranger."

"Hey, you."

There's an awkward moment before he ends it.

"How's everything in Italy? How's Violet and Chase?"

My smile seems to take over the screen. "They're great."

Then I explain everything.

"I'm sorry, Andi. Holly and I will get tested."

Feeling guilty, I say, "I didn't call you for that. I miss you guys."

"I know. We miss you too. But I want to help and I'm sure Holly would too."

"Is she around?"

My time is all mixed up when it comes to what time it is in Chicago.

"Yeah, do you want me to put her on?"

"Yes, I miss her so and Violet will want to see her." I take the iPad over to the living room. "Violet, see who's on the screen."

Owen waves at her and then Holly fits into the picture.

Violet waves and soon the two girls are talking and singing. The doorbell rings.

"Owen, I'll be right back."

The living room is in the sightline of the front door. I can hear Violet and Holly with their garbled speak. Violet is showing her a new doll she got from Chase, who spoils her rotten.

When I open the door, I'm shocked to see Lucia there. I'd convinced the security guy he could make a quick run to grab lunch, and I halt the door opening and move to make sure she can't see inside.

She lifts her chin and asks, "Is Chase here?"

"He's not," I say, hating that she can hear my daughter.

The woman doesn't deserve it. Why can't she just walk away gracefully?

She glances down at her belly bump, which I ignore. "I have to talk to him."

I move to step outside, but leave the door cracked open behind me so I can hear Violet. Owen is talking to the girls and I know I have a few minutes.

"Can I offer you a piece of advice?" I ask.

She rolls her eyes. "Why? You are only jealous."

"Actually, I'm not. Yes, you are more beautiful than I am, which puzzles me. Why chase after a man who doesn't want you?"

"Because I am better than you. He should want me."

Her accent is thick, but I understand every word she says.

"The thing is, men don't marry a woman to look at. They marry a woman to live with. For whatever reason, Chase wants me. That doesn't take away anything about you. It just means you aren't for him. But there are probably a million men out there who would walk over crushed glass to kneel at your feet. You deserve a man like that."

"I deserve Chase."

"Look, I get it. He's a great catch. But we both know he tells it like it is. If he finds you here with that fake baby bump around your waist—" Her eyes grow wide. "—Yes, I'm a neonatal nurse. I've seen lots of baby bumps, especially after women give birth. And I myself tried one on when buying maternity clothes. I know the difference. Anyway, Chase won't be happy. And he's done so much for you already. You'd do well to find a man that cherishes you."

I'm not sure if what I said did the trick or if the sound and sight of Chase's car coming up the drive chases her away. She flees to her car, turning on the engine just as he parks. I glance back and see Violet singing into the iPad, so Owen and Holly are still there.

Chase's narrowed gaze follows the car as it speeds off before he heads over to me.

"Why was she here?"

I shrug. "She wanted to talk to you." He blows out a breath and I see steam forming. I hold up a hand. "I handled it. I'm hopeful that's the last we'll see of her."

"I should talk to her."

"Don't." I shake my head. "You'll encourage her. Your best bet is to ignore her. She knows how you feel. She's just finding a way to initiate contact."

"Did she look pregnant?"

"She's not. It's fake."

His jaw tightens. "Trust me. I called her on it. That's why she left so fast. She knows she has nothing you want."

He kisses me then glances over my head since he's taller than me. "Who is Violet talking to?"

"Holly and Owen."

His brow arches. I step back into the house, giving me another inch or two. Then I draw him close. On my toes, I plant a kiss on his lips.

"Don't be jealous. He's just a friend and that's all he's ever been. He asked about you. Besides, you're home early."

"I can't stay away from my girls."

I grin and he smiles back, gracing me with another kiss before he goes to Violet and chats with Owen. I watch in fascination as they actually get into a conversation when Violet and Holly have said all they want to.

When I pull out the roast, I finally get why Mom never worked outside the home. There's something satisfying about taking care of my family. Yes, I miss working as a nurse. But I don't feel bored like I thought I would.

Chase surprises me while I lift the lid of the pot to smell the gravy I've worked up for our smashed potatoes.

"God, woman, is there anything you can't do?" he asks as he puts his arms around me from behind.

"I can't play soccer." I glance at him over my shoulder and offer up a wink.

"Football," he groans. "Not you too."

I turn in his arms.

"Do you want to teach me the difference?" I tease. "One is a full-contact sport, right?"

He tugs me flush against him. "You're killing me. I want you right here."

We both glance over at Violet. Then he gives me a wicked grin. "I will have you later and you'll pay for teasing me."

He slaps my ass and I yelp. Then he's back over with our daughter. She hands him a doll and I stifle a giggle. When he does his little girl's voice, it's so endearing.

"Team Wilde," I say to myself.

Things go so great the next week, Violet and I go to Chase's last regular season game. Though they are slated to go to the playoffs.

Violet cheers as I try to explain what's going on. "Dada ball." She points.

Sure enough, Chase dribbles, as it's called, down the field to the goal. When he called it that once, I thought he was talking about basketball. *Boys and their sports.*

Violet jumps up in my lap. "Goal."

She says it perfectly as her dad scores. It's one of those moments I wish for two more hands and clairvoyance. I would have liked to get that on camera. But someone taps me and points to the big screen. There Violet is on her feet with a fist in the air saying the word again and again.

It's exhilarating and unnerving at the same time. Have they found us? Would we be targets for the paparazzi?

But all of that is moot when time runs out and fans storm the field. Chase is surrounded, having scored the last goal to break the tie. I stand there and watch my man. He pushes his way through the crowd, hops over the barrier, and treads up the stands to us. If there had been any doubt who we are to him, that's all gone. He kisses Violet first and then me.

Later that night, when it's just the two of us, I ask the question.

"Did the press ask you about us?"

He couldn't stay with us after the game. His contract requires he speak to the press after games. We'd gone home and waited for him to arrive.

"They did. But it's fine. It's time the world knows that I'm yours. Maybe Lucia won't try anything else."

I hope so.

It must've worked, because after that, Lucia never shows her face again.

Two mornings later, he's gone again. With the playoffs beginning, they didn't get but a day's break, which we spent taking Violet to the zoo.

He's gone to practice and I've let Violet sleep because we had a long day yesterday. When I check the time, it's well past ten and Violet still hasn't gotten up.

When I enter her room, my heart stops. Her cheeks are flushed and her skin is hot—too hot. I don't need a thermometer. I rush to my bathroom and turn on the shower. She's barely opened her eyes when I scoop her up.

"Mama, feel bad."

There's no time to call Chase yet. I need to bring her fever down and call the doctor before I call him. It could be nothing, but deep in my heart, I know better.

THIRTY-EIGHT

Chase

THE TEAM IS ELATED when I score the winning goal. It's the second round in the playoffs, which means we'll be advancing to the finals. Neither team had scored the entire match, and we were wondering whether we would go into overtime. But my big break came in the final minutes. The left midfielder passed me the ball and I saw an opening between the sweeper and the stopper, so I took the shot and fired. Since I'm the team's striker, they were counting on me, and I was able to deliver. The ball sailed into the goal for a perfect score.

After the match, the media tries to interview me, but the coaches are great in fielding all questions. They know the players need to escape, because we face another game in two days.

I head to the locker room with the other players and check my phone. I'm more than a little surprised when there isn't a congratulatory text from Andi. I know she watched the game. What's going on here? Then it hits me: Something must've happened.

I tap her name on my phone and wait, but nothing. All the circuits must be busy since there are so many people here.

"Fuck!"

"What's up?" One of my teammates hears me and asks.

"I can't get a line here. All circuits are busy or something."

"Try the landline in the coach's office. They must have one."

"Great idea. Thanks."

Jogging over there, I barge inside. All the coaches' heads snap up as I enter.

"Hey, can I use the phone in here? I can't get a line out," I explain.

"Sure." They all look at me strangely. I'm in the *I don't give a fuck* moment. Picking up the phone, I dial Andi's number. It rings and I breathe again.

"Hello?" she says hesitantly.

"Hey, baby, it's me. I couldn't call from my cell phone. There are too many people here."

"Oh."

"I was worried when you didn't text me."

"Chase."

It's the way she says my name that clues me in. "It's Violet, isn't it?"

"We're in the hospital. She spiked a fever and things went south."

"I'm coming home."

"You can't come home."

"You wanna bet?" I hang up the phone before she can say anything else. Then I approach the coaching staff.

"My daughter is in the hospital. Things are really bad. I have to leave."

"Leave? You can't leave. We have a game in three days. We're in the finals."

"I'm sorry. If she's better, I'll be back. If not, then you'll have to compete without me. My daughter's life is much more important than any football match will ever be."

"You have a contract with us, Wilde. You'll breach it."

"Then I guess you'll have to do what you have to do, but my

daughter is extremely sick and I have to go. I'm sorry. I never meant to let the team down, but I also have an obligation to my family."

Not wasting another second, I run to the locker room to quickly shower so I can get to the airport. It's going to be hell getting out of the stadium as it is, but getting a flight is going to be another problem.

As I'm packing up my bag, I call Max. Luckily this time, the call goes through. "Max, I need your help. I need a flight back to Rome. Violet is in the hospital. I don't care how you have to do it, but get me back there as soon as you can."

"I'll do my best. What did the coaches say?"

"You don't want to know."

Max arranges for a car to pick me up and charters a flight to get me back to Rome. All of my teammates send their prayers with me. I arrive at the hospital at a reasonable hour. Even though I'm a mess when I walk into Violet's room, I put on the best front possible. I have to be strong for my girls.

Andi runs into my arms as soon as she sees me. Violet looks like the wilted tiny flower that she is. I rarely get the urge to cry … but this is one of those times. When I gaze at her miniscule form lying in that hospital bed, all I want to do is break down and bawl like a baby. But I don't dare. I'm the captain of Team Wilde, and I will not let any weakness show.

"How is she?" I whisper, because Violet is asleep.

Andi motions me toward the hall. Once outside, she fills me in.

"Not good. All her counts are extremely low. The doctors say she stopped responding to the drugs. They're talking bone marrow transplant."

"How much time does she have before that?"

"They're not saying. They're going to start blood transfusions in the morning. We can donate."

"Okay."

"She's on antibiotics to get her infection under control."

"Why didn't they do a blood transfusion today?"

"Oh, they did a white cell transfusion. Tomorrow they're doing the whole blood. I'm not sure the reasoning. I have to be honest. My brain hasn't been quite here. I was so upset when she woke up so sick."

I pull her close into my arms. "It's too much for one person to handle alone, Andi. That's why I came."

We stand together in silence for a few minutes, and then I say, "Babe, I think we need to go home."

"Home?"

"Back to the States. If Violet needs bone marrow, it's time. We need our families close by. Even if none of them are matches. It's all about them being our support system."

"Are you sure? This is your career."

I take her shoulders in my hands and catch her gaze. "You and Violet are my life. Not my career in football. If I lost either of you, I'd have nothing. Football is temporary. You and Violet are permanent. Football is a job. You and Violet are my family. Am I getting through?"

"Yeah, you are."

"Then the decision is made. We'll talk to the doctors. We also need to find out about who is a match. A lot of people got tested. Hopefully, one of them is at least a fifty percent."

In the morning, Violet wakes up and tries to grin when she sees me, but it never quite makes it. She's cranky and it's no wonder. The poor thing is ill.

The doctor comes in and we inform him of our decision.

"I don't recommend that she flies on a commercial airliner. With her immune system, all the germs floating around the recirculated air could pose a problem for her."

"That won't be a problem. I was planning on chartering a flight anyway," I say.

Andi adds, "And I'm a nurse, so I can give her any medications that might be required on the flight."

"Good," the doctor replies. "Then let's get this transfusion underway."

It gives us great relief to know that my blood is O negative and I'm able to provide Violet the blood she needs, along with Andi, who is A positive, which is Violet's blood type. At first we were worried about her getting blood from a random donor, but after they assured us we could be the donors, we felt much more at ease about her transfusions.

"Doctor, did you ever get the results of the bone marrow testing?" I ask. "I'm talking about whether anyone is at least a partial match."

"Ah, yes. I'll give all that to you before you travel. I believe one of your family members ended up being a match. I don't recall the name, but you're very lucky. A parent only has a one in two hundred chance of being a match, and a sibling only twenty-five percent. Seventy percent of donors come from the registry program. This has worked to your benefit indeed. The other thing I'll need is which hospital you'll want her to go to. I believe we discussed Children's Hospital in Nashville, Ms. James. Is that still your decision?"

"Yes, we think that's the best choice. And you agree?" Andi asks.

"I do. They have state-of-the-art treatment for aplastic anemia in children," the doctor answers.

"Then can you make the arrangements?"

"I'll be happy to. I should have that completed by this afternoon, so if you want to make your flight arrangements for tomorrow, that would be fine."

"Thank you, doctor," Andi says.

We have a lot to do in a day. I place a call to Max, asking him to charter a flight for us for tomorrow. And then I ask him to book us a hotel in Nashville close to the hospital. I'm sure we'll be staying with Violet, but one of us may need a break to sleep and our family may need to have a room or something.

Then there's the matter of packing our things and closing up the house.

"Chase, don't worry about all that. I can pack up what you leave behind, or you can come back and retrieve it when Violet gets better."

"But, Max, it doesn't make sense to pay for the house if we're not going to be there."

"I'll handle it. I can have someone come in, pack up your things, move them to storage until you return. Just pack up what you'll be needing for the next few months and I'll handle the rest."

"Good idea. Thanks, Max. My mind is spinning."

"I'm sure it is. And you know you'll be hearing about your contract."

"I do. I'll let you field everything until the crisis with Violet has passed. I don't want to be disturbed with this unless it's an emergency."

"Understood. I'll get to work on your flight."

"You're a lifesaver, Max."

I relay everything to Andi and she seems more relaxed about it. "It does ease my mind, but can you afford that flight?"

"Stop worrying about the money. I've already told you I can afford it. Did you know that European football players make much more than American football players do? Well, the good ones, anyway."

"Seriously?"

"Yeah, so let's worry about getting our things together."

She's standing next to Violet's bed, smoothing the little one's hair back. Violet is holding her favorite stuffed bunny. Her coloring is nearly ashen. It's scary. I want her to be laughing and running around the house again. Hopefully, the bone marrow transplant will do exactly that and we can have our giggling little girl back.

Andi slips into the bathroom for a minute, and while she's in there, the nurse comes in to hook Violet up with her blood transfusion. Now I'm more than happy Andi was a go for the port. All they have to do is basically plug the line into the port in Violet's chest. No needle stick for my little one. She doesn't miss a beat as she lies there. But she's so listless, it scares me. The nurse leaves and Andi walks out of the bathroom. I expect to see a sign of relief on her face when she notices the transfusion running into our daughter. Instead, Andi covers her face and cries.

Immediately, I rush to her side and wrap her in my arms. I think she's sad seeing Violet so ill, but then I hear her words.

"I'm not pregnant. I just started my period."

Shit.

"It's okay, baby. We'll have many more opportunities to try. Don't be sad. It's all going to work out. I promise." She sobs within the circle of my arms and I only hope I can fulfill the promise I just made to her.

THIRTY-NINE

Andi

_____

AFTER CHASE EXPLAINS THE PLANS, I shake my head. "They're just things. Most of it I don't really care about. But Violet's going to want her bear, Mr. Giggles, and CoCo, the doll you bought her."

"Max can get those."

"He can," I admit. "I don't have anything worth that much but my grandmother's ring. I can't lose it."

Tears burst from my eyes and I cover my face, feeling stupid for wanting a ring when my daughter is ill.

Chase tugs me against him and strokes a hand down my back.

"It's fine. I can go get it. The doc says Violet is stable. Plus, she's sleeping."

I step out of his embrace. Because it had been wishful thinking, I wasn't prepared.

"I'll go. There are things I need."

I give him a knowing look I hope he gets so I don't have to spell it out again about my body's failures. I've failed Violet twice. Maybe it's fate for me not to be a mother again. I turn

277

from Chase. It's selfish of me to cry in front of him when I should be putting up a brave front for them both.

Chase comes over. "Max is coming to pick you up." He tips my chin. "It's going to be fine."

I nod slowly, feeling the weight of the world on my shoulders.

By the time I make it back to the house, I don't hear what Max says. I drift through the door like a lone tumbleweed over cracked earth on a desert plain.

First, I pack a few things for Violet, including clothes and her favorite toys and books. When I'm done, I stand in the doorway and remember when I first arrived and how the room had become a home.

Covering my mouth, I escape the thoughts of long-past happy times and go into my room. It looks exactly like the day I arrived. I grab the handful of jewelry I own and a few other things for myself. Then I take a shower and cry. I let it all out so that when I go back to the hospital I can be strong again.

"Are you okay?" Max, a good-looking older man, asks.

He isn't ancient, just some years older than we are. He has a kind smile and eyes that see more than I want him to.

"I will be. I'm going to get a few things for Chase just in case."

He agrees and I go into our room. I look at the tangle of sheets and remember how happy I'd been. I quickly get a bag together for him and I'm reminded how I'm not sure if I got all his favorite things.

Suck it up, I chide myself. In the back of my mind I worry that Chase is thinking about all the time from his daughter I stole from him. Or maybe that's my guilt.

I inhale and let it all out before walking out.

"I'm ready."

I glance around and hate that Chase is letting this place go. It's where we found each other again. I'm not going to tell him.

It's just sentiment that's not important. Home is where the heart is and all that.

When we arrive back, Violet is awake and asking for food. She has a smile on her face that takes all my worries away. The doctor stops me before we enter.

"We can only take so much blood from you in any given week. And Chase as well. Do you want to use donor blood?"

I meet his gaze. "Is it necessary? I don't want to add any more risks."

He nods. "She should be fine with what we have, but I'm not sure how long the good effects will last. When you get to the States, she may need more. If you unwisely donate again, you'll be putting yourself at risk."

Though I nod, I would give my life for hers if necessary.

"Look who's here. It's Mama," Chase says.

Violet holds out her hands and I go over to hug her.

"I brought Mr. Giggles and CoCo."

She takes my offerings and hugs them and gives them each a kiss. Chase grins at me. Though I smile along with them, I know this good feeling won't last.

By the time we get on the plane, I'm exhausted. With Violet cradled to my chest, I close my eyes and drift off. I wake with Chase taking our sleeping daughter from my arms.

"There's a bed in the back. She'll be more comfortable," he says.

I nod and close my eyes just for a second. When Chase wakes me up again, I'm surprised and alarmed. I hadn't meant to fall back asleep, but the worry in his eyes has me trying to jump out of my seat only to be tethered by the seat belt.

"What's wrong?" I ask while trying to get the damn thing off.

It's a stupid question. I know what's wrong.

"I'm sorry to wake you, but she's getting warm."

"No, it's fine. It's fine," I add and take a breath. The dark circles under his eyes say that he's tired too. "Get some rest. I'll give her some medicine and she'll be better soon." I'm proud of how sure I sound. But I need him to get some sleep.

When I stand, I kiss him soundly on his lips and then pat his arm, urging him into the seat. Reluctantly he does, but I'm not sure how long he'll stay. I make my way to the back of the plane I'd barely taken notice of when we boarded.

I pass a table flanked by leather benches and wood grain cabinetry so fine I'm not sure I can touch it. It's certainly fancy. Through the open door, I see Violet curled up with a light blanket covering her. Mr. Giggles is tucked under her arm. She hadn't clung to toys before Chase bought her some. Now she hangs on to the bear like a lifesaver.

Brushing hair from her flushed face, I feel the beginnings of a fever. For a minute, I can't remember where I stashed the medicine, but then I spot the mini backpack I'd tucked everything she'd need in. I ignore the thermometer and pull out the small notebook where I'd recorded the time she'd gotten her last dose of medicine. I hadn't put it on my phone so it would be accessible for both Chase and me.

I check the time. I'd slept most of the flight. I wake her and give her a dose of Tylenol, which should hold her off for another few hours until we reach Nashville. She quickly falls back asleep, barely up long enough to swallow the medicine. I press a kiss to her head, and when I turn, Chase is there.

"You scared me," I say with my hand to my heart.

"Is she okay?"

I run a hand over my head and sigh. "She'll be fine. You should rest."

"I'm good."

I close the distance between us. "You haven't slept. I can take this watch. Why don't you lie down next to her? I'm sure you'll both sleep better."

He draws me on the bed with him. We sandwich our daughter between us as he threads his fingers through mine.

"Tell me it will all work out," he says.

To hear him say that freaks me out. He's been the strong one, and now he's asking me.

"It will. They will need to make her stable before any bone marrow transplant. She'll need chemo before that, so they need her as healthy as possible before they tear down her immune system."

"Sometimes I forget you're a nurse. That wasn't exactly reassuring," he says.

I squeeze his hand. "I'm sorry. It's—" I blow out a frustrating breath. "I'm scared, but this is something that happens every day, unfortunately, and is a tried-and-true practice. I have faith in our daughter's recovery because I can't survive any other outcome."

He says nothing and we lie there quietly. Gratefully, exhaustion pulls him under. Gently, I get up because I can't sleep. I need to watch over her to make sure the medicine takes hold. Otherwise, I'll need to sponge her down with a cool cloth to keep the fever at bay.

When we land, it's too soon for Chase. He hasn't had enough rest.

"I'll be fine," he says when I put a hand to his cheek.

He carries Violet to our car service not too far from the plane. We land at a private airport to streamline everything. Still, we have to show passports to get cleared.

When we arrive at the hospital, there is an overwhelming amount of paperwork. Gratefully, our families are here waiting for us. Tears I've held at bay rain down my cheeks when I see Mom. Her arms wrap around me briefly and I wish she could make things better like she used to when I was a kid. Chase's mom gives him the third degree for not getting enough rest. But I can see the worry in her eyes, just like in my mom's.

"I can take care of all this," Chase says.

"I've got this. Go see to our families."

I have health insurance through my job's Cobra program.

Chase can pay, but why not use the benefits we have available to us? Whatever it doesn't cover, he can take care of.

After she's settled in her large private room and once again asleep, I stand with the family huddled at the opposite end.

About that time, my brother Mark rushes into the room. He's alone because his girlfriend is on tour and couldn't leave to come with him. His eyes have a wild look about them as he searches the room, but when they land on me, he relaxes a bit.

I'm grateful he's here. He's Violet's savior, her best match for a donor.

"Tell me what you need me to do. I'm here for as long as you need," he says. Then I run into his arms and have a major breakdown.

FORTY

Chase

THIS HELPLESS STATE is as bad as it's ever been. Now that we've found out that I can't donate my own bone marrow to save my daughter's life, it's even worse. At least before there was a spark of hope that I could contribute at least something. But not now. Even Andi's brother is of more use than I am.

My brother, Fletcher, and his wife, Cassidy, arrive soon after. We man-hug and Violet's room is bursting with our combined families. The nurse comes in and tells us to keep it down. We're being entirely too noisy, and then she tells us there's a family room right down the hall where we can all talk if we want.

Andi looks at me and motions with her head.

"No, I'm not leaving your side," I say.

"You need to explain everything to the families so they know where we stand."

"Andi, I think you're the more knowledgeable one to do that. Why don't you go and I'll stay here with Violet?"

The worry in her eyes tells me she doesn't want to leave our daughter. "You'll only be gone a few minutes. I think I'm capable of handling her for that long." I wink at her.

"Okay. But I'll be right back."

Violet holds out CoCo to me and I sit on the bed with her. "Do you want me to kiss CoCo?"

She nods and her curls go flying. I comply and she's suddenly smiling. "Dada in bed."

"Okay." I slide my large frame next to her tiny one and we play games with her stuffed toys. She likes to have fake fights. For some reason, this makes her laugh. It's in the old *Sesame Street* fashion, where one animal goes after the other, only it ends up with both of us laughing.

I place my hand on her forehead and she seems much cooler than she was earlier.

"Thirsty," she says.

I hand her the cup of ice water and she sucks it down.

A nurse comes into the room and hooks up another bag of blood. She takes Violet's temperature and says it's only ninety-nine degrees.

"That's good. I'm not sure what it was earlier, but it was high on the flight."

"Let's get this transfusion going. I think Dr. Rosenberg will be dropping by soon. He's already ordered some supplementation for her to get her built up for the immune suppression. But he'll explain all of that."

"Good, because my partner is the nurse and expert, not me. And she's down the hall with the family right now."

All of a sudden, Violet yells, "Hungy!"

The nurse laughs. "Let's see what we can do about that, shall we?"

"That's probably a good idea."

Not much after that, the whole Team Wilde enters the room. Violet stares at everyone. Andi walks up to her bed and asks, "Violet, remember Nana and Grammy?"

Both of our moms walk up to her as she stares. Then her sweet grin spreads across her face as she repeats, "Nana, Gammy."

They sit on the bed and chat with her as I tell Andi what the nurse said. It's only a few minutes later when the doctor arrives.

He scans the room and then wants to know who the parents are. Andi and I greet him and he warmly introduces himself. The others want to know if they should leave, but we tell them no, especially Mark, since he will be Violet's donor. After all the introductions are made, Dr. Rosenberg goes to Violet's bed and asks to meet her friends.

"I'd really like to get to know them."

She holds out Mr. Giggles and CoCo and he talks to them like they are his long-lost buddies. It's easy to see he's a likable person. I'm beginning to build trust in him already and he hasn't even talked about her treatment regimen yet. He has Violet laughing and he tickles her exactly as though he knows what her funny spots are.

When he's spent a good amount of time with Violet, he turns his attention to us.

"Now then, let's discuss her treatment plan. I've reviewed her chart and all her tests. Her case is extremely puzzling to us due to her age. It's unusual to get one so young. The good news is that she responded so well at first to the stimulants. That's encouraging. We have every reason to believe she'll do well with the stem cell transplant."

"Stem cell? I thought she was getting bone marrow?" I ask.

"She is. We use the terms interchangeably. The stem cells are what she actually needs and they are found in the bone marrow."

"I see."

"Our journey begins today. We start by getting her as strong as possible. We give her nourishment through her port in the form of vitamins and minerals, along with liquid nutrition. She can also eat as much as she wants. For the next week, it's crucial for her to get strong. Because then comes the tough part."

Looking across the room, I notice everyone is hanging onto each of his words.

Andi stops him there. "Do we need to be wearing masks or gloves?"

"Good question. And yes. I would like you all to start doing that, along with gowns. That will continue until she's out of the woods. And another thing. Aside from immediate family, she is to have no visitors. The fewer the germs we introduce to her, the better the outcome."

Processing everything he's telling us is a bitch. "Will this scare her? Seeing us in masks, gloves, and gowns?" I ask.

"At first. But we handle it well up here. We make a game out of it. She'll have her own set so she can play too." He winks.

Andi half-smiles. It doesn't reach her eyes, but it's a start.

"Then what?"

"Let me just fill you in on something about me. I won't sugarcoat anything. I don't believe in it. The following week is going to be a bear."

Violet hollers, "Bear."

Dr. Rosenberg turns to her and holds out a fist. "That's right. Bear!" She holds her tiny one out and they bump theirs together. I've never seen her do that before and I want to pick her up and swing her around, but I can't because she's getting that damn transfusion.

"Go, Violet!" I yell instead.

In turn, she hollers, "Bear!" again.

We all laugh.

Dr. Rosenberg takes a seat on her bed and continues. "Every day she'll get a round of what's basically chemotherapy and we tear down her immune system. That's why it's critical we don't introduce her to any germs and she stays in a sterile environment. She'll feel like someone beat her to a pulp. I'm not going to lie. It's the worst, and you're going to hate me for it. That's when her donor comes in. Who is it?"

Mark steps forward. "That would be me."

"You're our superstar. If I could only tell you how incredible this is to have a family member be a match, you wouldn't believe it. The odds aren't in your favor."

Andi interrupts the conversation by saying, "We're not actually blood relatives. I was adopted by these amazing people and somehow it's turned into a miracle."

Dr. Rosenberg's eyes bug out. "Wow. In all my years, I've never heard of this. This truly is a miracle."

"Yes, it is," Andi agrees, smiling.

Mark puts his arm over her shoulders and hugs her. Then he asks, "So where do I fit in?"

"Ah, yes. Once we deem Violet ready, we extract your marrow, which we do under anesthesia, and then we transfuse it into her. It's as easy as that. Afterward, we watch for graft versus host disease, which was why we have to kill her immune system. We want to remove the possibility of her rejecting all of that lovely marrow you so lovingly donated."

"Sounds like a breeze," Mark says.

"It is for you. It's an entirely different chapter for this one." The doctor motions toward Violet. Andi crosses her arms and hugs her body. Anxiousness is written all over her expression. I'm sure my own mirrors hers. This has to work. I refuse to think of the other option.

Dr. Rosenberg stands and asks, "Does anyone have any questions for me before I leave?"

"None for me. Andi?" I ask her.

"Not now. I'm sure I will later. So as of now, we're on schedule to begin her chemo in a week, and then when you think her immune system is crashed, she'll get the bone marrow, correct?"

"That's correct."

Andi turns to Mark and says, "Looks like you're here for a while. Or, you can leave and come back."

Dr. Rosenberg steps forward. "We'd like to run some tests on him to make sure he's completely healthy. It's routine, so I don't think leaving is an option at this time."

"Andi, I wouldn't think of leaving anyway. It's not more than a couple of weeks."

"But what about Riley?" Andi asks.

"She's perfectly fine and sends her love, as does Ryder, her brother."

Fletcher pipes in and says, "Oh, yeah, I forgot. Ryder told me to tell you if you needed him here to give a shout-out."

Riley and Ryder are twins and my cousins. Riley is a golfer in the LPGA and on tour right now, and Ryder is an ace pitcher in the MLB. There isn't a damn thing either one can do, so I won't pull them away from their games. They are both in the middle of their seasons and need to keep their concentration steady.

"Thanks. I need to give him a call."

"No, you have more important things at hand now. It can wait," Fletcher says.

He's right. I stare at my daughter and know I would give both my feet—hell, my life, for her to be well.

The next week is amazing. Violet thrives. Whatever they are slipping into her port must be magic. She has more energy than I've ever seen. Andi and I both are thrilled. Only we know the bottom will be falling out soon. We make fun with the masks and gowns and I pretend to be Mama and Andi pretends to be me. Violet even pretends to be her Grampie and Grammy. It is hilarious. She loves the damn things.

Until ... they start her chemo. The first day isn't bad. They'd warned us what would happen. They warned us not to delude ourselves into thinking she'd be okay. Because the first treatment sort of gives you that false sense of security. Violet doesn't feel bad at all afterward. She is her old happy self, yapping on about this or that. She plays with her things as usual. Until nighttime when the side effects hit. They've given her the preemptive doses of anti-nausea drugs, and they keep her from throwing up, but she becomes very lethargic. We'd gotten so used to her energy, it's a bucket of ice water to witness the change.

Day two is much the same. She starts out like she'd gone to bed—lethargic and listless. They come and hook up the evil drugs. She is okay for a while, but the decline continues. Her pink skin begins to lose its color. And at night, she is ghostly.

Andi asks the nurse.

"It's perfectly normal. Remember, we're killing her immune system. The main thing is she doesn't spike a fever."

Andi and I settle in for another long night. We're both strong; we can do this. But by day six, we are two broken people trying to bolster each other up. Her beautiful curls falling out of the tiny head that she can barely lift off her pillow is my undoing. I storm out of the room, ready to kill anyone in my path. And that anyone happens to be my brother, Fletcher. He grabs me and pulls me into the closest bathroom. I sag in his arms as I cry like a baby.

Words that don't even make sense to me gush out of my mouth as Fletcher tries to calm me. "I've tried to hold it together. I have, Fletch. But I'm not sure I can do this. It's breaking my heart."

"I know. But you don't have a choice. That little girl in there needs you now more than ever. And so does her mother. You're going to have to dig deep, Chase. You'll figure out a way. You're a Wilde, and Wildes never give up."

He's right. We never do.

Nodding, I take several deep breaths, then move to the sink where I splash ice-cold water onto my face.

"When was the last time you slept?" he asks.

"I have no idea."

"You're stressed to the max and zero sleep isn't doing you any favors."

"Yeah, well, that ship has sailed."

"No, it hasn't. You and Andi should go back to the hotel and get some rest. Cassie and I can keep watch for you. Violet is mostly sleeping now anyway. There isn't anything you can do."

"I can't leave. I could never leave her side."

"You have to sleep or you won't make it through this. Why don't you and Andi do shifts? I can stay with you while she goes, and Cassie can stay with her while you go."

That makes a little more sense.

"That way one of you will be with her at all times. If something were to come up, you'd only be a phone call away. And the hotel is a five-minute walk from here."

"Let me talk to Andi about it."

When I do, she agrees it will help. I have her go first. We do six-hour intervals for sleep. We decide if it works, we'll extend it to eight.

Andi and I hug for a long time before I promise to call if anything happens. Nothing does. The doctor makes his visit while she's gone.

"Okay, we're on day minus two. One more day and we'll be ready. I can share this news with you because your donor has you on the HIPAA agreement. As you're aware, all of his tests checked out, so we're a go. The day after tomorrow, day zero, he'll report to outpatient surgery for the bone marrow extraction. That shouldn't take long at all. They use a short-acting anesthesia and then observe him for a while. Usually, the patient is in recovery for only a couple of hours and then released. He'll be able to go back to the hotel—not alone, of course. And then Violet will get the transfusion. Only one more day of the bad stuff. And then we monitor her for rejection and side effects."

"I'll be honest. This treatment has been awful on her mother and me."

"It usually is. The patient has it bad, but on so many meds they don't understand what's going on. She's done extremely well so far. Let's keep our fingers crossed it holds out until she receives the bone marrow."

Fletcher keeps my mind occupied until Andi returns with

Cassie. She looks somewhat better so maybe I'll feel a bit better after a nap. I relay what Dr. Rosenberg said and then Fletcher and I leave.

When I get back to the hotel, I take a long, hot shower, my first real one in days. It relaxes me so I crawl into the bed I haven't slept in since we've arrived. It seems like I've only been asleep for a few minutes when my ringing phone awakens me.

"Andi," I say, alarm clinging to every pore.

"Violet has spiked a low-grade fever. The antibiotics she's been on should be enough to handle it, but they're switching things up a bit."

"I'm on the way."

FORTY-ONE

Andi

─────────

It's hard to watch your child sick or hurt. I sit in a chair with my gloved hand stroking Chase's silky hair. Exhausted as we both are, he falls asleep talking. At least I'd gotten a nap, so I don't move where I sit in fear I'll wake him or Violet.

I use the back of my free hand to wipe at my silent tears. The latex doesn't exactly do a great job of removing the moisture, but it'll have to do since Chase and I have to wear gloves, masks, and gowns to be around Violet now that her immune system is basically nonexistent. Since they are both resting at the moment, I don't have to be strong in front of either of them.

We send Fletcher and Cassie home. She has a business to run and there's nothing they can do at the moment. My parents and Chase's are both retired. They are back at the hotel with Mark, who can work from anywhere.

I get off the phone from telling them about Violet's fever, which had spiked, but finally they've gotten it under control. I pray for nothing short of a miracle with the bone marrow transplant. I don't want Violet to have to undergo this procedure again.

Then I think about my baby or lack thereof, which only

makes me cry harder. There hasn't been time for Chase and me to even think about sex or another child.

As if he hears my thoughts, he stirs.

"Sorry," he mutters, sitting up from where his head had rested on my shoulder.

Then he notices my tears, and before I can wipe them away, he's there leaning in and kissing my temple, or doing his best imitation of it through his mask.

"She's going to make it," he says and uses the pads of his thumbs to remove the moisture from my face.

His conviction is as strong as ever. I pull on a brave face and nod.

My phone vibrates in my pocket. It's Beth. I signal to Chase I'm going to take the call outside.

"Hey," I say into the phone as the door clicks shut behind me.

"Andi, oh, girlie. I wish I could be there for you."

"I know, but there's nothing you can really do."

There's nothing I can do either, but I keep my feeling of helplessness to myself.

"It's awesome your brother is a match."

I don't go into the details. I'd texted her the details about how he's only a fifty percent match.

"Yes, it's like a miracle."

Though the odds were in our favor that a nonblood-related person would be a match, the odds of that person somehow being a part of my family was one in a million.

"You know if you need me, I'll drop everything and come."

I laugh, though it's with little humor. "And get fired? What about Joshua?"

"We don't have to talk about me," she says.

"No, really, give me something else to think about."

She distracts me for five minutes with a tale that has my head spinning.

"No way," I say.

"Yes."

Just when I think she's about to explain, Chase pokes his head out and I hear Violet murmuring something.

"She's asking for you."

Guilt rushes in that I wasn't there when she woke up.

"I have to go," I tell Beth.

"Yes, I hear. Give her my love and call me anytime."

I agree and end the call, hurrying over to Violet's side, just in time for her to throw up. I don't get horrified. Instead, I tell her all is fine when it isn't.

The next few days are horrific, but the doc has cleared her for the procedure.

"Everything looks good. We'll take your brother back in the next hour," the doc says before leaving the room.

"I'm going to go talk to him."

Chase nods and I lightly kiss Violet's cheek through the mask I'm required to wear before leaving. She's out at the moment and it's a good time for me to sneak off and talk to my brother.

He lies in bed with Mom and Dad huddled nearby. I take his hand and remember all the times my big brother took care of me, and here he is doing it again.

"Mark, there are no words for what this means to Chase and me."

He squeezes my hand. "There's nothing I wouldn't do for you, sis, and especially for my niece."

I lean in and hug him. For so long, I felt lost, like not knowing who my biological parents were mattered. In the end, it hasn't. They gave me the greatest gift, a family: one who loves me unconditionally.

"I love you so much, big brother. I always have, even when I'm pissed at you."

He grins and the door opens. I turn to see Riley, who looks flushed like she's been running.

"You're here."

She and I had talked the night before. She'd sworn me to secrecy that she was coming in case she didn't make it in time because of her tournament.

"Hey," my brother says with moon eyes at the woman I suspect he's loved since they were little. "I didn't think you could come."

I give her a quick hug and step away so he can have time with her. When she leans in to kiss him, I indicate to him and my parents that I'm leaving.

The procedure is free of a lot of risks, I tell myself. I have nothing to worry about. Mark will be fine.

A couple of hours later, a nurse comes into Violet's room and hangs the bag filled with Mark's precious gift of bone marrow. Chase and I watch as it runs down the line into her port where the engraftment will begin.

I turn in his arms and a sob escapes me. His hold tightens and silently we take comfort in each other.

"Oh, sorry."

I glance up to see Riley poke her head into the room. Chase lets go of me and hugs his cousin. "Thank you for coming," he murmurs through the open door.

"I just wish there was more I could do," she says.

He nods. "Is Mark awake?"

"He is. I had to know he was okay before …"

I walk over to the door.

"I'm glad you were there. I couldn't be in two places at once."

We were both torn between two people we love.

"They're both strong. And Violet's getting his marrow that will make her even stronger."

Overcome with emotion, I walk over and hug her. When we pull apart, Chase says, "Do you mind staying with Andi for a few minutes? I'd like to talk to Mark."

We watch him walk away. Riley enters the room and goes through the procedure of putting on gloves, mask, and gown.

Her mask moves and I'm not sure what she's going to say. "You know I'm hopelessly and utterly in love with your brother."

The giggle that escapes me is a sure indication that I need this respite from all the worries I have.

"I know. When you would come for the holidays, I caught you both sneaking glances at each other. At first, Chase and I thought it was so gross, especially when we caught his brother and Cassie making out."

She laughs. "It was never the right time. When he finally made that first move, we were moving to California. Then when I came back, he was with someone or I was."

"You didn't miss much." I point my finger to my mouth and mime gagging. "Those girls were ..." I roll my eyes and we both giggle again. Then I sober. "I'll let you in on a little secret."

Her face is alight with humor. "What's that?"

"Never once have I seen him look at someone like he looks at you."

Her hand moves over her heart. "He's amazing."

I nod. "He is. He's one of the best guys I know. And I'm glad you two found each other."

She takes my hand. "And you ... Chase. I've never seen him so happy."

We laugh. "Isn't it funny how everything worked out? When Fletcher left and Cassie married that other guy, I thought if it couldn't work for them, how could it work for Chase and me? She asked him to choose between his career and her and he chose football. I didn't want to make that same mistake."

I can tell by the look Riley's giving me that she knows what I've never admitted out loud before. "So when Chase got the chance to go play soccer."

"Football," I correct.

She grins. "Okay, football. You encouraged him to go because you were afraid he wouldn't choose you either."

"Yes." It feels like such a weight is lifted off my shoulders to admit it. "Though I have to say, I think he wanted me to go with him. But I had dreams of my own, college and nursing school."

Neither means anything now. All that time had been wasted when I could have had him. In the end, he and Violet have always been my choice.

"But you found each other again, like I have your brother. Now it's up to the both of us not to mess that up."

She's right. There is nothing I wouldn't do for either of them. Nothing. So I sit and curl my hands around the Styrofoam cup. I vaguely wonder what Chase is saying to my brother.

FORTY-TWO

Chase

As I WALK to visit Mark, I can't help the fear that crawls up my spine. The next few weeks are going to be brutal. Only I'll have to contain the terror that grips me because no way in hell will I ever let Andi see how frightened I am.

The elevator dings and the doors whoosh open. I'm accompanied by a half dozen or more people. But I've never felt more alone than I have today. Day 0. Transplant day. I should be excited, right? I do my best to thrum it up, as I would before an important game. Except nothing happens. There is no excitement, only dread. Why do I feel like this? Is this a premonition? Is God going to steal my baby girl from me after this short period of time? Would He be that cruel?

The elevator stops at another floor and I glance up to see which one. Unfortunately, it's not Mark's. I have two more to go until we get to the first floor where the outpatient center is. What would we have done without Mark and his matching Violet's marrow? How bizarre. Maybe that is a sign from God that everything will work out. Maybe God is testing me. I'm not sure what to think anymore, other than I'd do anything to see that Violet makes it out of here alive.

I finally get to the recovery area and ask the receptionist where I might find him. She directs me to the correct area and I see Mark's parents and then Mark. He's wearing a lopsided grin and looks half-looped.

"Dude," he yells. "I did it!"

His parents try to shush him, but he's too drunk on whatever they gave him for pain and it does no good.

"You sure did, and I owe you big." I bend over him and we man-hug.

"Nah, you don't owe me a thing. You'd have done the same for me if the situation were reversed."

"You know it. But still. This is something we will never be able to pay you back for."

He slashes his hand through the air. "Yeah, you will. When I see her walking out of this hospital will be payment enough. Oh, and maybe some World Cup tickets."

"Greedy bastard, aren't you?"

"You know it."

"When are you getting out of here?"

"I don't know. Mom? Dad?"

"I think they'll let you leave pretty soon now," his mother says. "They were making sure he wouldn't get sick from the anesthesia."

"They gave me some pretty good shit," Mark says, winking.

"Mark, language, please," his mom admonishes him.

Laughing, I say, "I can tell. You're going to feel like you got kicked by a mule, so take it easy, man."

"I know, I know."

"The doctor was just in here giving him that lecture," his dad says.

"Good." I pat his shoulder again and say, "Thanks again. You don't know how much this means to—I ..."

"Hey, you have to stop. I did it for Violet. Got it?"

"Okay, yeah. Sure." I turn away so he doesn't see me wipe the drop of water out of the corner of my eye. Using my thumb,

I aim it at the ceiling. "So, I'm gonna head back on up there. I left your sister with my cousin and no telling what they're up to."

"That's true. And can you send my girl back down? I want her to tuck me in when I go back to the hotel."

"Oh, boy. I will not tell her that. You can." I hug his parents before I head out the door.

On the way back upstairs, I can't help but feel the love of family and friends. We are so fortunate to have such a close-knit support group to surround us in our time of need. As I near Violet's room, I pass the waiting room and see Mom and Dad as they watch the TV in there. I stop and let them know about Mark.

"He's great. And I'm a lucky man."

"Fletcher and Cass are too. He's a great friend," Mom adds.

"Yeah. Hey, why don't you two head back to the hotel and get some rest? I'll call if anything happens."

"Are you sure?" Dad asks.

"Yeah. She received the marrow and will be asleep, I'm sure. It's all about the wait and see now."

They gather up their things and make me promise to call if anything happens.

"Even if she so much as scratches her nose, Chase. I mean it," Mom says.

"I will. I swear."

When they're gone, I walk the rest of the way to Violet's new home for the next several weeks. I observe Andi and Riley talking and then Violet as she sleeps. The two women are chatting away, and for the first time in weeks, I notice Andi's eyes light up. I'm happy Riley is able to take her mind off this terrible thing, even if it's only for a few lousy minutes. Then I remember that I'm supposed to send Riley down to Mark.

"Psst. I hate to break up the little party but, Riley, your presence is requested by a certain someone downstairs," I say from the doorway.

"Oh," Riley answers. "I guess I'd better go down and see what his Royal Highness wants."

"Hey, do treat him like a prince. After what he did for us, he deserves it," Andi says.

"Rest assured, he will be spoiled by me," Riley answers. Then she hugs Andi and walks toward me. When she gets out of the room, she takes off her mask, gloves, and gown and hugs me.

"We'll see you soon. Call me if you need anything. Coffee, a sandwich, vodka. Whatever."

"Thanks, cuz."

Now it's my turn to put the gear back on after I scrub my hands. Andi sits and waits.

"She's been sound asleep. The marrow is in and the nurse just came in and checked. All is well."

"Good. I thanked Mark. He was looped. It was damn funny."

"Oh, God. I can only imagine."

I put my arm around her. "I don't know what we would've done without him."

"Neither do I."

In silence, we both sit and watch our daughter as she peacefully sleeps. Eventually, we both drift off until sometime later when a nurse comes in to check on Violet.

"Mr. Wilde, you and Ms. James may want to open up the recliner into the bed. The sheets are in the closet there."

"Yeah, we know. We didn't intend to sleep this long." I check the clock to see it's after eight. Andi wakes up with all the chatting.

"Hey."

"Hey. Are you hungry?"

"Yeah, are you?"

"Starving. Why don't I run down and get us a bite to eat?"

"I think the cafeteria is closed."

"Damn. Let me call my mom. She'll get us something."

"Or mine."

I quickly text my mom and they are actually out eating and say they'll bring us something on their way back. I let Andi know.

"That was great timing on our part."

Violet wakes up then and starts to cry. Andi is on it like lightning.

"Hey, sweets. I'm right here."

"Thirsty."

Andi hands her the cup filled with ice water and she eagerly takes it. She's been asleep for quite a while now.

"Hey, superstar. Are you hungry?"

Her eyes don't look so hot to me. They're shaded in purple and I hate it.

Her head bobs up and down. "Waffles." Only it doesn't sound exactly like that.

Andi laughs. "Waffles? It's dinnertime."

Violet does her best at smiling. "Waffles," she repeats.

"I'll see if I can work some waffle-ific magic." I run down the hall to the nurses' station and ask one of the nurses, "Hey, what are the chances of getting my little girl a waffle to eat?"

"You are in luck. We cater to kids up here. Didn't you know that? They eat at all hours and we aim to please. There's one thing we do best here and it's giving them what they want to eat when they want it."

"You're serious?" I ask.

"You bet. She hasn't eaten in a few hours and she needs to eat. If she wants waffles, I think we can work up a waffle for her. It won't be homemade, now."

I laugh. "She likes the frozen kind. Butter and syrup, please."

"Coming right up."

"Oh, and …"

"What is it?"

"Do you have any orange juice boxes?"

"Follow me." I do as she tells me and she shows me the secret stash. There is a refrigerator/freezer combo with all sorts of food in there. She pulls out an orange juice box and hands it to me, then checks for the frozen waffles. "We're out of waffles in this one, but I'm sure one of the freezers has some. They're a popular item up here. Help yourself to whatever you see in there." She points to the appliance. "I'll be back."

I grab a couple of different juice boxes and take them back to the room. "Andi." She glances up and sees me in the doorway. "Here." I hand them off to her and tell her I'll be back.

When I get back to the little room with the kitchen, the nurse has returned with pay dirt. A box of frozen waffles is in her hand.

"I owe you big."

"Nah, just replace the box. It's kind of how it works. We handle all the drinks. The food is where you use it, you give it back."

"Oh, I'll buy this place a year's supply of them if you want."

She only stares at me, then says, "Toaster is in there, and don't forget the butter and syrup. Plates, plastic forks, and knives are in there. Wash them before she uses them."

"Got it." I go to work creating her waffle, and when I return to her room, I am rewarded with a half-smile. It's the best thing I've seen all day. She only eats half the damn waffle, but who cares? That she ate something is all that counts, and I was able to make her happy by giving her something she asked for. The little things in life …

That's how day 0 goes. Day +1 is much the same. Andi and I draw pictures for her and she is a bit perkier, nibbling at her food and drinking. Watching her do that makes us happy. Who would've known a year ago that me sitting in a hospital and watching a little kid eat like a bird would make me happier than winning the World Cup?

Day +2 and Day +3 are equally good. Andi and I are getting comfortable with things. We even go back to the hotel, leaving Violet with the grandmothers so we can take long, leisurely showers.

But Day +7 is when the shit hits the fan and she starts running a low-grade fever and gets a rash. Both of our spirits crash because we had been so positive she was out of the woods, which had clearly been stupid on our parts. This is only the very beginning and she has weeks, even months to go before that happens.

FORTY-THREE

Andi

PANIC SETS in like an old friend. I feel like I can't breathe as I stroke Violet's head and pray to the man upstairs that it's nothing when it's anything but.

I recognize the look on the nurse's face when she comes in to get Violet's vitals. It's too kind, like she knows a secret but can't be the one to break it to the family. I remember wearing that face many times in the NICU.

"This can be normal. We've alerted the doctor. He'll be down as soon as he can."

The worry on her face tells a different story.

Chase is voicing his displeasure and I place a hand on his arm to stop him. I shake my head when he looks at me. Though he's frustrated beyond measure, he silences his protest.

When she leaves, I say, "Violet isn't the doctor's only patient. It's just a low-grade fever."

I take his hand in mine and squeeze. When he draws me in a hug, I take a moment to let the mask on my face drop and breathe in his scent.

"I can't lose her," Chase says.

It frightens me to the core. He's been the strong one,

keeping the Team Wilde mantra going when I had moments of weakness.

"You won't," I say, meaning it like I can trade my life for hers.

The truth is, I'd planned to pray to anyone listening for just that. This man above anyone deserves the time I stole from him.

"Mama."

Violet's voice is weak and I leave Chase's comfort to give it to our daughter.

She's asleep when the doctor finally comes in, which feels like hours later.

"I'll be honest with you. The fever is concerning." *Duh*, I want to scream, but it would disturb our little girl. Chase must sense it, but he wraps a protective arm around me. "It may not be anything more than a minor reaction to the marrow or the drug we administered. I'm going to change the drug and see if that helps before we jump to any conclusions."

We nod and he leaves as silently as he arrived.

"You should go to the hotel," Chase suggests.

"No, I can't leave." Though I'm ripe for the picking and need a shower in the worst way, I can't leave yet. "But you should," I say.

In the end, we tough it out, neither of us speaking, lost in our thoughts in separate chairs. We are both on edge and a divide begins to form between us, or maybe it's just me imagining it.

I miss his touch and stare at him from what feels like miles away. Finally, he looks at me.

As if in slow motion, his hand rises and a finger points at me. "This is your fault. You did this."

All the air is sucked from my lungs, making it impossible to breathe. I'm trying to say his name when I'm jolted awake.

"I'm here," Chase says.

And he is. His eyes are kind and not the accusing ones from

the nightmare I had experienced. I pull him close, needing his warmth to wash away the dream that was so real.

"Violet's fine. Her fever is gone."

"What?" I separate us and glance at my daughter's sleeping form. "How long have I been sleeping?"

"A couple of hours."

I blink away that realization.

"Chase, I'm—"

His hand is on my lips. "You need rest." When I glare at him, he adds, "We both do. Our moms have spoken. They are sending us to the hotel—" He lifts a finger to his lips and I suck in the words I'd been about to say. "—Just for a few hours."

I lift my head and spot both of our mothers outside the glass. Mom's eyebrow lifts in that stern way that brooks no argument.

"Fine, I could use a shower, but I'm not staying long," I say.

"Agreed."

We ditch our gear after warning them to contact us the moment Violet wakes or any sign of the smallest of problems.

Though guilt weighs upon me, I reluctantly leave, remembering the many times I've had to shoo parents away. *We need a recharge*, I tell myself.

As soon as we are in the hotel, I'm determined to get in and out.

"I'll shower first," I say over my shoulder, studiously ignoring the bed.

I rip off my clothes, flinging them to the floor as I walk. The bath isn't huge. I head straight for the walk-in shower, holding the glass as I reach for the knob. I'm turning the water on when a warm body presses to my back.

He spins me around and he's just as naked.

"Chase—"

"Taking one together will save time."

And he's right. When his mouth crashes down on mine, all

the demons that have been whispering in my ear that he hates me disappear.

I gasp as he steps me back into the tepid spray. Though the water is cool, his feverish kiss has set all my nerve endings on fire. It's been weeks of not a touch between us, and it's this connection that reminds me of how much I need him this way.

He crushes me against the tile wall as warmer water rains down on us.

"I need you," he says, just as he hikes me up, my back sliding up the wall.

"Please," I beg, not needing to be primed.

I'm wet and ready in more ways than one. His lips leave mine and glide down my neck to that spot that causes me to squirm.

I feel the heavy weight of his cock pressed between us as his mouth finds one of my breasts.

"Now," I cry out. "Now."

Then it's there probing my entrance, and when he slams home, I feel almost virginal it's been so long.

He stills, his head buried in my neck, breathing hard.

"Damn, you're tight."

It's true and I feel every inch of him as my body adjusts to his presence.

He teases me by pulling out devilishly slow, before just as patiently sliding back in.

"You're killing me," I complain.

I'm held up, gripped in his hold, unable to move on my own above a wiggle, which I do.

"Stop." His voice is gritty like his jaw is tightly clenched. "Or it will be over before it begins."

I freeze because I'm close, but not that close, and I want this as much as he does.

He bucks his hips, once then twice before gliding into a rhythm that has my pulse rising. It's hard and fast and everything we both need. I cry out as I spasm around him and he pulses inside me.

It's true what they say about sex. I'd been tired and cranky when I walked into the bathroom. Every one of my muscles had been tense. Now, I feel like a noodle, loose and limber in his arms, breathing hard.

"You're mine," he finally says. His voice bounces off the walls in a growl. "This is mine, and when Violet gets out, tell me you'll walk down that aisle and make this official."

I giggle a little, dizzy post-sex. "Haven't we already talked about this?"

He's not amused when he says, "I need you to say it again."

And I realize, much as I've been, he's scared about our daughter too. I meet his wary stare. "I'm yours. I always have been. And when we take our daughter from this hospital and she's well enough to participate in our small wedding—" I eye him. I'm not really interested in a huge wedding, just big enough for family and close friends. "—I will be your wife, something I've dreamed about since I was old enough."

His frown tips up into a smile. He lets me get to my feet where he worships me with soap and his hands. Just when I think I'm lathered up, head to toe, he rinses off my inner thighs and uses his tongue to make me scream his name. When he's done, it's my turn.

I'm on my knees, his cock buried in my throat when he frees himself, tugs me to my feet, spins me around, and drives into me from behind. My pussy is slick from working him and he easily drives home. This time is longer, a little rougher, and every bit as pleasurable. His thrusts hit every magic button in my body and I have liftoff twice before he comes long and hard inside me.

We are both panting and trying to steady ourselves when we hear not one, but both of our phones buzz from the other room.

FORTY-FOUR

Chase

_____

WE BOTH SCRAMBLE TO grab towels and then run to answer our phones. Andi nearly crashes to the floor on the slippery tile, but I steady her with my hands on her hips. Water drips from both of us, but neither of us gives a damn. All we care about is what the news on the other end of those buzzing phones has for us.

Andi is the first one to yell, "What is it? What's happened?"

I grab mine next and shout the same thing. Mom's calm voice steadies my galloping heart rate.

"Chase, honey, everything's fine. Take a deep breath. I'm only calling to let you know Violet's awake and grinning. She's even asking to eat."

"What?" I shout.

"Honey, if you don't stop yelling, I'm going to need a hearing aid. I said your daughter appears to be feeling much better. I thought you would want to know."

My ass hits the bed because my legs basically give out. All the tension instantly drains out of me, leaving me as weak as a baby bird. I'm so choked up I can't speak.

"Chase? Honey, are you still there?"

Clearing my throat, it takes a few deep breaths before I can respond. "Yeah, Mom, I'm here. It's just that's such great news. Such a relief, you know?" My entire body is trembling and I can't figure out why. I glance across the room and see that Andi is crying. I want to go over and hug her, but I'm too weak to get up at this time.

"Chase, Violet wants to talk to you now."

"Yeah, that's good." I'm dimly aware of what's happening. What's wrong with me?

"Dada. I hungy." I hear her giggle after she says that.

"That's great, sweetie. Is your nana going to get you something to eat?"

"Popsicle."

"A Popsicle?"

"And waffle."

"That sounds exactly like something you'd eat." I laugh at her choice of a meal and then realize the weird sensations in my body are easing up. "Make sure you eat the waffle before the Popsicle, okay?"

"Okay."

"And Mama and I will be back soon."

Mom's voice hits my ear. "Chase, you and Andi need to sleep. You don't sound normal to me. I think you've hit the wall and you'll be no good to anyone, especially Violet, if you don't rest. The last thing we need is for you and Andi to get sick too."

"Okay, Mom."

"Now get some rest."

"I will." We end the call and I think maybe she's right. I'm feeling a little better, but for a minute there I was in the crash zone.

"Chase."

I hear Andi calling me. I stand up, and on wobbly legs, walk to her where she sits in a chair.

"Come to bed with me. We need sleep."

"She's good, right?"

"Yeah. She's going to have a waffle and a Popsicle." I laugh.

It's with relief as much as humor. Andi stands and I notice she's as weak as I am.

"Look at us. This is definitely a sign we need sleep. Mom made a good point. We're both near the point of exhaustion. If we don't take care of ourselves, we won't be able to take care of our daughter."

Andi grabs my hand. "Yes. Let's sleep and then go back. Make sure our phones are on, though."

"They are." We climb into the bed and I turn off the light. The blackout curtains are drawn and I put the *Do Not Disturb* sign out when we came in. Hopefully, we can catch a few hours and then go back to the hospital to relieve our moms.

When I stretch, every muscle is tight as though it hasn't been moved for a week. Sitting in a chair in that hospital is harder on a body than a grueling practice on a football field. Rubbing the sleep out of my eyes, I notice that Andi is still breathing softly. I slip out of bed, not wanting to disturb her. She needs this time, and even though we've only been asleep for probably a few hours, I want to let her get as much as she needs. I grab my phone to check the time and then take a second look. We went to sleep at four in the afternoon. It's now noon. Noon of the following day! We almost slept around the clock. About that time, my stomach lets out a gigantic roar. No damn wonder. We haven't eaten in an entire day. How the hell did we sleep this long?

I trudge into the bathroom on stiff legs, and pee, and pee, and pee. Jesus, how did I hold it for this long? We must've been in a coma.

I decide to take a shower and then run down and grab some food for us. As I'm showering, a thought plows into me. Our daughter's beautiful curls have all fallen out due to the potent chemo they had to give her before the bone marrow transplant.

To show her my support, I'm going to shave my head. I grab my electric shaver and go to town. It takes longer than I thought, as my hair is as thick as a damn hedge. When I'm done, I check it out with a mirror to ensure I didn't miss any spots and don't look like some weird animal. Then I shower. As I'm getting dressed, Andi lifts up her head.

"What the hell, Chase! What happened to your hair?"

"Nothing, other than I'm supporting our daughter. By the time mine grows back, so will hers."

"Oh, my God." Her hand covers her mouth. "Come here." Then her arms are around me, holding me tight. "That's the sweetest, kindest thing I've ever heard."

"No, it's not. It's nothing really. Just a shaved head, babe."

She's still hugging me when she asks, "You do realize it will take hers longer to grow back than yours? Yours is just shaved, but hers is pretty much destroyed down to the follicle. And where are you going? Did something happen?"

Chuckling, I say, "Nothing, other than we both slept like lazy dogs. I'm running down to grab us some coffees and a bite to eat."

"Oh? What time is it?"

This time I laugh. Super hard. "It's noon."

"Okay." She releases me and plops back down, but then springs up like a jack-in-the-box. "What the fuck! Noon! How the hell did we sleep that long?"

"Must've been bone weary. Why don't you shower and I'll have food by the time you're out?"

"Ugh, I'm so lazy now."

"Stay in bed then. We've gotten no phone calls or texts, so all is good, babe." I bend down to kiss her sweet lips. "I'll be back."

The hotel lobby has a coffee shop, so I load up on her favorite latte and then grab an assortment of muffins and pastries for us to munch on until we feel like heading out for a real, honest-to-goodness meal. I'm going to convince her that's what we need to do for our health and sanity.

By the time I get back to our room, Andi is emerging from the steamy bathroom with a robe on. She looks yummier than the goodies in the paper bag I brought up to the room.

"Here." I hand her a latte.

Her face morphs into one of pure happiness as she sips the concoction. "Oh, is this good."

"I knew you'd love it."

We both sip our drinks and nibble on the muffins for a minute. Then I make a suggestion. "I think we should go to lunch. A nice lunch before we head back to the hospital."

Andi gets ready to object, but I stop her before she gets the opportunity.

"Hear me out, please. Yesterday, after Mom called, I sat on the bed and literally could not move. My legs were gone, Andi. I was out of juice. At first, I was really scared there was something major going on with me. But then I realized I'd hit the wall. I do that sometimes when I play too hard in a game, but it wasn't computing yesterday because my brain was malfunctioning. We were both so tired and weary. When was the last time you slept twenty hours straight? I don't think I ever have."

"I haven't, either."

"We need this break, babe, or we're going to break. And we can't afford that. Are you with me on this?"

"Yeah. As much as I want to rush back there, we do need to refuel. Our moms are right. Let's take a leisurely lunch and then go back. Violet probably isn't even aware we're not there."

"You're right. I'm sure they are spoiling her to pieces."

No sooner do the words leave my mouth than both our phones buzz. Fuck!

I grab mine as she grabs hers.

"What?" I scream.

"Calm down, Chase. It's just me letting you know all is fine."

I exhale a tank full of air. "Sorry, Mom. It's just that every call …"

"You don't have to explain, son, but stop thinking so negatively. We hadn't heard anything from you two so I figured I'd give you a call."

"We didn't wake up until noon."

"Honey, that's wonderful."

"And we're going to go out and eat a nice lunch for a change before we head back up there, if that's okay."

"That's a great idea. Your daughter is having a great time. She's with her grandfathers now and they are spoiling her. She had ice cream for lunch."

"Mom, will you see if they can at least feed her something nutritious?"

"You mean ice cream isn't nutritious?"

"You're so funny."

"Chase, take your time and come back when you're ready. We're all fine here."

"Thanks, Mom. I love you."

"Love you too, son."

Andi is shaking her head when I look over at her.

"What is it?"

"That was Mark. He wanted to crash our lunch."

"He did? What did you tell him?"

"I told him no way. That I wanted time with my sexy boyfriend because I hadn't had enough of that lately."

"You did?"

"Damn right, I did."

"What did he say?"

"He laughed and said go for it and that it took me long enough."

"Then why are you shaking your head?"

"Because then the jerk wanted to know when we're getting married. He said we had a daughter and it was time you did right by me. I told him I was the holdout, so he cussed me out."

I throw back my head and laugh.

"It's not funny."

"Yeah, it is."

"You only think so because he's Team Chase."

I reach over my shoulder and pat myself on the back. Andi scowls at me. I can't have that so I make a mad dash for her and toss her on the bed as she screeches.

"He might be Team Chase, but I'm Team Andi." Then my mouth doesn't waste any time as my lips home in on hers and make sure she knows she's mine.

Her purrs of delight tell me everything I need to hear, and I follow through as I untie her robe. Then I slip it off her shoulders. Her thong comes next and my tongue finds her hot and silky slit as she moans my name. Her taste is sweet and salty as I tunnel inside of her and then circle around and around on her little nub. She moans and arches into me, begging for more.

"I need you inside. Now."

That won't do. Not until she gives me an orgasm. So I add one finger, then two, and find that spot that makes her go crazy for me. Her hands grab my head and I know she's close. But when her legs clamp against my head and I feel her inner muscles quiver against my hand, it's all over.

I quickly drop my pants and spread her legs. Then I'm pressing my cock into her opening as though it calls my name. She looks more beautiful than anything I've ever seen as she waits for me.

With one long thrust, I'm home, in deep, my mouth on hers, and we find the rhythm that we both love. Hard and fast strokes that hit her deepest places, she wraps her legs tightly around me until we're locked together.

"I love you, Andi James. Never forget I'm always Team Andi."

"I love you, Chase Wilde. Never forget we're Team Wilde."

I can't tear myself away from her eyes. I pull her up until she sits on my lap and we make love slowly this way until we both climax deliriously in each other's arms. It's strange really, but I sense something different this time, something new between us blossoming. A deeper love, maybe. I'm not quite sure what it is. I only know I never want to be without this woman again.

"I don't care what tomorrow brings. I only know I can face anything as long as I have you by my side. You are my strength, my world, Andi. Without you and Violet, my life isn't worth a thing."

FORTY-FIVE

Andi

THE NEXT FEW WEEKS, we watch as our daughter grows stronger and has a few setbacks here and there. In the end, it's all worth it when the doctor declares she's recovered enough to go home.

"Home," Violet cheers.

I smile at Chase, but in the back of my mind I wonder where home is. Chase gave up the villa in Italy. I have my apartment in Chicago, but …

"Yes, home," the doctor says, interrupting my drifting thoughts.

He gives us a laundry list of dos and don'ts and things to watch out for. I take notes, but I'm grateful when he hands us a packet that has all the things he's said written down.

"I'll need to see her for a follow-up in a few weeks."

I nod. It answers one question. We can't exactly leave the States or even go to Chicago because we need to be close in the event something happens.

Because Violet doesn't need isolation, our family comes in for the good news.

Chase startles me when he tips up my chin. "What's wrong?"

I shake my head, plaster on a smile, and say, "I'll tell you later," because lying to him isn't an option and he's already picked up on my mood.

Violet wants ice cream and Mark and Riley offer to take her.

When we arrive at the hotel, Chase doesn't give me a second.

"Tell me," he demands.

I drop my head to study my fingernails. "It's just I don't know where home is anymore."

The idea pains me so, I feel tears prick the back of my eyes. He forces me to face him.

"My home is with you, no matter where in the world we are. You, me, Violet are a unit."

I nod. "So we stay here."

"Fletcher's going to training camp. He's offered his house," he says, taking me by surprise.

He's obviously already thought about this.

"What about Cassie?"

"She's taking the baby and bunking with him. She has someone else handling her practice for another few months."

"Then what?"

He's my home too, and I'm willing to go wherever he wants. I've taken too much away from him as it is.

He shrugs. "Chicago?"

I stare at him, agape. "For what?"

"You have a place there."

My heart bursts for this man. How could I have ever given him up? "No, the next time I go to Chicago is to pack up. I want to know when we have to go back to Italy."

It's his turn to stare at me with wonder.

"We don't have to. I had Max secretly looking at potential contracts in the U.S."

"When?" I ask, yet again amazed.

He stares at me a second and runs a hand through his hair. "Before I went to Chicago that first time to find you. I decided then that you were more important than any career." As I just stand there stupefied, he says, "You have to know it's only ever been you for me since that first kiss we shared. It doesn't matter where I play as long as we are together."

I lift onto my toes to meet him halfway for a kiss. Before I do, I say, "I'll go wherever you want to play. You are my home too." The kiss that ensues scorches the carpet below our feet. I cup his face as I back us toward the bed.

"You are my sunshine, Andi. Every day has been cloudy without you in it."

Then we are falling in a tangle of naked limbs. He eases his way on top of me. Every kiss from my lips to my clit leaves me breathless and melting. His tongue is everywhere, swirling and making me boneless. Gentle suction, probing and thrusting fingers take me to the edge. But before I can come, he stops, leaving me aching and silently protesting with fisted hands in sheets. His sly smile grows as he slides his hands between my legs and parts my thighs. When he enters me in one powerful thrust, I detonate around him, unable to hold it off.

Things don't end there. He knows how to get me to rise to the occasion again. The pads of his fingers slip down to stroke my sensitive nub, awakening a growing storm inside me once again. I grind myself against him, needing to be closer, needing more of him. He rotates his hips, hitting that spot deep inside until I cry out with release, but I'm not the only one as he roars his pleasure.

As we lie cocooned in one another, sweat cooling off our skin, I ask, "So where will we live?"

"Are you sure you're okay with Italy?"

I bite my lip and smile up at him. "Italy, France, Germany, London, wherever you want to be. It's your career."

"And your career. You love being a neonatal nurse."

I lift my shoulders. "I can do that anywhere. Once we decide a place where we're going to be, I can look into that."

Then I close my mouth, not sure if I should voice my other thoughts.

"What is it?" he asks knowingly.

I meet his gaze. "It's just I kind of like being a mom. This whole thing reminds me what I would have regretted missing. I'm hopeful Violet is fine ..." I bite off my next words as the possibility of losing her still haunts me. He only stares at me, waiting for me to finish. "But if ..." I don't finish that thought. Instead, I say, "For now, I'd be happy just being at home with her."

"I'll support you no matter what you decide. You can always change your mind."

He strokes my back and I fall asleep. I wake at the sound of a phone ringing. Chase answers.

"Dinner?" he says into the phone.

The one word has me launching out of the bed and making a dash for the bathroom. I barely make it before the muffin and dredges of coffee I'd had that morning all come up.

Chase is there, moving my hair out of the way with concern etched on his face.

"I think I got the stomach bug," I say once the heaves of my stomach die down. Our nurse had told us about the emergency room being packed with people with the bug. I hope I have the twenty-four hour kind.

"I guess dinner is out? That was Mark."

That word again sends me to gag again. When I can finally sit on my butt in the bathroom, ignoring that it is a hotel, I say, "You should go. I can't see Violet until this runs its course."

His lips purse, but he nods. "You're right, but I can't go either." He grins. "I've been swapping spit with you, thus I'm infected as well."

His wink draws out a half-smile from me. "I'm sorry."

He shakes his head. "There's no one I rather be quarantined with."

After talking with the moms, they decide to drive Violet

home so she can get home-cooked meals. Plus, they bring up the fact that if the bug is in the area, it is best to not have Violet exposed to people in restaurants. Mark and Riley plan to bunk at Fletcher's until we can come and keep her overnight since that's where we'll be staying. Everyone thinks it's best to get Violet in a routine. The moms will trade time spending with her.

It's a few days of nausea and vomiting before I feel well enough to possibly go home.

"Maybe I should stay and you go," I tell Chase.

He never caught it. Lucky bastard.

He shakes his head. "Doc thinks you're not contagious anymore and Violet misses her mom."

"And her dad," I add.

We pack up and drive, but I make a stop at a drugstore before we pull up to Fletcher's. Mark is outside with Violet and he has to stop her from running to the car when she sees us. I have the same problem. I've missed her like crazy. When Chase finally stops the car, I'm out like lightning. I wrap my arms around her and she feels so small in my embrace. She has lost some weight, but I close my eyes, running a hand through her still bald head.

"Mama, silly." She points at my face. "Mask?"

I'd gotten those sterile masks, not wanting to take a chance that she'd catch anything from me. I'd even used hand sanitizer before getting out of the car.

"To make sure you aren't sick."

Then Chase is there. He scoops her up.

Mark comes over and pulls me aside. "This probably isn't the right time, but I imagine you are going to spend a lot of time with Violet." I nod. "I asked Riley to marry me." I gasp and hug my brother.

"Congratulations. I assume she said yes."

"She did. She wants to get married on Valentine's Day next year." More hugs. "I made everyone promise not to spill the beans until I could tell you myself."

"I'm so happy for you."

His face turns serious. "Now it's time for you to put Chase out of his misery and marry him."

"What? Misery?"

His brow arches. "As long as I can remember, Chase has been hung up on one girl."

"How do you know?" He gives me a *duh* expression. "Fletcher?"

"We didn't know who she was. He wouldn't tell us."

I laugh. "We couldn't. You would have kicked his ass."

"I would have."

"See, then Fletcher would have kicked yours."

His eyes narrow. "Fletcher can't kick my ass."

"Keep telling yourself that, big brother."

"Anyway, now I know it was you. If you take my advice, know that there isn't another guy in the world I would approve of more than him."

I launch myself in his arms again, thinking how lucky I am to be surrounded by the people in my life. Silently, I thank my parents for giving me up. Though I would have loved to know them, they had given me the greatest gift.

When he lets me go, Chase is there, hand outstretched. Mark pats my arm and I move forward to take Chase's hand. We walk up to the modern farmhouse with a wraparound porch. Fletcher built a one-bedroom suite with kitchen and bath and its own front side entrance, though you can access it through the house as well. Fletcher says it is for guests, but we all know he built it in mind for his brother coming into town. Now we are using it.

Walking inside, I remember Chase's words about our family unit. Though there is something niggling at me. Something I need to figure out.

One thing I'm certain of is Chase. I love him more than life, always have, always will.

FORTY-SIX

Chase

ANDI HAD AGREED to marry me a while back, but we never talked about a formal date. I want to do this right because she's the woman I've always wanted, the woman of my dreams. It's a warm late summer's night, and Violet is sleeping. We're sitting on the porch that overlooks the view, the one that Fletcher and Cassie love so much. The ring I've been carrying around for months now is practically burning a hole in my pocket. I wanted to do this a long time ago, but with the way Violet's condition was so precarious at the time, I figured it would be best to wait it out. Tonight is the night, I've decided.

Abruptly, I push to my feet and she stares at me, right before I drop to one knee.

"Andrea James, you are my path to happiness, my path to joy in this world. Without you and Violet, I am nothing. Even though we're together and you've promised yourself to me, I'd like to make this official. Will you do me the honor of making me the happiest man alive and becoming my wife? Oh, and just so you know, I've asked your father for his permission."

"You did?"

"Of course I did. Even though we're sort of doing this backward, I wanted him to be on Team Wilde too. So what do you say?"

Her eyes flick between my hands, which hold hers, and my eyes. She doesn't say anything for a second or two, which seems like a million years to me.

"Andi, do you not want to marry me?"

"Chase, I'm pregnant." And suddenly she's beaming. Her radiant smile pretty much lights up the entire porch.

"Oh, God." I grab her, pulling her to her feet and then lifting her into my arms. "Are you sure?"

"Yes, positive. You know how I thought I had a virus? It's a pregnancy virus."

"Seriously?" I gently set her down. "Do you need to sit, or maybe lie down?"

"Chase, I'm pregnant, not an invalid."

"Yeah, right. Okay then."

"And I'll gladly marry you."

"Marry me?"

"Yes. Didn't you just ask me to be your wife?"

I scratch my head where the thick hair is growing back already. "Uh, yeah. Oh! Marry me. Yes!" I dig into my pocket and drop back down to my knee so I can slide the ring onto her finger. I'm numb with the news of her pregnancy. It's overshadowed anything I was planning to say to her. "Andi, you've surprised me more than I can say. I was going to sweep you off your feet with my proposal, but you've managed to do that to me with your news. I'm a bit speechless here."

Her hands frame my face as she leans in close to mine. "Chase, it's the best of surprises for the both of us. How can we possibly be any happier? We have the two of us, and Violet is getting stronger every day. Her energy is bounding back faster than I ever imagined it would. And now this. Another baby on the way. Our Team Wilde is getting larger, isn't it?"

A breath huffs out of me. "Yeah, it is. But now are you sure you want to go back to Europe?"

"Why wouldn't I?"

"You'd be farther away from your mom."

"Um, aren't you forgetting something?"

"Like what?"

"I had Violet and I was completely alone. I could've been on Antarctica for all intents and purposes. I did everything on my own. So, being in Europe with you will be a breeze."

"When you put it that way, I guess so."

Her sweet lips press to mine, but I stop her before things get a chance to heat up. There are a few things that need to be discussed first.

"Can we talk wedding plans?" I ask.

"Small and intimate," she says.

"I know, but I was thinking timing."

"Next week?"

I bark out a laugh. "You're joking?"

"Nope. Let's do it. I only want the family, so what does it matter?"

When she puts it like that, it doesn't matter at all.

She grabs my arm and says, "We can do it right over there." She points to where there's a gorgeous view during the day. "And afterward, we can have drinks and appetizers. That's all I want."

"Well, we would need to ask the owners of the place if that's okay."

She grimaces. "Oh, yeah. I sort of forgot about that."

"I'm sure it'll be cool."

"I hope. But would that be okay with you?"

"I'd love it. We need to check about the marriage license."

"It takes twenty-four hours, I believe. I remember when Ryder and Gina got married. Someone mentioned it."

"Then let's call our parents and get the show moving. Oh, there is something else. Max called. He said Germany is still interested in talking with me at the end of the season in July. We can discuss this later, though."

"Chase, this is your career. You— I mean, we—would be foolish not to listen to what they have to offer."

I can't stop the smile from extending across my face. This woman is everything to me. I pull her into my arms and kiss her, slowly and passionately. Then we go and make the calls. Our parents couldn't be more excited for us. It makes us both so happy to know we have their love and support. When we tell them about our wedding plans, they agree with us in thinking it's a great plan. And then Andi lets them know that baby number two is on the way. You would think by the way they cheer and celebrate they were standing in the room with us. My ears are ringing by the time we end the call.

"I don't think I've ever heard my mom that excited. And that includes when Fletcher and I both ended up with professional contracts. Now I know where her priorities are," I say.

"Where they should be. A mom always looks out for her child's best interest, and in sports there is always that chance a kid could get injured. That's why she's like that."

"You think she worries about us?"

"No, I know she does. I would be frightened to death. So just know if our kids decide to play professional sports, I will be walking on pins and needles the entire time."

Another thought occurs to me. "Do you worry about me like that?"

"Of course I do. But you're doing what you love and I know you're careful."

I'm not careful. I'm aggressive as hell out there. That gives me pause because I have two kids to worry about now.

"So what if we bought a house here, so when we come back we'd have our own place to plop down in?" I ask.

"Really? You'd do that?"

"Not at all. We'd do that. What's mine is ours now. We're Team Wilde, remember?"

"I guess. It seems weird though."

"You'll have to get over that and get used to it. One other

thing. If we stay in Italy, would you like to go back to our villa? Maybe buy it? Or would you rather build something?"

"I liked that villa. It was awesome."

"Yes, but we could get something closer to the stadium."

"If it makes it easier for you, then yes."

"Okay, I'll check into it."

A week and a half later, Andi and I say our "I dos" on a gorgeous summer's evening. She wears a plain white lacy dress. It isn't fancy, but it is sexy, with one bared shoulder showing off the glowing tan she's gotten since we've been here. Her hair is twisted into a bun at the nape of her neck with flowers tucked into it. Violet wears a matching dress, only hers isn't off the shoulder. Her hair is growing back and the soft downy fuzz tops her head and crowning it is a halo of summer flowers. She looks like the little princess that she is. She leads the way down the aisle for her mama, tossing petals to pave the way. When she gets to me, she says, "Pick up, Dada." How can I possibly resist?

So it's the three of us together as the minister says the vows and we all promise our love to each other, Violet piping in now and again. At the end, he finally says, "I now pronounce you husband, wife, and Violet." Our families break into a huge round of applause, but it's Violet who gets the biggest charge out of it. "You may kiss the bride," the minister says.

"Kiss Mama," Violet says. I don't waste any time with that order. But soon, she yells, "Now me."

Now that she's well, I have a strong feeling this kid's gonna be a handful. A very loving handful. And I'll gladly take it.

Epilogue

THE DAY IS warm with spring giving way to summer. I sit out back in the chair swing that's tethered to a tree, watching the kids playing with bubbles. Everyone is here at our newly renovated farmhouse in Waynesville to celebrate my birthday, a surprise from my husband.

Things didn't work out with the Germany deal and we've only been back from Italy a few days and haven't seen the family yet. We are getting over jet lag and trying to get our two kids back on schedule. I wasn't expecting a big to-do for my birthday.

With the Wildes all involved in different professional sports, it's rare when they all can get together without a conflict. But somehow, everyone is here—Fletcher and Cassidy, Ryder and Gina, Riley and Mark. Even Chase's cousins, Kaycee and Landon, who both are heavily into winter sports, are here and all the parents. We haven't all been together since my brother's wedding back in February.

Colt wiggles in my arms. He's been patient, almost to the point of sleeping after being fed, but with his sister and the cousins all playing, he wants in on the action.

"Okay, bud. Here you go."

I set him down on chubby legs and he takes off in that awkward run a boy at his age does after only learning to walk a few months ago.

The happiness inside me is almost to the point of bursting. How close did I come to missing out on this?

"Hey, you."

I look up to see Gina, Ryder's wife, waddling over. Her belly looks huge and I glance down at my flat stomach, reminiscing about my pregnancy with Colt and how different it was than with Violet. Chase had been there every step of the way with his *What to Expect When You're Expecting* book he'd kept close like it was a Bible.

"Hey," I say, scooting over so she can sit next to me. "How's it going?"

She shrugs. "My back hurts. My feet hurt."

We laugh.

"Just wait until the baby comes. Your back and feet will hurt because you'll be chasing the little guy. I don't need Zumba with Colt."

Our chortles have the guys looking in our direction. She cups a hand over her mouth and lowers her voice.

"Watch this. Ryder's eyes are going to narrow. He thinks I'm talking about him."

I can't help but snicker when he does precisely that.

"What exactly does he think we're talking about?" I ask.

"He probably thinks I'm telling you about the room we put in our house."

I giggle. "You just did. Besides, I've heard about the swing."

She winks at me. "Yeah, Mr. Vanilla over there has crossed over to the dark side."

"Really?"

She nods. "Not completely, he has limits." She sighs wistfully. "But he prefers giving me what I want in our house instead of going to a club."

"Good luck on finding the time when the baby arrives."

She glances over and tips her head in Ryder's parents' direction. "Their first grandchild. Pfft. Now that they've moved back since Riley and your brother's wedding, we have built-in babysitters. His mom has already told me she wants to be a large part of the baby's life."

"What does Ryder think about having a daughter?"

They'd announced this at her baby shower.

She snorts. "He's freaked the fuck out. I think it's cute."

Cassidy walks over with a sleeping baby swaddled in her arms. "What are the two of you talking about?"

"The room," I say dramatically.

We practically wet ourselves laughing so hard at poor Ryder, who's either red with embarrassment or pissed as hell.

"I hear you're considering going back to work," Cassidy says.

"Chase and Fletcher gossip like girls," I tease. "But yes, I've considered it. How do you manage it with two boys?"

She doesn't hesitate with an answer. "I cut back my hours after the first was born. I only go in three days a week when the oldest is in preschool, and my mother-in-law takes the baby. But since Fletcher has been off, he's taken on a larger role. So I'm able to go in five days, but still, I don't do full days."

I nod and her eyebrow lifts. She continues. "But you said you considered it?"

Shrugging, I say, "There's a lot to consider." I change the subject because I want to talk more to Chase about it first. "What is it like being the only girl in the house?"

Cassidy is about to answer when Riley joins us.

"We're considering trying again for a girl so I'm not the lone one," she says.

We then turn to Riley. She holds up her hands. "Don't look at me. Yes, I want kids, but not yet. Mark and I are going to wait a few more years."

Her career as a professional golfer has taken off. She's the number one ladies' golfer in the world.

Cassidy says, "Don't you want your kids to be able to play with ours?"

Riley's eyebrow lifts. "I don't see any of you stopping the baby making any time soon." Her eyes land on me and then the other girls stare at me too.

Uncomfortable with the scrutiny, I get to my feet. "I need to find Chase."

"Sure." Riley smirks.

I'm going to kill my brother. He can't keep a secret. "Besides, Gina needs to put Ryder out of his misery."

Gina curls a finger at her husband. His frown flattens and he heads in our direction.

I tease, "Just don't scare the kids with any public displays. We have more than enough guest rooms if you can't contain yourselves until you get home."

Owen, Fletcher, and Chase are all playing with the kids. Owen's presence is another surprise Chase had for me. Holly and Violet have been thick as thieves since they showed up.

When Chase sees me coming, he breaks off from the group.

"Are you happy?"

He presses a quick kiss to my lips.

"Deliriously." I snuggle to his side and watch as Fletcher loops an arm around the shoulder of his wife, Cassidy.

He's one of the nicest guys you can ever meet. I'm glad that he and his high school sweetheart worked things out.

As Violet organizes the kids in a circle, they begin playing Duck, Duck, Goose.

The bone marrow transplant has done the trick. Violet has been fine, though blood work is done at every routine visit. And by the grace of God, Colt doesn't have the dreadful disease. We've had him tested to be sure.

"Chase," I begin.

"You see it too," he says, looking at Owen, who is now in a conversation with a smiling Kaycee.

Owen and Chase have become fast friends, having sports in common.

"Isn't he seeing someone?"

Last we spoke, he'd been dating a woman he'd met from Holly's preschool.

Chase shrugs. "I don't think it's serious."

We watch as Kaycee blushes and I leave it because I want to talk to him before we get inundated by family again.

I meet his beautiful gray eyes before glancing at my nails, suddenly tongue-tied. His beauty inside and out floors me on a daily basis.

"How did I get so lucky?" The words spill out of my mouth instead of remaining in my head.

"The luck is all mine."

He bends down and presses our lips together.

"Hey, you two."

I yank back because I know that voice. Chase's mouth splits in a grin. "Surprise."

Then I'm enveloped in a hug from my best friend, Beth. Tears leak from my eyes because I haven't seen her since I formally moved out of my apartment in Chicago and gave her and the city a final goodbye.

We screech and bounce on our toes as we spin.

"I've missed you," I say through sobs.

I'm not sure she's heard me until she says, "Me too."

Violet tugs on my shirt. "Mama okay?"

I reluctantly separate from my friend, still a little surprised she's really here. Then I bend down.

"I'm okay. These are happy tears."

My little girl leans in and kisses my cheek. Then she turns to Beth and holds up her arms. "Bef."

Beth picks her up and swings her around, gracing her with loads of kisses.

I knock on Chase's shoulders. "You got me."

He smiles. "Anything for my girl."

There is no time to say more because my mom comes out with a cake and everyone is singing "Happy Birthday" to me.

I don't hold back on emotions. For once, I let it all pour out, unafraid because everyone here is family, blood or not.

Chase and I don't get another moment alone until after I've fed Colt and Chase has tucked in Violet. We've left Owen and Beth downstairs watching a movie with a promise to return.

"Wait," I say before Chase tugs me out the door. "I've been wanting to talk to you all day."

He cups my chin and rubs a thumb lovingly across my cheek. "Worried about the trip to see your aunt?"

Though my parents have passed, I made contact with my mom's sister months ago. With Colt's birth and going back to Italy, I haven't had a chance to meet her yet. But judging by everything I've gotten to know about her, she's a lovely woman.

She'd told me how Mom struggled with the decision to give me up for adoption. When my dad died in service of the U.S. Army, she'd taken it hard and didn't have the means to take care of me. So she'd given me up. I will forever be grateful for her decision. If she hadn't, I might never have met Chase and have two beautiful children with him. Not to mention Mom, Dad, and Mark.

"No, not about that. Actually, I'm looking forward to it."

She'd said she had lots of pictures of her family and some of my father.

He brushes his lips over mine. "It's okay to be nervous."

I nod because I am, just not for the reason he thinks.

Though the door is cracked, we are far enough away not to be overheard.

I lift my head and gaze at the man who's made my life a fairytale.

"I'm pregnant."

We've never really talked about how many kids we wanted, just that we wanted them.

His eyes drop to my belly. I try not to let insecurity rise, as it's not as flat as the first day he put his hands on me. And just like the first time, when his big hand splays over my stomach, butterflies take flight. I cover his with my own.

"Say something," I whisper.

He stares at me with wonder. "Every day I wonder how I could ever be happier than I am. But you've done it again. You've made me the happiest man alive."

"Are you sure? We've never really—"

His finger stops me from saying more. "If I didn't want more kids with you, I would have pulled out, worn a condom, or asked you to go on the pill. Any child we have will be lucky to have you as a mother."

"And you as a father."

"We can have twenty kids."

I laugh. "Yeah, no," I say firmly.

His hand lifts and gently closes the door. His hooded eyes are a dead giveaway to his mood shift.

I playfully back away with two hesitant steps.

"What about our company?"

The corner of his mouth lifts in a sly half-grin as he prowls forward. "They're adults. They can take care of themselves."

For a mere millisecond, I think about Owen and all of the female attention he's gotten. He's given them all equal time, which includes Beth. I'm not sure where things stand between her and Joshua. They've had a few dates, but nothing has turned serious yet.

All thoughts disappear as Chase scoops me up and tosses me onto our bed. When he crawls across the mattress, my insides boil and drench in anticipation. I vaguely wonder if the door is locked before his hungry kiss completely turns my brain into mush. My last thought before I'm consumed is how he was very much worth every risk to my heart. The reward is priceless.

The End

We'd like to thank you for taking the time out of your busy life to read our novel. Above all we hope you loved it. If you did, we would love it back if you could spare just a minutes or two to leave a review wherever you purchased this book. If you do, could you be so kind and **not leave any spoilers** about the story? Thanks so much!

Acknowledgments

You guys ROCK! Your continued support means the world to us. So Thank You!

A book may start with words, but it takes a team to bring it altogether.

We begin with our beta readers, Kelly and Samantha. A huge THANK YOU. Your feedback was so important to help smooth out the bumps in the words. You ladies are amazing!

Once that's a wrap, we move onto to the shine. For that we want to thank Paige for editing and Sydnee Thompson for proofing. Your suggestions and corrections made everything better.

For every great book, you need a great cover. We owe are gratitude to Lauren at Perrywinkle for her stunning photography. You make it seem so effortless. Then onto Letitia at Romantic Book Affairs, for designing a gorgeous cover.

And we find ourselves back to our amazing readers. So again thank you. We couldn't do what we do without you.

About Terri E. Laine

Terri E. Laine, USA Today bestselling author, left a lucrative career as a CPA to pursue her love for writing. Outside of her roles as a wife and mother of three, she's always been a dreamer and as such became an avid reader at a young age.

Many years later, she got a crazy idea to write a novel and set out to try to publish it. With over a dozen titles published under various pen names, the rest is history. Her journey has been a blessing, and a dream realized. She looks forward to many more memories to come.

I have several upcoming releases, make sure to sign up for my newsletter
http://eepurl.com/bDJ9kb
or check my website for details.
www.terrielaine.com

If you are a fan of me, make sure you join my fan group. Terri's Butterflies:
https://www.facebook.com/groups/671789082985465/

And you can join my reader group to talk books. Terri E. Laine Bad Girl Group:
https://www.facebook.com/groups/1738725283032502/

About A.M. Hargrove

One day, on her way home from work as a sales manager, USA Today bestselling author, A. M. Hargrove, realized her life was on fast forward and if she didn't do something soon, it would be too late to write that work of fiction she had been dreaming of her whole life. So she made a quick decision to quit her job and reinvented herself as a Naughty and Nice Romance Author.

Annie fancies herself all of the following: Reader, Writer, Dark Chocolate Lover, Ice Cream Worshipper, Coffee Drinker (swears the coffee, chocolate, and ice cream should be added as part of the USDA food groups), Lover of Grey Goose (and an extra dirty martini), #WalterThePuppy Lover, and if you're ever around her for more than five minutes, you'll find out she's a non-stop talker. Other than loving writing about romance, she loves hanging out with her family and binge watching TV with her husband. You can find out more about her books www.amhargrove.com.

Stalk Annie

If you would like to hear more about what's going on in my world, please subscribe to my mailing list on my website at amhargrove.com.

You can also join my private group—Hargrove's Hangout— on Facebook if you're up to some crazy shenanigans!

Please stalk me. I'll love you forever if you do. Seriously.

www.amhargrove.com

Twitter @amhargrove1

www.facebook.com/amhargroveauthor

www.facebook.com/anne.m.hargrove

www.goodreads.com/amhargrove1

Instagram: amhargroveauthor

Pinterest: amhargrove1

annie@amhargrove.com

For Other Books by A.M. Hargrove visit www.amhargrove.com

For The Love of English

For The Love of My Sexy Geek (The Vault)

A Special Obsession

Chasing Vivi

Craving Midnight

I'll Be Waiting (The Vault—April 2018)

From Ashes to Flames (May 2018)

From Ice to Flames (July 2018)

From Smoke to Flames (October 2018)

Cruel and Beautiful

A Mess of a Man

One Wrong Choice

A Beautiful Sin

The Wilde Players Dirty Romance Series:

Sidelined

Fastball

Hooked

Worth Every Risk

The Edge Series:

Edge of Disaster

Shattered Edge

Kissing Fire

The Tragic Duet:

Tragically Flawed, Tragic 1

Tragic Desires, Tragic 2

The Hart Brothers Series:

Freeing Her, Book 1

Freeing Him, Book 2

Kestrel, Book 3

The Fall and Rise of Kade Hart

Sabin, A Seven Novel

The Guardians of Vesturon Series

Stalk Terri

I love to hear from my readers. Follow, Stalk, and Contact me at one of these places:

Website: terrielaine.com

Facebook: terrielainebooks

Facebook Page: TerriELaineAuthor

Twitter: @TerriLaineBooks

Instagram @terrielaineauthor

Goodreads: terri e laine

Newsletter Signup: http://eepurl.com/bDJ9kb

Join my fan group
Terri's Butterflies or Terri's Bad Girls Group on Facebook.

BOOKS ALSO BY ME

Because of Him

Captivated By Him

Taming of Him (TBA - July 2018)

Ride or Die

<u>Chasing Butterflies Standalone Series</u>

Chasing Butterflies

Catching Fireflies

Changing Hearts

Craving Dragonflies (TBA - April 2018)

Chasing Butterflies Standalone Spinoff Series

Songs for Cricket (TBA - August 2018)

Other Books

Sex, Alcohol, and My Neighbor (Beer Goggles Anthology)

Honey (The Vault Anthology)

Sugar

Other Co-authored Books

Cruel & Beautiful

A Mess of A Man

One Wrong Choice

A Beautiful Sin

Worth Every Risk

The Wilde Players Dirty Romance Series:

Sidelined

Fastball

Hooked

Made in the USA
San Bernardino, CA
29 March 2018